THE LONG ISLAND SERIAL KILLER MURDERS
GILGO BEACH and BEYOND

by Robert Banfelder

BB
~
BROADWATER BOOKS
Riverhead, New York

Broadwater Books
141 Riverside Drive
Riverhead, New York 11901

broadwaterbooksinfo@gmail.com

ISBN: 978-1-7326025-9-5

Printed in the United States of America
10 9 8 7 6 5 4 3 2 1

This novel is dedicated to Donna, who, by now, absolutely and positively knows the meaning of the word *sacrifice*.

Books by Robert Banfelder

FICTION:

A Trilogy
[A Three-Book Series of Madness and Evil in the Making]

Dicky, Richard, and I
The Signing
The Triumvirate

Tetralogy
[A Justin Barnes Four-Book Series]

The Author
The Teacher
Knots
The Good Samaritans

Trace Evidence
A novel inspired by the Robert Shulman serial-killer trial
Riverhead, Long Island, New York

Battered
A novel based on the true story of a woman sent to prison for
murdering her physically abusive husband

Reviews for all of the above works may be viewed on
www.Amazon.com.

NONFICTION:

The Fishing Smart *Anywhere* Handbook for Salt Water
& Fresh Water

Spin Casting, Baitcasting, Fly Casting ~ Lethal Lures & Live
Baits ~ Kayaking/Canoeing ~ Seafood Recipes ~ Smoking Fish

The North American Hunting Smart Handbook
with Bonus Feature:

Hunting Africa's Five Most Dangerous Game Animals

Bull's Eye! The Smart Bowhunter's Handbook
with Bonus Feature:

Bowfishing on a Budget

The Essential Guide to Writing Well and Getting Published
with Bonus Feature:

Making Decent Dollars Writing, Plus Little-Known Reward-
Reaping Benefits

On Your Way to Gourmet Cooking

ACKNOWLEDGMENTS

My heartfelt gratitude goes out to Donna Derasmo, whose indefatigable efforts were an invaluable source as advisor, editor, formatter, and life's partner.

A special thanks to Bob Hartz and Mary Ann Price for many a fine meal at the Iron Skillet Restaurant in Mattituck, Long Island, New York. Also, Bob, thanks for introducing me to umami.

A notable thank you goes out to my son, Jason Banfelder, for his computer expertise and advice over the course of many, many years.

I'd be remiss if I didn't mention my son's significant other, Luce Skrabanek, for unwittingly lending her surname with respect to one of my favorite characters in the novel.

IN MEMORIAL TO THE MURDER VICTIMS OF GILGO BEACH, ET AL

The following is a list of six victims who are suspected of being murdered by one or more serial killers and whose remains were found along a narrow, isolated stretch of thick and thorny underbrush running parallel between Ocean Parkway and Gilgo Beach, bordering Suffolk and Nassau Counties on Long Island. The discovery of their remains, and others, was precipitated by the search for Shannan Gilbert, a sex worker who went missing in that general area after a twenty-three-minute 911 call to police at 4:51 a.m. on May 1, 2010—screaming for her life. As of this publication, that tape has not been released to the public. Shannan's body was discovered on December 3, 2011, nineteen (19) months later! The initial finding of the medical examiner's autopsy stated that the cause of death was undetermined. An independent autopsy performed by a renowned pathologist hired by the family determined that the cause of Shannan's death was consistent with strangulation. Police, however, speculate that her death was an accident, that she had drowned.

#1 ~ Barthelemy, Melissa – age 24

#2 ~ Costello, Amber Lynn – age 27

#3 ~ Brainard-Barnes, Maureen – age 25

#4 ~ Waterman, Megan – 22

#5 ~ Taylor, Jessica – age 20

#6 ~ "Jane Doe" – head, hands, and right foot found on Gilgo Beach; her torso found 47 miles away in Manorville. Identified in May

2020 as 24-year-old Valerie Mack.

Next, is the list of four <u>unidentified</u> victims who are suspected of being murdered by one or more serial killers and whose remains were found in the areas of Gilgo Beach, Fire Island, Tobay Beach, and Manorville.

#7 ~ toddler-age female

#8 ~ Asian male – believed to be a sex worker, found in women's clothing.

#9 ~ woman linked by DNA to above toddler.

#10 ~ skull of women found at Tobay Beach; linked by DNA to a pair of legs found on Fire Island.

Additionally, the bodies of seven identified/unidentified women found on Long Island, "suspected by some" as having been murdered by a serial killer, are as follows:

#11 ~ "Peaches" – woman with a heart-shaped peach tattoo on her left breast found in Hempstead Lake State Park, disappeared 1997.

#12 ~ "Cherries" – female with two cherries tattooed on left breast, Mamaroneck, disappeared 2007.

#13 ~ Tanya Rush – a prostitute who was found in a small suitcase off the Southern State Parkway in Bellmore, disappeared 2008.

#14 ~ Unidentified woman

#15 ~ Unidentified woman

#16 ~ Natacha Jungo from Queens – body washed up on Gilgo Beach, disappeared 2013.

#17 ~ Shannan Gilbert, disappeared May 1, 2010.

Robert Banfelder

CHAPTER ONE

Before continuing his tutelage, the man smiled down warmly at Charlotte Endicott who sat sullenly silent.

"Therefore, a brown sauce is the most versatile of the famed five-star French *mother* sauces used in cooking, Charlotte . . . ." He paused then laughed loudly. "Do you see the importance of a pause in speaking or a comma in writing, Charlotte? Otherwise, it would come out, 'A brown sauce is the most versatile of the famed five-star French mother sauces used in cooking Charlotte.' In other words, I'd be speaking about cooking *you*." The man nodded affirmatively and grinned broadly.

"Yes, a brown sauce is a basic sauce for so many gourmet and derivative dishes. But basic is not at all what we'll be dealing with here this morning as well as into the wee hours. No, indeed! And when I say *we'll*, I mean you and me because we are going to create. Like artists! Yes. We are going to be elaborating on the fundamental foundation of that most inviting, versatile brown sauce, bringing it to its pinnacle, referred to as Espagnole sauce, for Espagnole sauce is the quintessence of the purest form of a true brown sauce. Espagnole," the man repeated. "It's the French pronunciation as well as the spelling of the word Spanish." The well-built man slowly spelled out the word. "E·S·P·A·G·N·O·L·E.

"Don't ask me how all that came about exactly. Something about King Louis the thirteenth and his fiancée, Anne, being influenced by some Spanish chefs who didn't quite find favor with the flavor of the traditional French sauce being prepared for the king's and queen's wedding banquet. And, so, the Spanish chefs added tomatoes to the recipe to enhance richness and flavor. The ceremonial dinner was a huge success. So, out of respect, that country was honored by having the Spanish name, Espagnole, adopted as the altered French sauce.

"Anyhow, the sauce is first prepared with a vegetable base stock referred to as mirepoix before being transformed into a rich brown sauce. The magic is the flavor of the marrow from the bones and added meat. With a bit of meat left on the bones from the necks, shanks, ribs and knuckles of pork, beef, veal, and lamb, we'll slather the bones with olive oil and tomato paste before roasting them in order to create Espagnole sauce. But in order to create that decadent, savory, brown gelatin-like liquid, we are going to thicken it, reducing it by half over a low flame to simmer for eighteen hours. If we have time, we'll make a port wine mushroom based demi-glace; demi meaning half; glace meaning icing. Do you see how all these things come together so neatly, Charlotte? The sauce and demi-glace will be the finishing touches to our Chateaubriand. Needless to say, we have a lot of work to do. The key to making life easier is to do as much preparation as possible well ahead of time. We'll make about a quart of Espagnole sauce, and I'll freeze the rest in ice cube trays to have on hand when I invite other guests—just like you. So, let's get busy."

Charlotte sat seated in a corner, now trembling.

"The first thing we have to do is to create that mirepoix stock/brown sauce because it takes the longest to prepare. Simmering for eighteen hours over a low flame for a superb flavor. A mirepoix is an aromatic vegetable base, which will enhance the taste of many sauces, soups and so forth. It's basically a mixture of coarsely cut onions, carrots and celery. But again, basic is not at all what we'll be dealing with here. No, indeed! We'll be striving for perfection and creating the extraordinary, like so many innovative chefs throughout the world. Working wisely with spices, herbs and seasonings is part of the magic, too, Charlotte. Condiments like rosemary, thyme, tarragon, parsley, cloves of garlic, peppercorns, and bay leaves are key—oh, and lots and lots of leek."

The man unstrapped Charlotte from the metal chair bolted in the center of the concrete floor, leading her to a counter in the kitchen area.

"So, what I'd like you to start doing, Charlotte, is to coarsely chop up the onions, carrots, and celery on the cutting board before you. I'll take care of the leeks and the rest. And be careful not to cut your fingers with that knife and cleaver because they're very, very sharp," he assured her and smiled coyly.

Charlotte cringed.

"You'll note that I separated and heavily salted the center-cut section from each end of the length of prime beef tenderloin for our Chateaubriand. The salt will help dry the meat for a reverse-searing process we'll be employing, rather than the traditional method of initially searing it in a hot pan atop the stove then cooking it in a relatively hot oven. No. What we'll be doing first is cooking the meat slowly in the oven set at a very low temperature. Slow-and-low is the name of the game for several good reasons. Namely, the roast will cook evenly from edge-to-edge throughout, without leaving you with that grayish overcooked outer edge. Served either rare or medium rare, the roast will be the desired color throughout. A medium-rare pink coloring is what I prefer. I used to like my beef served rare. 'Walk it in, sit it down, and wipe its horns off,' I'd joke around. But quite seriously, Charlotte, utilizing the reverse-searing method and having the roast served medium-rare, folks are pleasantly surprised to learn that the meat is actually juicier and more flavorful. Truly it is.

"So, I'm going to put this piece of heavily salted center-cut beef tenderloin in the refrigerator to sit overnight, which will create a pellicle, meaning a skin or film that will aid in producing a nice thin brown crust while cooking in the oven. Then we'll finish off the roast in a hot cast iron skillet atop the stove, basting it with our *drop-dead* savory sauce and butter," he emphasized.

Charlotte began to weep bitterly.

"Please don't cry, dear. You'll be around long enough to enjoy the first course and maybe even partake in the main event. Now, I suggest that you start cutting up those vegetables. And remember that the knife and cleaver are extremely sharp. What I like to call scary sharp. I'm going to stand over here away from you in case you get any crazy ideas." Charlotte's tormentor smirked then giggled quietly behind a cupped hand, brushing back his bushy blond head of hair.

Charlotte tried desperately to steady her nerves as she began to cut and chop the vegetables.

CHAPTER TWO

Working closely with the district attorney's office, eight squads comprise the Suffolk County Homicide Unit, performing an around-the-clock rotating schedule. Detective Sergeant Brenden Reilly and his partner Detective Mike D'Angelo were part of a team, headquartered in Yaphank, Long Island.

After a lengthy conversation with forensics, Brenden hung up the phone. "We got another one, buddy," he said to Mike.

"Where?"

"Corner of East Main Street and Riverside Drive, Riverhead. Railroad tracks, and in plain sight."

"Again with the fucking railroad tracks. Male or female?"

"Female this time around. Guy walking his dog found her and called 911."

"She I.D.'d?"

"Charlotte Endicott. Twenty-two-year-old seamstress. Worked at Vojvoda's Dry Cleaners."

"That's right across the street from the tracks."

"Right."

"Same MO, I trust."

"But with a twist this time."

"How so?"

"Perp broke her neck. Twisted it like a rag doll," Brenden elaborated. "Cleanly cut off her earlobes, not the ears themselves. Harold thinks they found food stains on her clothing."

"Christ! Same as the Gilmore guy in Nassau."

"Yup."

"That makes eighteen women, an Asian male found in women's clothing, and an infant. I'd say we have a serial killer back in play after all these years." Mike D'Angelo was alluding to the Gilgo Beach/Oak Beach/Manorville area murders and the victims' remains discovered years ago in Nassau and Suffolk Counties. "You think these last two are connected to the others from decades ago?"

"Two murders in December to close out our year—after all this time? Hard to say. We'll have to wait and see."

"I'll bet we're looking at a serial, Brenden. Dormant or not, a continuation of the same. Maybe even the same killer."

"The problem with that theory is most of the women were found back west in Gilgo."

"Yeah, but three were found in Manorville, and one of the torsos wound up in Gilgo, which lead some folks to believe there are two killers, maybe more, working in concert. You yourself considered the possibility some years ago," Mike reminded his partner.

"Let's just focus our attention on what we have now and see where this takes us."

"You said food stains. Endicott woman have stains similar to Gilmore's?"

"Harold seems to think so, but it's too early to determine. Hopefully, forensics can tell us what kind of food stains, or what it is exactly the ME can find in her stomach."

"Any guess at this point?"

"Tomato sauce or tomato paste like on Gilmore's clothing, Harold's saying in his preliminary. Alan will likely corroborate."

"You really believe four-eyed Harold could distinguish tomato stains from blood stains at a crime scene at first blush?" Mike kidded. "Myopic prick. You note the size and thickness of those lenses?" he went on.

"I guess there were more tomato stains than blood stains this time around than at the Gilmore scene," Brenden bantered back. "Anyhow, Harold says he'll have Alan notify us immediately after the autopsy. Troy and Trevor are on top of this, but I think we should shoot over and take a peek for ourselves."

Mike stood up from his seat. "Tomato sauce. I'm telling you that we've got to get eyes on that sous-chef at the new Michelangelo's Restaurant in Riverhead," Mike continued with the kidding.

Brenden smiled and got up. "Why, because he didn't give you a dozen littlenecks on that clam dish the last time out?"

"No, because he mixed up my order between Clams Oreganata and Clams Luciana. The menu clearly said that with the Clams Oreganata you get six littlenecks. With Clams Luciana you're supposed to get close to a dozen littlenecks sautéed in white wine, garlic and oil, not six overcooked, rubbery cherrystone clams. 'Take it back and bring me the dish with littlenecks—spaghetti with red sauce on the side,' you'll recall I told the waiter. And what does he tell me? They're all out of littlenecks. Like his boss, the chef was out shopping. Out to lunch was more like it."

"Look, the guy apologized and told you in a nice way that they just opened the week before. They hadn't even advertised yet. What they call a soft opening."

"Yeah, so my wife and I go back a month later and I order the Pasta e Fagiole Soup. What comes out is a pasta *stew*. No broth. Mostly pasta and very little beans."

"I think you got Italian food on the brain."

"Is there any other kind?"

Brenden smiled. "I keep telling you to try Cucina 25 right down the street. Their Monday and Tuesday specials after four p.m. can't be beat; $14.95. Fairly good selection. Delicious food."

The two detectives headed down the stairwell and out the building toward their vehicle, heading for Hauppauge where Charlotte Endicott's body had been taken for autopsy.

CHAPTER THREE

Whenever Josh Billings and his wife dined out, they'd have dinner at the Iron Skillet Restaurant in Mattituck, a cozy 12-person limited-seating, 170-year-old farmhouse on the North Fork of Long Island, just north of the railroad station. What Josh loved about the quaint eatery, besides the fine fare, was that you could BYOB: wine, beer or other beverages. Its owners, Bob Hartz and Mary Ann Price, offer a limited menu comprised of several hearty soups and scrumptious appetizers, a dozen enticing entrées, and a trio of decadent desserts.

If you dined at the Iron Skillet for the very first time, having failed to check out their online menu beforehand, you'd immediately size up Bob and Mary as minimalists. Josh Billings and his wife loved the place and dined there once a month on average. On special holidays, Josh and Claire would invite family and special friends.

Josh was not a heavy hitter in any sense of that phraseology. He was a salesman for a software company. Josh occasionally wound up with and enjoyed extra cash because he was a prudent man, making his own coffee in the morning before leaving for work, brown-bagging his lunch, limiting himself to one glass of overpriced wine in local restaurants, and saving a specified percentage of his salary. Those savings, coupled to a nice yearly bonus, allowed Josh to splurge every now and then, spoiling family and folks close to him.

For being a fairly successful salesman as well as a powerfully-built man, Josh Billings was a rather quiet soul. Normally. Always the perfect gentleman. Family and friends attributed Josh's sales career success to his unassuming demeanor. His clients loved him.

If one could name but a single weakness ascribed to that well-liked man, it would unquestionably be *food*. And of the endless selection from which to choose, Josh Billing's choice would invariably be steak, steak pizzaiola style being one of his favorite dishes at the Iron Skillet, especially the way Bob Hartz prepared a fully trimmed, well marbled, 12-ounce plus prime New York strip steak. Josh would usually hold off ordering that dish until summer, when Bob would use his vine ripened sweet tomatoes to make the meal.

When cooking at home, Josh would always shop at Costco in Riverhead for their prime and choice cuts of meat: rib eye, filet mignon, T-bone, skirt steak, flank steak, hanger steak, short loin, flat iron steak and, of course, a nice New York strip steak. He never fancied himself a gourmet cook. Family, friends, and neighbors, however, deemed him a genius in the kitchen as well as a gifted gourmand around the grill. Josh's barbecues were legendary throughout the neighborhood, although limited to a small group of friends. However, that did not stop some folks who lived along the block from dropping by whenever Josh was grilling on the back deck. They always started a conversation with a similar greeting.

"Gosh, Josh. I just stepped out to grab the newspaper, and I could smell whatever it is you're cooking all the way down the block."

"Steaks to go, Bill," Josh replied. "Delivering these to the Jentzens across the street. Steve is laid up with a bad back," he fibbed. Not the part about Steve being laid up with a bad back, but the part about delivering the steaks across the street. "If you'll excuse me, I gotta run, otherwise they'll get cold."

"Oh, sure thing, Josh. Sorry to intrude. I was just taking a little walk." Bill Hammerhand held the Sunday newspaper awkwardly by his side. "Oh, look. Silly me. I forgot to bring the paper back in the house before I left. You believe this weather?"

"Have a nice afternoon, Bill," Josh said with a smile, removing the rib eye steaks and shutting off the burners on the barbecue grill before escaping into his home.

Once inside, Claire smiled at her husband. "Guy's got the nose of a bloodhound."

"Prevailing wind this time of year does help carry the aroma," he said with a grin.

"How did you manage to get away?"

"Told a tarradiddle; otherwise, he'd be here for the afternoon, go through a bottle of wine, not to mention half of *my* rib eye steak."

"That's because you're too nice a guy, Josh."

"An almost seventy-degree day in the middle of January, so I wasn't about to give up a Sunday chitchatting with Hammerhand."

"Shoot you later if you had."

"Ready to eat, darling?"

"Famished, oh chef of the past, present, and future."

"Good. Wait till you taste the sauce I made."

"Can't wait."

"It'll be almost as good as Bob Hartz's."

"It's been a good month since we've been there."

"I'll make a reservation for next weekend. All right?"

"Sounds great."

"What do you think you'll have this time around, Claire?"

"Bolognese sauce over fettuccine."

"Creature of habit."

"Right you are."

"I think I'll go for the half rack of Australian lamb, roast potatoes Anna, which you know I love."

"I know."

"It's a special-order item, so I better call Bob right after we eat before I forget."

"You won't forget."

"Why is that, dear?" Josh questioned, pretending that he didn't know the answer.

"Because when it comes to meat and potatoes, actually, food in general, you don't forget anything."

CHAPTER FOUR

Janet Johnsen sat where Charlotte Endicott had sat—strapped to a metal chair in the center of a clean, commodious basement apartment with a well-equipped kitchen. The blond bushy-haired man busied himself at a table in the opposite corner of the room, sharpening an expensive chef's knife on a manually-operated, controlled-angle knife-sharpening system.

"You will never ever in a million years get away with this, you fucking piece of shit. My husband will find you and kill you, you filthy bastard. My husband is a cop, and he will hunt you down. DO YOU HEAR ME?"

The man kept his back toward the woman as he worked. "Oh, I hear you all right. It's not so much your profanity that's coming in loud and clear, Janet. It's your exaggerated use of clichés and claims. First off, your husband is not a cop. Well, not in the sense that you'd like me to believe. Your husband is a New York City Transit Officer. So, unless you were abducted on a city subway, dear, which of course you weren't, and screamed out his name for everyone to hear, he wouldn't even have an inkling that you're missing at this hour. He won't miss you until late tonight because you're scheduled to have dinner with your mother at eight p.m. So, maybe by ten or eleven he'd start to worry."

Janet looked down at the concrete floor in sheer frustration and disbelief. *How does this man know all this?* she wondered. *How? He's been watching us,* she realized. *Studying Jeff's routine. Noting his regular daytime hours and the graveyard shift. Knowing the time I'd have dinner with Mom.*

"I'm sure you know, Janet, that the city is hiring over five hundred transit officers to merge with the New York Police Department in order to combat crime in and around the subways. I understand that Jeff is involved in their training. He's been a very busy boy these days. Indispensable. Actually, though, I'm sure they'll cut him a little slack when he learns that a crime's been committed practically on his doorstep. Not even a hundred yards from the Long Island Railroad station in Mattituck. Don't you ever get tired of that whistle and all that rumbling, Janet? It would drive me crazy; I kid you not. Then again, I guess you get used to anything after a while."

Janet raised her eyes from the floor, staring at the man's back, watching his arms and hands working forward and backward with rhythmic alternating strokes, like a cross-country skier or a person exercising his upper body on an aerobic machine.

"Do you know the secret to getting the blade of a knife not sharp but scary sharp, Janet? Precise angle control. This knife-sharpening system I'm working with is the magic. As a matter of fact, it is truly the very best of the best in the whole wide world. That's not simply the boast of the company. It's the consensus of folks ranging from knife aficionados to skilled cutlery craftsmen throughout the world. Of course, there is a bit of a learning curve involved. But once you master the process, through practice, practice, practice, this manually-operated controlled-angle knife-sharpening system beats them all.

"As a matter of fact, it's far better than any of those electric knife sharpeners advertised for Harry and Harriet homeowner, like the Chef's Choice model that sits on your kitchen counter in Mattituck, right alongside your twenty-piece Wüsthof Classic knife set on which you spent over twelve-hundred dollars. No, Janet. A good many electric-type knife-sharpening machines destroy the temper of a blade, thereby limiting the longevity of expensive cutlery, deteriorating the bevel of a stout, sturdy blade, ultimately ruining its symmetrical edge. Yet people are duped into buying them for their so-called convenience, convinced that they can bring back a factory edge with just a couple of passes through a preset angle. Nonsense, Janet. Just can't happen. Actually, my knives are sharper than any knife sent directly from the factory because I take the time to sharpen them correctly. Sharpened and honed to pure perfection. I could slice your ear off in a nanosecond, and you wouldn't even know it until you saw the blood running down your cheeks, body, and into the drain beneath your feet."

Janet stretched her neck and gazed down at one of the circular drains in the concrete floor.

The bushy-haired man stopped sharpening a large chef's knife and got up from his seat. "You know, it's a shame you have such a bad attitude, Janet Johnsen. Most of my guests join me in the end with one last meal. You? I really don't know what I'm going to do with you. You're so unappreciative. You don't want to help me prepare an exquisite meal? Fine. What I might do is let you starve. Not starve to death but rather have you suffer to the brink of starvation and then feed you some of your own body parts. I think I'll start with your ears as an appetizer, and then we'll go from there. Why are you shaking your head in the negative? You don't think you'll eat your own ears if you're hungry enough? No? Well, we'll soon see, won't we, Janet? Oh, and by the way. The chef's knife I'm holding is an eight-inch Zwilling J.A. Henckels; seventy bucks. *Your* Wüsthof eight-inch chef's knife, if sold separately, would cost more than twice that amount. Mine is the workhorse in this kitchen. Yours, you've ruined the edge on that worthless electric sharpener. It would take me a good deal of time to bring that blade back to cutting-edge precision," the man commented with a smile.

"I know who you are!" Janet suddenly and firmly declared.

"You do?"

"You're the fucking monster who killed that woman by the tracks back in Riverhead."

"Wrong. I'm the monster who killed that woman back in Riverhead right here in the very seat you're sitting in."

Janet said nothing for the next half minute. "You're a very sick fucking, fucking puppy," she stated through a sneer.

"Wrong again. I *was* a very sick puppy with a pretty bad case of the flu. It's really going around, you know. But I'm all better now.

And when your hubby learns where the police will find your body—not fifty feet from the train station in Mattituck—I think he's going to have a shit fit. And get this, Janet. In months from now, I'm going to befriend him. No, it's true. I'm going to advise him on how to reprofile; that is, realign the beveled edges of those knives you ruined. And he's going to invite me over to show him how to do just that. At least that's the game plan as it stands now. Then again, he may want nothing whatsoever to do with knives after he learns or sees for himself how badly you've been butchered, and all because you refused to assist me in creating a beef Wellington. I would've taken care of the pâté de foie gras and the pastry. All you had to do was peel and cut some vegetables as sides, and we could have had a wonderful dinner, just the two of us."

"You're a *fucking* animal, and you'll burn in hell for this."

"That young woman you mentioned from Riverhead, she absolutely loved my Chateaubriand . . . to absolutely die for, Janet." The man raked the fingers of one hand through his bushy blond head of hair and smiled brightly.

Janet Johnsen did not want to cry. She willed herself not to shed tears. But she knew she was going to die at the hands of this maniac no matter what she said or did. "He'll know it was you if you ever go near him. Jeff will somehow know," she affirmed. "And he will kill you! And that's if the Suffolk police don't catch and kill you first," she swore and forced a crooked grin before she spat toward the man.

The man simply grinned and shook his head.

"The Suffolk County police are not like other police departments," she went on. "They truly protect their own. They avenge their own. Transit cop or not, they're still part of the police family. And if they don't kill you on the spot when they find you—and they will—you'll rot in a jail cell in upstate Dannemora until you take your own life because the guards—who are given incentives—will make life unbearable until you take your own life. Believe me."

But the bushy-haired man was shaking his head. "Wrong again, and again, and again. You see, I have something that only several of us have, Janet. I have a *monopoly* on life, insured with a get-out-of-jail-free card. So, unless they shoot me on the spot like you said, without my having the benefit of explaining what cards I genuinely hold, I'm really in the catbird seat."

16

CHAPTER FIVE

Suffolk County Police Chief James Burke had badly beaten a handcuffed/shackled man, Christopher Loeb, while in police custody. Loeb's lawyer had filed a lawsuit against Burke and others. Burke met with Suffolk County's District Attorney Thomas Spota and his top anticorruption prosecutor Christopher McPartland to discuss cover-up strategies. It didn't fly. Burke had served most of a 48-month sentence at a low-level federal prison in Pennsylvania. In a four-count federal corruption case, Spota and McPartland were found guilty of obstruction of justice, witness tampering, conspiracy, and the cover-up referencing Burke's assault of prisoner, Christopher Loeb. Postponements followed. Spota and McPartland were soon to be sentenced. A new date had been set for the end of June 2020.

As a teenager, Burke had been Spota's star witness in a murder trial that he was prosecuting, dating back to the late seventies. Years later, Spota hired Burke as an investigator, bringing him up through the ranks then promoting him to chief investigator, grooming him for chief of police of Suffolk County, to which he was appointed. Over the years, their close relationship and friendship raised many eyebrows. Spota is 78; Burke is 54.

The majority of bodies and remains that turned up along the narrow,

17

isolated stretch of thick and thorny underbrush running parallel between Ocean Parkway and Gilgo Beach was precipitated by the search for Shannan Gilbert, a sex worker who went missing after a twenty-three-minute 911 call to police, screaming for her life. "They're trying to kill me," she had shrieked. The search for Shannan eventually resulted in authorities discovering eleven bodies, inclusive of Shannan's. The murders, spanning more than a decade, are attributed to one or more serial killers using the deserted stretch of straggly scrubs and shrubs as a dumping ground. The narrow stretch of barrier beach where the ten bodies were uncovered is bordered by the Atlantic Ocean to the south and along Ocean Parkway just to the north. Its reach runs from west to east through Jones Beach, west Gilgo Beach, and on up to Oak Beach. Gilgo is a small gated community, a hamlet situated along the south shore of Long Island in the town of Babylon.

So-called 'persons of interest' interviewed as part of an ongoing criminal investigation were immediately eliminated as suspects: Joseph Brewer, owner of the home where Shannan Gilbert was solicited for her services via an advertisement posted on Craigslist; the driver of the hired vehicle who drove Shannan to that home and waited for her; and a neighbor of Brewer's, a former police surgeon for Suffolk County, Dr. Peter Hackett, whose sketchy background and explanation for inviting Shannan into his home that very evening after pounding on his door, begging for help, remains suspicious. Hackett had given Shannan medication to help calm her. These interviews were all downplayed by the Suffolk County police.

Subsequently, it was in the same neighborhood where Shannan Gilbert's body was found that Suffolk County Police Chief Burke had parked his vehicle before it was burglarized by the man Burke had later beaten at the 4th Precinct police headquarters in Smithtown. From an unlocked police department-issued vehicle, Christopher Loeb had stolen Burke's gun belt, ammunition, and a duffel bag (later referred to as the 'party bag') containing a box of cigars, a bottle of Viagra, sex toys, sex videos, along with a plethora of other pornography—some of homosexual content involving pubescent boys.

It wasn't long after the Gilgo Beach discovery of Shannan Gilbert and ten other bodies that the FBI entered the investigation.

18

Both District Attorney Thomas Spota and Chief of Police James Burke did what they could to initially block the investigation by keeping the feds at arm's length from the case. The reasons were twofold: Burke was to be protected at all cost from Loeb's charge of being assaulted by the chief while in handcuffs at the police station; also, accusations were being made by a female escort [Leanne ~ last name momentarily being withheld from the press] whom John Ray, a flamboyant Miller Place attorney, was representing. The woman had stated in an affidavit that Police Chief James Burke had solicited her for sex at a party in Oak Beach, a home just five miles from where Shannan Gilbert was last seen alive. The men at the party were prominent people from both Suffolk and Nassau Counties. John Ray was busy building upon a circumstantial case that named James Burke and Dr. Peter Hackett as possible suspects in the Gilgo Beach murders.

After a news conference that Ray and the woman had given, rumors flew about like a flock of birds in erratic flight. The acronym, **LISK**—Long Island Serial Killer—was linked to the police chief as well as those friends who were very close to him. Hence, the acronym, LISK, was expanded to LISKS—Long Island Serial Killers, plural, for many folks firmly believed that there was more than one serial killer responsible for the murders. Especially when it was learned that the skull, hands, and right foot of one woman's body were discovered in proximity to Gilgo Beach, her torso found earlier in time back in Manorville, a hamlet in the northeast corner in the town of Riverhead, a distance of 47 miles away. Two serial killers, perhaps more, working in concert, was but one of the many theories being bandied about. In 2014, John Bittrolff, a carpenter, had been arrested for the murders of two prostitutes whose remains were discovered in Manorville. Authorities speculate that Bittrolff may have been connected to at least one of the Gilgo Beach murders, and with good reason.

In addition to the discovery of the Gilgo Beach and Manorville victims, the remains of several other young women turned up in Hempstead Lake Park, Mamaroneck, Bellmore, Fire Island, and Lattington (an incorporated village in the town of Oyster Bay, Nassau County). One mutilated body was found in a suitcase, another in a Rubbermaid container, while other bodies were found wrapped in

19

burlap that presumably originated from Bissett Nursery in Holtsville, owned by Jimmy Bissett, a wealthy developer and co-owner of the Long Island Aquarium and Exhibition Center, in addition to the adjacent Hyatt Place Hotel in the heart of downtown Riverhead. Shortly before Christmas in 2011, Bissett committed suicide in his vehicle at Veteran's Memorial Park in Mattituck—the day after Shannan Gilbert's body was found. Gilbert's phone number was purportedly listed in Bissett's cell phone directory. An undisputed fact was that Jimmy Bissett and James Burke were very good friends. Savvy folks were beginning to connect the dots. Coincidentally, the same initials referencing some of the key players presented a curious conundrum: **J**oseph **B**rewer, **J**ames **B**urke, **J**immy **B**issett, and **J**ohn **B**ittrolff.

If one is of the belief that there are no coincidences, then one can have a field day with the facts. After summing up the similarities referencing those initials, an award-winning crime-thriller novelist/outdoors writer from Riverhead coined the phrase (shared strictly among friends, of course): "The Good Ol' Boys J.B. Sex Club," alluding to the circle of suspicious characters.

A year and a half after Bissett's suicide, Robert Lanieri, age 60, a food service executive for the Long Island Aquarium, committed suicide at his home in Jamesport.

On January 16th, 2020, former FBI Agent Geraldine Hart, then head of the Long Island field office and now the new police commissioner for the Suffolk County Police Department, gave a news conference announcing a previously undisclosed piece of evidence to be shared with the public referencing the Gilgo Beach, et al, murders. A black leather belt with embossed half-inch high letters depicting the initials W H or upside down H M had been discovered at one of the crime scenes. The police are confident that the belt did not belong to any of the victims but was handled by the suspect. At the end of the news conference, several obvious questions were raised by reporters; however, authorities were playing it close to the vest, revealing very little, hoping that someone with information would come forth. The commissioner, dressed in black as if in mourning, wearing a heavy gold necklace, gold earrings, and official gold badge pinned to her outfit, stood behind a podium. Four male members of the

20

investigative team stood behind her. Commissioner Hart stated that they were "launching a website dedicated to sharing information with the public about these unsolved murders and also providing a new way for the public to provide us with tips." GilgoNews.com.

Hart's office provided the FBI with DNA samples of the unidentified victims' remains in order to conduct genetic genealogy testing so as to deduce biological relationships among individuals. Case in point: The serial murderer referred to as the Golden State Killer, Joseph James DeAngelo—a retired California cop—was identified and apprehended through the scientific technique of genetic genealogy. In short, the police traced the killer through his family tree; that is, familial DNA searches. It did not matter that DeAngelo was not in any database because a distant relative of his was. The suspect pool was eventually narrowed down to a single family, then finally down to a single person: Joseph James DeAngelo. And the books were closed on another cold case file.

Amen.

CHAPTER SIX

Bob Hartz and Mary Ann Price were busy in the kitchen when Josh and Claire Billings stepped from their vehicle and moved promptly toward the entrance of the Iron Skillet Restaurant in Mattituck. The relatively mild days of January enjoyed by most everyone were drawing to a close. It suddenly turned cold and windy with a wind-chill factor plummeting temperatures down into the teens, reminding folks that it was still winter. Josh opened the front door for Claire, and Bob's cat brushed passed their legs.

"You won't be out there long," Claire called after Kitty.

Bob heard the front door open and quickly close. He stepped from the kitchen and greeted Josh and Claire. "You're early," the chef said pleasantly, wiping his hands on a dish towel then taking the couple's cold hands into his. "Frigging cold out there, no?"

"Frigging cold out there, yes," Josh answered assuredly, setting down a sheathed bottle of wine upon their table, about to help Claire off with her coat.

"I think I'll keep this on till I warm up a bit, thank you," she insisted.

Bob politely pulled the chair out for Claire, and Josh removed the bottle from its BYOB neoprene sleeve before removing his coat. Bob eyed the bottle approvingly, reaching into a sideboard for two

22

glasses. "That's a very nice selection. A Josh Cellars Cabernet Sauvignon for Josh. How appropriate."

"It's a 2015 vintage. Gift from a client."

"We were on a cruise with Holland America when first introduced to this nice wine," Claire explained.

"I went on and on about the wine when we returned home. Told everyone."

"I remember," Bob said through a broad smile.

"Next thing you know, I received a whole case at Christmastime."

"Pays to advertise, Josh," Bob put forth earnestly.

"Indeed," Josh agreed, uncorking the bottle then pouring two glasses for Claire and himself. "Grab a glass and join us," Josh offered.

"No, I've got to cook for you two. You know me. I'll join you later with my glass of Scotch. Josh, you preordered the stuffed mushrooms and the half rack of Australian lamb, roast potatoes Anna, and the vegetable tonight is broccoli."

"Sounds great."

"And what are you going to have tonight, Claire? But before you answer, I just made a hearty beef vegetable soup, cutting up and adding the end pieces from a prime New York strip steak that will positively melt in your mouth."

Claire smiled and nodded her head. "The soup and the Bolognese, please."

"Great. Josh, I know you're going to share a stuffed mushroom appetizer with Claire. Any soup for you?"

"Sure. The crab bisque."

"Excellent, excellent."

Bob, Josh and Claire chatted for a while. Claire removed her coat. The coziness and charm of the small restaurant was suddenly interrupted by the sound of sirens and flashing lights coming from the intersection of Love Lane and Pike Street, across from the Mattituck railroad station. Claire went over to a window as Josh folded her coat on the back of her chair.

"What's going on out there?" Josh asked.

"Don't know. Too dark out there, now. Can't really see anything except a zillion blinding lights."

In the distance, more sirens sounded, the cacophony steadily growing closer and closer.

"Must be a pretty bad accident," Bob offered in explanation.

"We didn't hear a crash or anything since we've been sitting here," Claire said, "and we didn't see anything driving here either."

"Probably the wind out of the north. She's been cranking. It would drown out the sound of a cannon."

"But not the ear-piercing sound of those sirens. Anyhow, I think your mushrooms are ready. I'll be but a second."

Claire returned to the table. "Famished."

"Good. You'll enjoy your meal," Josh said.

"I'd enjoy Bob and Mary Ann's cooking if I were replete," Claire kidded.

"What about my cooking?"

"You'll do in a pinch."

"You have complaints?"

"Only that we'd be eating steak eight days a week if I didn't say anything."

"That's not true. Look, tonight I'm having lamb, am I not?"

"Meat, meat, meat, and more meat. You know you're not exactly eating healthy. True?"

"And look at you. You practically salivated when Bob described the prime pieces of beef that he was putting in your barley soup."

"Beef *vegetable* barley soup," she emphasized, "with only *pieces* of beef," she stressed.

"Oh, not to mention Bolognese sauce that's made with *beef*, too, dear."

"Mere *morsels* of ground up chopped meat over pasta, *dear*. Not a solid slab of twelve-ounce marbled strip steak or half a rack of lamb that you'll be having tonight. And what about when you're home alone cooking in the kitchen, sweetheart. Prime bone-in rib eye smothered with gravy and mash potatoes drenched with butter. A heart attack waiting to happen. Moderation is the key, which you know nothing about."

The couple sat in silence and sipped their wine until Bob returned several minutes later with their mushroom appetizer for shares.

"They look great," Josh declared.

"Of course, they're great," Bob said immodestly. "You know they're great. How many times have you had them? Almost every time you two are here. That's how many."

Claire smiled.

"Enjoy. Your soups will be out shortly." Bob looked toward one of the windows. "Things finally quieted down out there?"

"Seem to be."

"There's certainly something going on out there, though," Claire said solemnly. "Those lights are like searching everywhere behind the hedges across the way."

"Yeah, both drivers are probably looking for their hubcaps or a missing fender. Car crash, I'm telling you."

Claire shook her head rather doubtfully. "It's lit up over there like a light show. Something is going on."

Bob peered out a window then walked over and opened the door to let the cat back inside. He held the door ajar as Kitty scurried passed the tables. Bob hesitated but for a second, anent the cold if not his curiosity, then abruptly closed the door. "You know, I think you're right, Claire. Something strange is going on over there."

Josh leaned back and glanced over his shoulder, staring out a side window for a better view. "Looks like they're closing the street, cordoning off the area with those wooden barriers at the intersection."

CHAPTER SEVEN

Homicide Detectives Brenden Reilly and Mike D'Angelo stood before the gruesome crime scene. Janet Johnsen's body, or what was left of it, was badly mutilated. She lay beside the railroad tracks, 50 feet east of the Mattituck train station, across from The Broken Down Valise bar on Pike Street.

"She's married to a transit cop," one of the officers explained. "Jeffrey Johnsen; that's s·e·n."

"He know yet?"

"Don't know. Not at home. We got a call into his Unit Shop, Manhattan."

"Excuse us a moment," D'Angelo said to the officer.

"Sure." The cop stepped away and headed toward a trio of other uniformed officers.

Brenden put away his notes, and his partner took him aside. "I got this guy figured to a degree," Mike asserted.

"The rookie officer?" Brenden kidded.

"Our fucking nutcase. He grabs this Johnsen woman, who happens to be married to a cop. A transit cop but a cop still trained like any of us. We'll find out she's no Charlotte Endicott, meaning meek and mild-mannered like all her neighbors, friends and family said about her. But this one. This one was a fighter," Mike affirmed, pointing to the victim's blanketed body. "I'll bet she got to him. I'll bet she knew she was going to die and really pissed him off. Think about it."

Brenden was thinking.

Mike went on. "The Wilbur Gilmore guy they found in Medford. A nice nerdy accountant type. Cut up, too, but not like this. Even less so with the Endicott woman because she was timid and probably did everything he asked. Went easy on her and simply cut off her earlobes before snapping her neck. But this one," Mike jabbed a thumb toward the shrouded body, "this one he carved up like a Thanksgiving turkey."

"Could be he's just escalating, getting more violent as he moves ahead."

Mike was shaking his head. "Not like this. The degree of torture he inflicts before he wastes them is in line with their personalities, I'm telling you. You'll see. This is over the top because she did not do what he asked her to do. The other two did exactly what they were told, I'll bet. And according to Sheffield, he fed them well. They had full stomachs, although he can't say with certainty exactly what they had to eat. Food and sauce either on their faces, on their clothing, or in their hair. They probably weren't even aware that a madman was on the prowl. Didn't hit the newspapers like it will now, a bit too late," Mike rambled on. "But with a husband as a cop, transit or not, Janet Johnsen probably knew the whole nine yards. Jeff probably told her stories that we know never made the headlines. And now that we have a new police commissioner, the focus is fully on Gilgo and *those* other victims."

"I know you think this guy is somehow a part of all that, either working as a lone wolf or perhaps working in concert like you said. But this is years later, Mike. I will give you though, that I feel we have a serial on our hands."

"Look, what I know for sure is what you know, and that is, he's not going to stop until we stop him in his tracks. Tracks. Get it, partner?" Mike punned, pointing to the railroad tracks beside which Janet Johnsen's mutilated covered body lie.

Brenden nodded gravely. "Got it."

At 5 p.m., Transit Officer Jeffery Johnsen changed out of his uniform and left the New York City Transit Bureau District building at 1 Central Park West. He headed straight for the subway and boarded the No. 1 train that took him to Penn Station. From there he rode the Long Island Railroad, changing at Ronkonkoma, traveling east toward his home in Mattituck. The train lumbered along until it reached Yaphank, where it was announced that there was difficulty getting into Mattituck Station because of an accident, but that busses would be waiting at the next stop, Riverhead, to transport riders to Mattituck, Southold, and on out east to Greenport. Everyone was assured that service would not be interrupted.

When the train pulled into Riverhead Station, there were no busses waiting. A second announcement said to expect delays of up to forty minutes, but that everyone could remain aboard until the busses arrived. The train wasn't going anywhere. "Sorry for any inconvenience," the conductor concluded.

A forty-minute delay turned out to be an hour and a quarter. Jeff was pissed. He didn't bother calling his wife to tell her he'd be late because he knew she was out shopping and then having dinner with her mother that evening. "Fucking busses," he complained bitterly. He hated the noise and noxious order of those outdated 21-year-old city diesel busses and was glad that he had been assigned to the subway system and the training of new recruits. The Transit Authority had declared that it would convert its entire fleet to fully electric busses by the year 2040. Jeff had smiled at that pronouncement some time ago. By 2040 he'd either be retired or dead, hopefully the former, he had told his boss.

Well at least the busses' windows were all closed this time of year, following the sudden drop in temperature, he mused. Then again, there was always some asshole who would open a window wide, if not for the sheer purpose of pissing people off. Jeff loved to encounter such troublesome creeps. He had a secret weapon—his wife, Janet. He smiled at the recollection of one particular incident.

"Hey, asshole," Jeff had entreated one such soul many a year ago as the temperature along with the wind-chill factor factored out to three degrees below zero in a 50-mile-an-hour moving bus. But the man simply closed his eyes and smiled broadly.

Jeff returned to his seat and smiled broadly, too.

Janet Johnsen had gotten up from her seat and immediately confronted the man. "Shut that fucking window, now, clown."

The man opened one eye and grinned, giving Janet the finger.

In a flash, Janet had broken the man's finger followed by two quick jabs to his nose. If it were not for the blood streaming down his face and onto his clothing, it seemed as though the man was sleeping peacefully. Janet closed the window then calmly returned to her seat. No one on the bus had uttered a single word.

When Jeff finally reached the Mattituck station by bus, he immediately knew that something was terribly wrong. Floodlights and flashlights filled the landscape, beaming and streaming everywhere, searching, presumably searching for evidence, for a shroud covering a body told the tale. Several official vehicles still lined Love Lane. Had it been a fatal vehicular accident, the body surely would have been removed from the time of the conductor's announcement that there would be a delay.

Jeff noted that a forensic team in hooded white coveralls was finishing up when his cell phone sounded. It was the Metropolitan Transit Authority. *Fuck,* he thought. *Work. Gotta be kidding. Assholes probably have no idea I've been riding the rails for hours . . . or maybe they do . . . shit.* Jeff answered the call. "Johnsen."

"Been trying to reach you, Jeff."

"No signal would be my guess," *asshole*, he wanted to add. "Been on a fucking subway, train, and bus for hours tryin' to get home. There's been a situation here in Mattituck—"

"That's why I'm calling. Pete got a call from Sal who said they want you to call Suffolk County P.D. headquarters, Yaphank, ASAP. Ask for Detective Reilly or D'Angelo, and give them your name. If they're not there, the desk sergeant will put you through to one of them. Got all that?"

"What's going on, Freddie?"

"Don't know. All I know is that they're setting up a staging area and an extensive inner and outer perimeter: Route 25 into Main Road, Love Lane, Pike Street, Westphalia Road, Sound Avenue, and —"

"And they probably want me to do overtime because I live out here. Fine."

"Probably something like that."

"Gotta go, Fred." Jeff folded his phone and walked toward the station.

"Hey! You can't be here; can't you see—"

Jeff removed his wallet and showed his badge, continuing toward the uniformed officer. "I was told to contact Detectives Reilly or D'Angelo. Either of them here?"

"Who told you?" the officer snapped.

"Your mother," Jeff Johnsen answered flatly.

"I'll ask you again."

"Came from headquarters, Yaphank."

"Your name."

"Jeff Johnsen, s·e·n," Jeff spelled out.

"You wait right there." The officer marched off in the direction of several suits, relaying the information. Four of the men suddenly huddled, looking over the shoulder of the uniformed officer, staring in Jeff's direction. One suit pulled out his cell phone and called Detective Reilly.

Jeff still figured that it was some assignment they were handing him because of the proximity to his Mattituck home and manpower needed to control the perimeters, pedestrian traffic, or whatever.

Seconds later, a tall, thin figure with dark brown hair headed straight toward Jeff. The homicide detective's face was taut and fraught with pure frustration. In that instant, Jeff knew. He turned abruptly away and ran full-bore in a given direction, directly toward where he had seen the shroud covering the victim. He absolutely knew.

Jeff was sent to the ground in a nanosecond and about to be handcuffed.

Brenden caught up and waved the others away. "Let him go!" The detective reached down and pulled Jeff to his feet, taking the man firmly into his arms. Jeff struggled fiercely to free himself. "You don't want to see her, Jeff. Trust me, please. You do not want to see her. Not now." *Not ever,* he truly wanted to add.

CHAPTER EIGHT

"Oh, you missed a fantastic meal," the blond bushy-haired man told his guest. "I had a young woman sitting right there where you are who gave me nothing but trouble. Absolutely nothing but trouble. I asked her to pitch in, but she wouldn't. She made a mockery of the meal I was preparing. I gave her chance after chance, but she would not cooperate in the least. Finally, I had to take matters into my own hands; my own two hands. A nine-and-a-quarter-inch folding knife with a four-inch blade in each. It's nice that I'm ambidextrous, Veronica. Makes the job go twice as fast. Finished with her in half the time.

"I had picked Janet Johnsen up in Mattituck after she went shopping for her mother. I mean literally picked her up and carried her then drove her here. She was to have dinner with her mother later that evening, so I thought to myself, maybe she was being obstinate about helping me or eating anything because she believed she was somehow going to keep her dinner date with dear ol' mom. That was not to be her destiny—not then or ever. Please tell me you're not going to be any trouble and that you'll do exactly what you're told. Tell me."

Veronica Severini nodded her head rapidly up and down as if it were a rubber ball attached to a short elastic string pounding upon a paddle. "I'll do any– anything you say," she stuttered. "Anything, just pl-please don't hurt me. Please."

"Now, that's just what I want to hear you say," the man said with a satisfying smile. "So just relax. You and I are going to have a fantastic meal together. You'll love the way I cook. I promise."

It was not the kind of promise Veronica wanted to hear. "Pl-please don't hurt me," she repeated.

"Just relax. What we are going to have tonight, Veronica, will be a combination Classic Italian/French lasagna that's made with a béchamel sauce instead of ricotta cheese, and a traditional ragù Bolognese sauce instead of your ordinary red, which, by the way, your dad likes to call gravy."

Veronica lifted her head and raised her eyebrows in surprise. *He knows my dad. But how?* she wondered. *How?*

"A French red sauce is known as one of your five mother sauces. Not *your* mother's sauce, Veronica," the man emphasized and grinned. "Therefore, with just this one dish you'll be learning two of the five mother sauces.

"The combination is outstanding," the man went on. "But first a tiny bit of history. Ragù was created in the 18th century by a man named Alberto Alvisi, a cook to the Cardinal of Imola, a city southeast of Bologna, Italy. Imola is well known for its tile. In short order, ragù Bolognese became known as the Cardinal's ragù. Do you see how neatly everything fits together, Veronica?"

Veronica nodded vigorously.

"Oh, speaking of Imola tile, did you happen to notice the soft colors I chose for the walls and backsplash behind the kitchen sink, Veronica? It's a combination of gray and beige called greige. Isn't that clever? I did all the work myself. No comment?"

"Yes, it's beautiful."

"And behind these walls and in the ceiling are fiberglass insulation batts for superior soundproofing quality, acoustic tiles over that, and laminate flooring upstairs covered with thick carpeting for sound absorption. And when you consider the distance from the main road to the house, no one could hear a sound coming from down here. I did all that by myself, too.

"Anyway, I tried to explain to my ungrateful guest the origin and preparation of certain dishes and how they differ from today, but she wasn't the least bit interested. She threw a tantrum along with a plate of hot pasta with her right hand halfway across the room. That's why I had secured her left hand to the arm of the chair you're sitting in. I had anticipated such behavior. Had she heaved her dish as a southpaw, she surely would have hit the far wall. As it was, I still had a mess to clean. It wasn't too bad though as you'll note the fire-hose hookup I have in the corner. I can wash away tomato or blood stains on the walls in a jiff, just so long as I don't let them dry; otherwise, it's scrub and rub-a-dub-dub. Know what I mean?"

"Yes."

"I imagine you'd like to eat your lasagna with both hands tonight. Yes?"

"Yes."

"Good. You do seem well behaved."

"I am. I won't cause you any trouble at all. I swear."

"I believe you, Veronica."

"How do you know my father?"

"How do I know your father?" the man recited rhetorically. "Let's just say that you know a lot more about people by observing them rather than interacting with them. The connection between your father and me would definitely have to be food. I'm sure you know that he fancies himself a wizard around a grill. Yes?"

"Yes."

"He's really not too bad a cook. I mean he's no pitmaster like Aaron Franklin or Myron Mixon, mind you, but he does know his barbecue when it comes to steaks and chops, although I did watch him butcher a brisket. Oh, I don't mean butcher in the sense of slaughtering," the man declared then absolutely roared with laughter. "I mean he bungled that brisket from the very start, he did. Why do you look so confused? Ah, I bet you don't even know the names Aaron Franklin or Myron Mixon. They're the world's finest pitmasters, Veronica."

"My father never made a brisket in his life. You must have the wrong person."

"Is that so?"

"I don't know the two men you're talking about, but my father never made brisket," she repeated with assurance.

"Are you sure?"

Veronica nodded nervously, instinctively realizing that she should not be addressing anything negative, which could set him off. "I mean I could be wrong," she quickly added.

"Well let me inform you that you are wrong. But tell me why you first seemed so certain."

Veronica hesitated.

"Tell me," he snapped.

"My father only buys expensive cuts of meat for our family. A brisket is an inexpensive cut of meat. That's why I said that. But like I said, I could be mistaken."

"And I'm about to tell you why you're very, very wrong, all right?"

Veronica said nothing.

"First off, I agree that your father only buys expensive cuts of meat for your family. Secondly, he buys *in*expensive cuts of meat," he emphasized, "when he visits his girlfriend in Shirley, brisket being one of them. He even bought and assembled the grill that he gave her as a gift last April on Easter Sunday. Your mother thought he was working out of town when he was actually gallivanting about town with his gal. That's when he botched the brisket by burning it."

Through her fear, Veronica was doing a slow burn. The things the man was saying seemed to fit. Her father did indeed do a disappearing act around most holidays, claiming that he was working out-of-town construction jobs.

"Well, they both thought that was terribly funny then made cheeseburgers on the grill. At first, I didn't know what your dad's attraction to the Mastic/Shirley area was as it has a very high crime rate. But then I followed him from a distance one evening. That's when she stepped out onto the deck of her modest beachfront home in Shirley. I could see the attraction. Quite a looker she is, she is."

Veronica began to cry.

"Oh, don't take it to heart. It's not like he lavishes her with gifts and spends most of his time with her. Just once in a while around the holidays. Otherwise, he's pretty much a family man. You can't say he's deprived you or your mother. Nice home. Nice cars. Nice clothing. Good schools. Oh, and good food," the man added for good measure, wearing a great big smile.

"So, are we ready to begin our sauces? You'll be attending to the béchamel, and I'll be working with a Bolognese sauce. I've already set out all the ingredients we'll need for both. The San Marzano tomatoes that are shipped here in the United States from Italy are ninety-five percent bogus. All kinds of games are played with the labeling. Authentic San Marzano tomatoes are labeled POMODORO S.MARZANO DELL'AGRO SARNESE-NOCERINO. See? You look for *that* labeling." The man held up a can. "The D.O.P. stands for *Denominazione di Origine controllata*, meaning Protected Designation of Origin. Truly grown and packed in the Valle de Sarno region of Italy. They're the real deal.

"Next, we have equal amounts of ground beef, pork, and veal; aromatic vegetables of onions, carrots, and celery, from which I already made a mirepoix/brown sauce well ahead of time. Takes hours to prepare. It's a killer, Veronica. So, most of the laborious work is already done. Let's see: olive oil, butter and flour, whole milk, nutmeg, salt and pepper, lasagna noodles of course. Forget about the no-boil kind. And I prefer the kind with those curly, wavy edges. See?" The man held up an open package. "The cheeses generally used are, of course, regular mozzarella for layering and Parmesan for finishing off. However, I use Parmigiano-Reggia no in lieu of cheese labeled just Parmesan. Parmesan is an imitation and lacks flavor. And for a truly creamy mozzarella cheese, I prefer burrata. Being that you're half Italian, you probably know some of these things. Yes?"

Veronica nodded a yes.

"So, I think we're good to go. You ready?"

Veronica nodded another yes.

"Good. What I'm going to do is unstrap you from the chair and have you walk over to the stove. You'll start by melting a stick of butter in that saucepan over a very low flame then mixing in twice the amount of flour, just a little bit at a time. The measurements of flour and butter actually go by weight, but our two-to-one ratio equals approximately the same. You'll keep stirring till there are no lumps, working from a rather pasty mix until it becomes nice and smooth and silky. The trick is not to burn the floury butter. You'll slowly add hot milk while mixing, whisking away all the lumps. But not to worry. You'll have me close at hand, looking over your shoulder." The bushy-haired man smiled broadly, sticking his meaty hands deep within the pockets of his khaki cargo pants.

CHAPTER NINE

After a wonderful dinner that evening at the Iron Skillet Restaurant in Mattituck, Josh and Claire Billings said their good nights to Bob and Mary Ann and headed briskly straight ahead through the palpable cold to the parking lot. Josh pressed the remote, opened and held the passenger door for Claire. Claire simply shook her head.

"What's the matter?"

"You think you're driving after what you had to drink?"

"I had a couple of glasses of wine."

"Wrong. You practically drank the whole bottle. I had half a glass."

"Did you see what I had to eat? It's practically all absorbed."

"Yeah, absorbed into your bloodstream."

"Did you know, Ms. Smarty Pants, that lamb, which as you know is what I had tonight, reduces the peak blood alcohol concentration in your body by fifty percent?"

"Yeah, relative to what's consumed on an empty stomach, Mister- Know-It-All."

"We've been sitting in there for almost two hours. I'm fine."

"You're not fine. You're slurring your words."

"I'm not slurring my words. I'm shivering."

"Are we going to stand out here in the freezing cold arguing about this? Just give me the keys."

Josh gave her the keys. "I suggest you make a right out of here and take Sound Avenue. I don't think you're going to get through that police barricade and traffic mess."

A series of forensic light sources still flooded the area in and around Love Lane and Pike Street, though the activity was considerably quieter than earlier in the evening.

As Claire headed north, a police officer suddenly stopped her at a vehicle checkpoint, signaling for the SUV to pull over to the right. Claire drove to the shoulder, sending down her window.

"Where are you headed, ma'am?"

"Home. What's going on, Officer?"

The police officer did not ask Claire for her driver's license, nor did he bother to check the windshield for an expired inspection or registration. "And where is home?" he asked pleasantly, glancing around the interior of the vehicle then fixing his eyes on Josh.

"Riverhead," the couple answered simultaneously.

"Where are you coming from?"

"We just had dinner back there at the Iron Skillet, around the corner," Josh answered soberly.

"May I ask how long you were dining at that restaurant?"

"Almost two hours. Why?" Claire pressed.

"So that would make it around 4:30 when you arrived."

"That's right. And then moments later we heard all this commotion. Sirens. Lights. Lots of activity. Was there a bad accident, I mean to take this long?"

"May I have your names, a phone number where you can be reached, and home address, assuming you two are together?" the cop asked and smiled congenially.

"Josh and Claire Billings," Josh snapped, reaching across Claire and handing the officer a business card. "Why do want our names, phone number, and address?" he questioned impatiently. Josh received a nudge from Claire from across the seat. "You could have asked for her license and registration. Wouldn't that have been proper protocol?" Josh received something more along the lines of a prominent poke from Claire.

"Well, I certainly could have had there been some sort of infraction. But what I'm really interested in at this point is the fact that the two of you wound up in the area about the same time that 'all this commotion' started. I'm going to pass along this information, and I'm sure detectives may want to speak with you about this evening."

"Detectives?" Josh stammered.

"Homicide detectives, Mr. Billings. Are the two of you going to be available later this evening or sometime early tomorrow?"

"We'll be home," Josh answered quietly.

"Great. One more thing. Had you been behind the wheel tonight, Mr. Billings, I'd have asked you to step out of the car. Know what I mean? It's good you have a designated driver." The officer smiled and winked at Claire. "Safe home, folks."

"Good evening, Officer," Claire said politely. "We'll be home," she said, repeating Josh's assurance, sending her window up then driving slowly past the roadblock where several other uniformed officers milled about. One of them waved an oncoming vehicle ahead.

Josh said nothing until they were a good distance away. "Fucking audacity. Fucking cavalier attitude of that cop. A murder in Mattituck, and he's all smiley, smiley. I knew it had to be something big. Car accident my ass is what Bob had believed. Multiple official vehicles; a dozen or so law enforcement personnel in uniforms and suits, others in white hooded coveralls, and lights that would light up MetLife Stadium."

"It's a damn good thing you weren't driving," Claire said with certain satisfaction.

"We're about to be questioned as part of a murder investigation, and you're going on about my driving."

"I was going on about your drinking."

"Well, when we get home, I'm going straight to bed. I'm not waiting up to answer a bunch of questions by detectives. If they do call or come tonight, you tell them tomorrow's another day. We didn't see anything that could help them solve a murder, for Christ's sake."

"Don't be so sure," Claire said in a quiet tone that surprised her in that very moment.

"What?"

"You had your eyes on the road when we came here. I caught something out of the corner of my eye when you drove by Love Lane and that street that's across from the railroad station."

"And what did you see?"

"A man in an SUV, like ours, pulling something out of the back."

"And you're just bringing this up now."

"I just thought of it now."

"Not during the two hours we were at the restaurant?"

"We were all thinking a horrific car accident. Not a murder."

"I think your imagination is running away with you."

"I didn't imagine what I just told you."

"A man in an SUV dumping something?"

"No. Pulling something out of the back."

"Pulling what?"

"I don't know."

"Let me tell you something that I do know. A man is not going to dump a body by a train station—"

"In back of the station."

"A man is not going to dump a body in back of a train station in broad daylight."

"It was getting dark, remember?"

"Let me tell you what probably happened. The guy you likely saw was dumping trash that he didn't want to bother carting off to the town dump. Out here, residents have to cart even their own household garbage and pay a per load fee. Otherwise they can hire a private garbage company serving the area. Point being is that one way or another, people out this way have to pay. Not like in Riverhead where our trash and household garbage are picked up curbside."

"Which we pay for in our taxes, dear."

"So, I don't believe it was a body being pulled or dumped or whatever the hell you think you saw."

"I didn't say it was a body, Josh."

"You're implying that it was."

"No, you're inferring."

"Boy, you do love to argue. Ever since we sat down for dinner you've been looking for an argument."

"Not up until your third glass of wine."

"You don't quit, do you?"

"Actually, I didn't say a word until you insisted on driving

40

home."

"No, just those dagger eyes you kept messaging from the middle of the meal through coffee and dessert."

"Glad you were paying attention. Maybe the message will sink in."

"You know they're going to ask you a million questions like 'Can you describe the vehicle: make, model, and/or color?'"

"It was dark."

"'Can you describe the man?'"

"It was dark, Josh," she repeated.

"'Can you tell us what he was wearing?'" Josh pressed as though he were the investigator.

"Yes."

Josh turned his head abruptly. "You serious?"

"Yes."

"Wearing what?"

"Cargo pants."

"Cargo pants?"

"Yes."

"Anything else?

"Is this a dress rehearsal, dear?"

"Facial features."

"Thin mustache and a harelip," she teased.

"Be serious."

"It was dark, I keep reminding you. That's all I noticed."

"If you're smart, you tell them you didn't see shit."

"What if he's one of them?"

"One of them what?"

"A serial killer, like the one who police kept saying was not necessarily a serial killer except for the fact that ten bodies turned up along Ocean Parkway in Gilgo Beach, and Shannan Gilbert's body turned up in Oak Beach, not to mention the remains of three bodies found in Manorville. And now, years later, we have three new bodies turn up in Suffolk County. One in Medford, one in Riverhead, and now a third body turns up in Mattituck—all by railroad tracks."

"The police don't want people to panic, Claire. That's why they downplay these things till they're sure."

"Yeah, downplay. Like the police downplayed those missing

persons as runaways or who intentionally chose to go off the grid to conceal their sex trade activities. That is, until a decade later the police found their bodies or scattered remains."

"But the women *were* involved in the sex trade, Claire. Escorts. Advertising their services on Craigslist or wherever. So, I can see why the police initially downplayed the serial-killer angle."

"Oh, really? And then there's the speculation by police brass arguing over whether there's one or two serial killers on the loose. And now we got three more bodies all found by railroad tracks?"

"First off, the man back in Medford was male."

"Men usually are male," Claire mocked playfully.

Josh ignored her gibe. "Secondly, the Gilgo Beach murders police believe were separate and apart from the woman they found years later at Oak Beach."

"Shannan Gilbert. You're making my case."

"But the police say that Shannan Gilbert was *not* the victim of foul play, that she probably drowned."

"That's bullshit."

"Maybe, maybe not."

"Shannan Gilbert's family hired that famed forensic pathologist, you know, Michael Baden, to perform an independent autopsy on Shannan. And what did he come away with? The fact that the woman's broken hyoid bone in her throat is consistent with strangulation. That's what. But the initial autopsy performed by the Suffolk County medical examiner determined that the cause of Shannan's death was undetermined. Don't you find that a bit more than suspicious?"

"Well, the police still speculate that she wandered off in the marshy area of Oak Beach and drowned."

"Yet Baden determined that there was no evidence of illegal drugs or drowning. Can't you see that this whole thing smells of a cover-up by the police?"

"Then why are you so anxious to speak to the police if you suspect them of underhandedness?"

"Look, I didn't ask to speak to the police. They want to speak to us, Josh, because we were dining in the area at the time of the crime."

"But you can't wait to tell them what you saw or what you think you saw. I don't get it. If you feel they're concealing something, why involve yourself? Why involve us?"

"Because there's a new team in town; the FBI. They're taking over the investigation of all these murders. If I can help in any way, I will. And just for the record, what I saw is what I saw, not what I *think* I saw. Got it?"

CHAPTER TEN

At 6:45 a.m. the following morning, Detectives Brenden Reilly and Mike D'Angelo drove into the driveway of the Billings residence on Riverside Drive in Riverhead. The unmarked beige Ford Taurus sat with its motor running for a good five minutes before Brenden cut the engine and the two men stepped from the four-door sedan.

"Kinda early, no?" Brenden said.

"Kinda early, yes."

"Maybe we should call first."

"They're up. Or at least one of them is. I saw movement in an upstairs window."

"Maybe they'll offer us coffee."

"I could certainly use a second caffeine fix. I'm beat."

"Been a long night, partner."

The pair walked up to the front door and rang the bell.

A moment later, Claire Billings opened the door. "Yes?" she asked, although she knew the answer as to who the men were standing before her on the front stoop.

Brenden held out his badge. "Detective Reilly, and this is my partner Detective D'Angelo. May we come in?"

Josh Billings peered above Claire's shoulder. "You tell them to show you each a badge and a second piece of identification. Anyone can flash a badge."

Claire turned to face her husband. "Why don't you tell them, dear." Claire stepped away from the door and walked into the living room.

Brenden smiled at Josh Billings. Mike did not. Both men obliged Josh's request.

"May we come in now, Mr. Billings?" Brenden asked politely.

Josh stepped away from the door, and the two men entered the home.

"An officer said that you might be calling. I thought you'd call first before coming," Josh stated flatly, his jaw muscles locked tight as he finished his sentence.

"Sorry for the inconvenience," Brenden said, taking in his surroundings. "Nice home." He directed both the apology and compliment at Claire.

"Please have a seat," Claire invited, pointing toward the sofa. "Would you gentlemen like a cup of coffee? If you don't mind my saying so, you both look like you need a cup of *strong* coffee—and maybe a good night's rest."

The detectives smiled at one another and then at Claire. "I'd love a cup of coffee, Mrs. Billings," Brenden said appreciatively. "It's been a long night."

"I can well imagine. Detective D'Angelo, coffee?"

"Yes, ma'am."

"Please call me Claire. And you can call my husband Grumpy."

Both detectives grinned.

"How do you fellows take your coffee? We have milk, half and half, and cream."

"Black, thank you," Brenden said.

"Same."

"Honey, please put up a pot of coffee for us," Claire instructed. "Oh, and use the big ten-cup pot. I think we're all going to be here for a while."

Brenden and Mike glanced surprisingly at one another, if not for the fact of ordering her husband around, but for her certainty that they would be sitting for a spell.

Josh stepped abruptly from the room.

"Josh does virtually all the cooking around here," she explained.

"I do most of the cleaning up. Although I will say he's not a sloppy cook. He does clean up after himself pretty much as he's working, but at the end there's always a bit of a mess. I don't mind though. I consider myself lucky. He does all the food shopping, too. He wouldn't dare let me pick out meat or vegetables," she babbled on.

Brenden politely covered his mouth and yawned. "Excuse me. It's been a long night," he repeated.

"We didn't get much sleep either. I know about the man in Medford who was murdered, and of course the young woman here in Riverhead. And now this."

Brenden took out a pad and looked down at his notes. "The officer you spoke to last night told us that you and your husband were dining at the Iron Skillet Restaurant in Mattituck from around 4:30 till almost 6:30."

"That's right."

"That's about the time you heard 'all the commotion,'?" he questioned, reciting Claire's words verbatim from last evening.

"Yes, that's right."

"You drove directly from here to Mattituck, last night? Is that correct?"

"Yes. I mean no. Josh drove. I drove back home after we left the restaurant."

"What route did you take to the Iron Skillet, Mrs. Billings?"

"Claire," Claire said with a bright smile.

"Claire. How did you and Mr. Billings travel to get to the Iron Skillet from Riverhead? Did you take Sound Avenue; that is, the North Road then make a right onto Love Lane? Or did you take Route 25—Main Road—making a left onto Love Lane?"

"The latter. We took Route 25, the Main Road, making a left onto Love Lane."

"So, you crossed the railroad tracks."

"Yes."

"Did you or your husband see or hear anything strange at that time, other than the 'commotion' that you later heard while dining at the restaurant?"

Claire hesitated before answering. "Detective Reilly. I want you and Detective D'Angelo to understand that it did not register with me at the time, but when Josh and I were stopped by that officer last night, and we learned that the incident was a murder and not a fatal car accident, I suddenly recalled something as we were driving home that I hadn't realized before." Claire hesitated anew.

"And that was?" Brenden asked, leaning forward in his seat.

"I saw something."

"Go on, please."

"I saw a man, or at least I thought it was a man, pull something out of the back of a vehicle to the far right of the railroad tracks at the Mattituck train station."

"What did he pull?"

Claire shook her head. "It was getting dark. I'm really not sure. Like maybe a carpet, all rolled up."

"Can you describe the person?"

Claire shook her head.

"Tall or short?"

"Again, it was getting dark, so it was really hard to tell. Maybe average height."

"Can you tell us *anything* else about this individual?"

Claire nodded in the affirmative. "I can tell you that the person was wearing cargo pants."

"Cargo pants?"

"Yes, cargo pants."

Detective Brenden Reilly tested the woman's veracity with his next question. "Were the cargo pants khaki colored or another color?" Brenden questioned." For if Claire had picked a specific color or shade with certainty, her attention to detail would negate the fact that it was 'getting dark' as she had twice maintained.

"I'm sorry, Detective, but once again, it was turning dark. I could only make out the bulging pockets. That's how I knew that they were cargo pants."

"Bulging pockets?"

"Yes. You know, bulky."

"You mean like they were filled or stuffed with something."

"Exactly."

Brenden made a notation. "Were the pockets just below the waist, or were they further down along the legs?"

"Definitely down along the sides of the legs."

"You could see that the pockets were bulging out from both sides of the legs?"

"Yes."

"Was this person facing in your direction, or turned away from you?"

"After he pulled something out of the back of the vehicle, he faced away. That's when I could see the bulging pockets."

"So, you obviously couldn't see his face at that point. What about at any other point?"

Claire shook her head. "No."

Brenden returned to the item being pulled from the vehicle. "What about what he pulled from the rear of the vehicle in terms of size or shape?"

"Like I said, it was like a rolled-up carpet. Maybe six or seven or so feet long. I'm really not sure."

"Can you tell us anything about the vehicle—make, model, color?"

"The only thing I can tell you is that it was definitely an SUV," Claire said with certainty, nodding her head assuredly.

"How do you know for sure?"

"Well, for one thing, we drive one. Number two, I could tell by the shape. It wasn't a van or truck where you'd drop or swing aside a tailgate. The hatch was open, angled up in the air, outlined against the sky. It was unmistakably an SUV."

"Compact, midsize, full-size SUV?"

"If I had to guess, I'd say midsize like ours. But I'm really not certain."

"Apart from the cargo pants, anything else about his clothing?"

Claire sat deep in concentration, slowly shaking her head from side to side. "That's all I can remember. It all happened so fast. Josh drove straight ahead on Love Lane toward the restaurant then crossed that street where the train station is. As we crossed the tracks, that's when I saw the man pulling something from the back of that vehicle. I'm sorry I can't be of more help."

Brendan smiled warmly. "Claire, you've been a big help. Believe me." The detective put away his notes and was making small talk while waiting for Josh to return from the kitchen with coffee.

"I have a question," Mike interjected.

"Yes, Detective D'Angelo?"

"Call me Mike," Mike uncharacteristically remarked.

Claire smiled. "Yes, Mike?"

"Getting back to that hour, Claire, you made it abundantly clear that it was turning dark. What you saw were shadowy silhouetted forms and shapes backdropped against a sky that was quickly losing light: the shape of those bulging pockets on a pair of cargo pants, the item the man was pulling from the back of the vehicle, the vehicle being an SUV. In other words, outlines, Claire. Can you close your eyes for a moment and focus on the outline of the man?"

Claire calmly closed her eyes.

"Good. Now, look at the top of his head. Is he wearing a hat, or can you see his hair? Short, long, wavy, anything at all?"

Claire still had her eyes closed. Tightly. The silky skin around them scrunched in concentration. "Not a hat exactly." Claire was shaking her head. "No. Not a hat; he's wearing a cap!" she exclaimed.

"What kind of a cap, Claire?"

"Like a ski cap, pulled down low over his ears."

"Keep your eyes closed, please. Focus in on the SUV and the man pulling something from the rear of that vehicle; the man's build: small, medium, large build?"

"Average build, I think, yet big across the shoulders. If that makes any sense. It's really hard to tell."

"Anything else you *see*?"

Claire concentrated fully, but nothing else came to mind. "No, sir."

"Mike," Mike reminded and smiled in satisfaction. "Open your eyes, Claire. You did well."

"I did, Mike," Claire said and knew. "I saw and see that dark cap pulled down over his ears for sure."

Detectives Brenden Reilly and Mike D'Angelo looked at one another then back at Claire. "You did extremely well," Brenden added as Mike got up and headed toward the kitchen where Josh Billings was setting cups and saucers upon a silver serving tray and pouring coffee.

"Here, let me get that," Mike offered.

"I got it. If you wouldn't mind pulling the plug on the pot."

Mike construed the comment to mean, 'I want you guys out of

here as soon as possible.' From the sour look on Josh's face, Mike felt sure that he was reading the man correctly.

Josh carried the tray into the living room, setting it down upon the coffee table in front of the sofa.

"No cake or muffins to put out for the detectives?" Claire asked her husband.

"All gone," Josh replied rather curtly.

Claire said nothing, lowering her head.

"We're fine with coffee," Brenden said appreciatively. "While you were busy in the kitchen, Mr. Billings, we had a nice chat with your wife."

"Yeah, I heard in part. Mr. Hypnotist, here, inducing his subject to respond to inane cryptic suggestions. Claire would see a hat on a cat if you told her you were looking for an animal instead of a person. She would see shit on a shingle if you told her to head on down the block then turn around and look back at our roof," Josh Billings added inanely with a sneer.

"Claire was very, very helpful. And although she clearly stated that you saw nothing, that your eyes were on the road as you traveled north on Love Lane, crossing the railroad tracks and turning into the restaurant, I'd still like to ask you a few questions. Would that be all right?" Brenden asked politely.

"Shoot."

Claire handed the detectives each a cup of coffee then did the same for Josh and herself.

Detective Brenden Reilly basically covered the same ground as he had with Claire Billings before asking Josh about work-related matters. After a second cup of coffee, Detective Mike D'Angelo studied the husband's reaction to certain questions along with the man's body language. If Brenden had been asked to describe Josh Billings' attitude in a single word throughout the entire interview, it would have to be BOREDOM, set in all caps, and certainly mixed in with a cup of annoyance.

Claire offered the detectives a third cup of coffee and tried to steer the conversation toward her theories on the serial murders when she saw an opening.

"All I have to do is plug this pot in for a few minutes, and it'll be ready."

The detectives smiled appreciatively but declined.

"We'll be on our way," Brenden said, shaking Claire's hand and handing her his card. "If you remember anything else, please call us."

The four were in the midst of exchanging civilities. Mike handed Josh his card, shook hands, and left with the feeling that had there been a proverbial smoking gun, Josh would have blanketed the evidence, poured himself the two remaining cups of coffee from the ten-cup pot, eaten whatever cake and muffins that were probably concealed somewhere within the kitchen, then return to his bed for the rest of the morning.

CHAPTER ELEVEN

Thomas Spota, ex-district attorney for Suffolk County, was still awaiting sentencing along with his chief aide, Christopher McPartland. The pair had been arrested and indicted by a federal grand jury. Paradoxically, McPartland had been Suffolk County's top anticorruption prosecutor.

Christopher Loeb, the victim of the cover-up, had been severely beaten and kicked while handcuffed and shackled to the floor at the 4th Precinct police station by then Suffolk County's Chief of Police James Burke. In the end, Loeb won a 1.5 million-dollar judgment.

Thomas Spota's protégé, James Burke, had been under the microscope since the early days when he was Spota's star witness in the 1979 murder of Johnny Pius, a 13-year-old boy from Smithtown. Four youths were charged with the murder: 14-year-old Michael Quartararo, his older brother 15-year-old Peter Quartararo, 17-year-old Robert Brensic, and 17-year-old Thomas Ryan. All the boys knew one another. They were charged with beating then sadistically stuffing stones into Johnny Pius' mouth and throat, resulting in traumatic asphyxia. Johnny's body had been found the following day under two logs and a heap of branches and leaves.

The story goes that the boys had stolen a motor-less minibike (valued at $5 dollars) and believed that Johnny Pius had witnessed the theft. In order to ensure his silence, the foursome killed Pius, each participating in the 13-year-old's death.

James Burke, 14 years old at the time and Spota's star witness at trial, gave testimony that Michael Quartararo had told him when asked why he (and the other three boys) had killed Johnny, Michael responded, "If you were drunk and stoned, and you didn't want to get caught, you would do the same thing." The conversation between Quartararo and Burke took place following John Pius' funeral mass. Burke also said that Michael Quartararo had told him "I didn't touch the kid. All I did was put the bike against the tree," referring to Pius' own bike. At trial, however, the prosecutor (Thomas Spota) had convinced the jury that the four youths had chased after and caught up to Johnny Pius, beating and killing the boy, believing that Pius would rat them out for stealing the minibike.

The trial and its aftermath were the beginning of Thomas Spota and James Burke's long-lasting friendship. There are those who speculate to this very day that their unusually close 42-year relationship was something more than just a father figure and protégé —a 24-year difference in age between them notwithstanding—nor the fact that Spota had groomed Burke from beat cop to the chief of police while protecting and covering for him in several scandalous situations along the way.

One incident involved a prostitute on crack cocaine having sex with Burke in his patrol car while he was an officer on duty. The event had triggered an internal investigation and charges were filed. Spota, a police union lawyer at the time, defended Burke and negotiated a plea deal, saving his protégé's career.

Years later, when Burke was appointed chief of police, he brought the wrath of God down on Patrick Cuff, the police official who had led the internal investigation against Burke. Pat Cuff was demoted four ranks and sent off to work in a property warehouse.

Earlier in time, Pat Cuff's 18-year-old son had been seen outside with his father's handgun. Christopher McPartland of Spota's office immediately tried to upgrade the son's charges from a misdemeanor to a felony.

The trio, Spota, Burke, and McPartland, were ostensibly autonomous, referring to themselves as The Administration, punishing all those who challenged their authority.

CHAPTER TWELVE

The serial killer sat with Veronica Severini at a table in the basement apartment. The two had shared classic French/Italian lasagna made with the combined ingredients of béchamel and ragù Bolognese. That was well over a week ago, dining on derivative cuisine created from those leftover sauces: fettuccine Alfredo covered with clams and shrimp; spaghetti and meat sauce; macaroni and cheese; béchamel sauce transformed into a Mornay sauce by adding a cheese and preparing a chicken Mornay casserole; filets of whiting baked in a white wine sauce with capers. The possibilities proved endless. Veronica, at given moments, temporarily forgot that she was being held captive by a madman . . . a madman yet a genius in the kitchen. She prayed nightly and believed that he would eventually let her go. A week had turned into two.

From the evening he anesthetized Veronica with chloroform and put the young woman over his shoulder and into his SUV, he never made sexual advances toward her. During the day, he'd strap her into the metal chair positioned in the center of the large basement apartment. In the evening, he'd loosely strap her into the lower bunk bed using two-inch wide utility belts with center-spring cam buckles, which he would then slide beneath the metal box frame and out of her reach. Sewn to the straps were strips of thick one-inch wide webbing that bound her hands and feet. She could turn her body left or right, but she could not get out of bed.

If Veronica had to go to the bathroom in the middle of the night, which he warned would make him very, very angry, she was to announce her need in a normal tone, for he was a very light sleeper and slept in the bunk right above her. Veronica made sure that she attended to those needs right before she went to bed. As not to upset her captor after the lights were out, she'd turn on her side in the fetal position, put her face into the pillow, and cry herself to sleep.

The man truly enjoyed listening to her witless whimpering while he drifted off peacefully into a relaxed state of rest.

Early one morning, the man scooted down the bunk bed ladder, startling Veronica, waking her from a restless sleep.

"It's a beautiful sunny morning, Veronica. We're already into February and the temperature is supposed to climb into the high sixties, maybe even hit seventy degrees. You can't say we're not having a very mild winter."

The blond bushy-haired man slipped into a pair of khaki cargo pants, put on a freshly ironed shirt hanging in a nearby closet, unbuckled the straps from beneath the bottom box frame, then unfastened the strips of webbing that bound Veronica's hands and feet.

"Get up, sleepyhead, and get into the shower."

Wearing a matching set of oversized men's pajamas and slipping into a pair of two-sizes-too-large slippers, Veronica noisily flip-flopped over to the alcove shower stall and basin located in a far corner of the room. She went to the bathroom, flushed, washed her hands, brushed her teeth, took a leisurely shower, shampooing and thoroughly washing then towel-drying her lustrous long brown hair. He listened for every sound, never rushing Veronica when she was attending to her hygiene.

The killer's mother, on the other hand, had been an absolute slob all her adult life. Unkempt. Rarely combing her messy long gray hair; a state of disorder and disgust. Hardly ever brushing her yellow teeth except for when she had food stuck between them, causing her discomfort. Occasionally, she'd floss, leaving pieces of food particles clinging to the bathroom mirror. Never-ever flushing the toilet after going to the bathroom.

One evening, a little more than a decade ago, when his mother was fast asleep, the 16-year-old stealthily slipped into her bedroom and bludgeoned her before cutting her throat from ear to ear—just below the jaw line—working the blade of his folding knife precisely through the omohyoid muscles, thyroid cartilage, spinal accessory nerve, hypoglassal nerve, external carotid artery, jugular vein, vague nerve, the common carotid artery, including the cervical vertebral column, which took some finessing, before her head finally fell off. Picking up the bloody pate by its filthy gray hair, he carried it to the bathroom of their single-story home.

"Hey, Mom! You're a fucking redhead now," he swore, placing the bloody head face down in the toilet then flushed. "See," he noted to no surprise, "it won't go down. Even in death, you won't go down, Mother—mother of all five sauces."

At first, the teenage boy giggled like a girl before he positively roared with laughter.

At 16 years of age, the killer of his mother had not an inkling of how to sever a head from its neck but knew to Google the anatomy by searching "anatomy of the head and neck" for images and general information. By 28, the bushy-haired man knew most every bone and muscle in the body, but more importantly, he knew how to inflict pain. He did not learn the latter from the Internet; he learned it through experimentation. His very first murder had been the murder of his mother. Up until the murders of the Medford man (Wilber Gilmore) and the Riverhead woman (Charlotte Endicott), his 96th and 97th victims, respectively, the serial killer kept accurate records in a black and white composition notebook, like the kind students use in the lower grades. The notebook was written in code and kept in a safe deposit box in another state under the pseudonym Joseph Baker. **J**oseph **B**aker, just for giggles.

Veronica reappeared from the bathroom as fresh as the morning sun. She crossed the room and asked permission to get dressed.

"You certainly may," the bushy-haired man answered quite pleasantly. Her abductor had washed, dried, and neatly folded her clothing as he had the week before. "Your clothes are on the bed. Get dressed, and I'll tell you what sauce we'll be preparing today."

Veronica immediately did as she was told.

When the young woman was dressed, her captor led her to the

metal chair bolted to the floor, but he did not strap her in this time. With hands clasped in back of him, he stood before her like an instructor lecturing a student.

"Today, Veronica, we are going to prepare another white sauce, a velouté, one of the five mother sauces of French cuisine. It is made from a blond roux and a light stock. Velouté is the French word for velvety. As it applies to the sauce we'll be preparing, it will be of a very smooth and delicate texture, lighter than our béchamel sauce as a rule. The chief difference between the two is that velouté is made from a stock, be it chicken, fish, veal or pork, whereas béchamel calls for milk to thin it.

"Velouté, as well as the other four French sauces, was popularized by Georges Auguste Escoffier, a 19th century famed French chef and culinary writer who was referred to as the 'king of chefs and the chef of kings.' He was the head chef of such famed hotels as the Savoy and Carlton in London, having made many a contribution to the culinary arts. Chief among them would have to be what is known as the 'brigade system of organization,' which is still used today."

Veronica feigned rapt attention. Hypothetically, had she been quizzed on the history of culinary information that the man had imparted over the past two weeks, she probably would not have received a grade greater than a C. However, had Veronica been given a practical exam referencing a fortnight of cooking with this professor-type madman, she surely would have received an A+.

But Veronica's focus was neither on culinary history nor her skill in and around the kitchen; her focus was on receiving her freedom. She promised maybe a hundred times that she would not tell a solitary soul of her abduction from the parking lot of the Jamesport Commons shopping center on the night she had picked up a large pizza from Lenny's of Jamesport, a pizza/pasta bistro on Main Road in Jamesport, town of Riverhead. She swore up and down that she would not utter a single syllable about her kidnapper's SUV, the basement apartment, or the man himself.

"*I promise, I promise, I promise,*" she would repeat endlessly, until he finally relented and promised Veronica later that morning that he would let her go after they completed the last two sauces: the velouté that they would be preparing this evening, and the hollandaise sauce shortly thereafter.

"What will you say happened to you, Veronica, when I let you go?" the man tested her later in the day.

"I've been thinking about that since the moment you promised me my freedom. I'm going to say that after I picked up the pizza that evening, I met a friend in the parking lot when I was leaving the restaurant and that I decided to go for a drive with him."

"And when they ask you why you just left your car in the parking lot without calling someone, or who this guy is, what are you going to say?"

Veronica thought quickly. "I'll just say that the guy told me he made arrangements to have the car picked up and brought to the house and to let my parents know that I'm all right and that I'll be home soon, which I guess he never did, I'll tell them. How's that?"

"And what about this fictitious guy? I'm sure your parents filed a missing persons report, and the police will surely want to know what happened and where you stayed."

"An old boyfriend, I'll say. We drove off together and spent the time at his apartment, that he was home on leave from the military for a short time and was being deployed back to Iraq for a fourth tour of duty."

"And if they want to see the place where you stayed?"

"Why would they?"

Her captor just let the question hang there.

"I'll just say that I don't know where the apartment is, that when he drove me there it was dark, and when he drove me home it was dark. What do you think?" she asked nervously.

The man smiled. "I think you're very devious, Veronica."

"Seriously, what do you think?"

"Hope springs eternal, Veronica. Hope springs eternal," the serial killer repeated and smiled warmly.

For the very first time in weeks, Veronica shed tears of sheer happiness.

CHAPTER THIRTEEN

All Claire Billings could think about was the body found brutally murdered beside the railroad tracks near the Mattituck train station, across from The Broken Down Valise pub. Claire was pretty sure that the person she saw pulling something from the rear of the SUV was the killer. The local newspapers as well as *Newsday* initially had very little information, apart from an elderly man walking his dog who found a body in a rolled-up carpet on the far side of the tracks, just east of the train station.

Curious, the man had rolled the carpet open with his foot and fell. Within the carpet was a large clear plastic bag with what first appeared to be bloody butchered meat. On his hands and knees, with the dog's leash in one hand, he closely inspected the bag at one end. What he saw at the other end was a person's head. The man screamed, and the dog went wild, drawing the attention of a young couple who helped the man to his feet and called 911 when they, too, saw the butchered body within the bloodied transparent trash bag. The body was later identified as that of Janet Johnsen.

Claire Billings instinctively knew, as did the police, that there would soon be other bodies. Claire was now certain that she had, indeed, seen the serial killer the night that she and her husband had dined at the Iron Skillet. What Claire didn't know was that a local female teenager from the area had been missing for more than two weeks.

Homicide Detectives Brenden Reilly and Mike D'Angelo had good reason to believe that the missing girl, Veronica Severini, had been abducted by the serial killer. They did not wait for Claire Billings to call them in the event that she had remembered something further that might help with the investigation. Without phoning ahead, they drove directly to the Billings' residence, knowing that her husband, Josh Billings, was not at home.

The two detectives went over Claire's statements anew. Once again, she told them everything she had seen that evening, making it very clear that she could recall nothing further, that she had read the newspapers and pondered the matter till her head hurt, and that she would have called them the moment had anything jogged her memory. It hadn't.

Detective Mike D'Angelo later asked Claire, in a roundabout way, questions about her husband, as if he were making small talk instead of opening a pertinent avenue of inquiry into the man's hobbies and habits relating to fishing, hunting, and cooking—picking up cues from a wall decorated with pictures of trophy fish, deer, and Josh Billings standing beside a smoking barbecue grill.

"Those are some magnificent photos, Claire," Mike put forth. "Did he catch all those fish and harvest that, what, twelve-point buck?"

Claire smiled. "Interesting euphemism, Detective."

"I thought we were on a first name basis, Claire," Mike teased.

"Interesting euphemism, Mike. Harvesting. Yes, he shot and killed that twelve-pointer with a handgun from thirty-five yards away. Of course, the distance gets greater every time he retells the story."

"I'm surprised he didn't have that one mounted. That's some rack."

"Interesting you should mention it. Most all those fish you see there are catch-and-release. Josh doesn't enjoy killing anything for the sake of killing. That deer, on the other hand, is a different story altogether. He shot, field dressed, skinned, and butchered that big buck all by himself. We gave venison away to half the neighborhood that year. Actually, Josh likes to *harvest* the smaller ones," Claire said with a smile, "because they're far more tender; like veal. We had backstraps last season that positively melted in your mouth."

"Where does Josh do his hunting?"

"Well, he used to do his hunting right here on the Island, but it gets tougher and tougher each and every year. Farmers lease out their property to sportsmen come the hunting season for big bucks—I mean money." Claire giggled and waved away the nonsense. "Anyway, he generally hunts upstate."

"Does he hunt with a friend or friends? I mean because it can be dangerous not to hunt with someone for safety reasons." The detective knew he was pushing the envelope but took the chance. Mike didn't want Claire thinking that he and Brenden were looking deeply into Josh's activities.

"I must have mentioned it a hundred times, but you can't talk sense to that man sometimes."

Mike simply nodded his head.

Josh Billings had been locked onto Brenden and Mike's radar for the better part of a week and for a number of reasons. Chief among them was the fact that he and Claire had been in very close proximity to the scene of the crime at approximately the same time that Janet Johnsen's body had been discovered by the elderly gentleman walking his dog. Another coincidental but perhaps silly reason was that the man's initials, J.B., were indelibly stamped upon the minds of not only Detectives Brenden Reilly and Mike D'Angelo, but upon the minds of homicide detectives who were working the case both night and day. Yet, still another consideration was the fact that neither Brenden nor Mike could shake the notion that Josh Billings was hiding something, notwithstanding the obvious fact that neither of them liked the man. Eliminating the man as a suspect was the furthest thing from their minds.

Claire broached the subject of serial killers as she had wanted to do during the first interview with the two detectives and was now able to capture their attention this time around. She spoke about her theories concerning the possibilities of two or more serial killers with regard to the Gilgo Beach/Manorville murders and now the TRAIN TRACK KILLER as headlined in the press.

"I believe that somehow they're all connected," Claire

continued. "Of course, it's only supposition, conjecture on my part." Claire went on connecting the dots, elaborating on the association among several key players. When she finished venting, Claire took a deep breath. "I guess you think I'm one of those conspiracy nuts," she concluded, wearing a sorrowful frown.

"No, not at all," Mike said truthfully. "What I think is that you're very well informed. Any reasonable person could draw the same conclusions as you have, Claire. But we, as police, do not have the luxury of second-guessing and drawing conclusions based on assumptions. Of course, we're only human and sometimes tend to veer off in another direction. But ultimately, we return to follow a straight line, and that line, Claire, is a course that follows the facts— straight and narrow though it may be."

Brenden was impressed in the way his partner couched and summed up their job in a nutshell to a civilian, candidly and to the point.

"Well," Claire declared, slapping both palms down hard upon her knees, "sometimes you just have to use abductive rather than deductive reasoning, gentlemen."

"Meaning?" Brenden fell for the bait.

"If it walks like a duck, swims like a duck, and quacks like a duck, it's a frigging duck," Claire declared with the widest grin plastered upon her pretty puss.

Brenden and Mike laughed and shook their heads simultaneously.

"Does your husband ever win an argument?" Mike questioned in all seriousness.

"Rarely."

"What I thought," Mike said rather quietly.

The two detectives stood up from the couch and were about to take their leave, grabbing their coats draped over the back of a club chair recliner.

"Before you go, fellows, can I ask you something?"

"You can ask," Brenden answered.

"Has there been another abduction like that Janet Johnsen woman and the others that I won't read about in the papers until they're found murdered?"

Brenden and Mike glanced at one another before locking their eyes on Claire.

Brenden addressed her question diplomatically and officially. "Now, you know perfectly well, Claire, that we can't discuss an—"

"—an ongoing investigation, blah-blah-blah. I know, I know. I've watched *Law & Order* a zillion times; reruns, too. SVU. That's Special Victims Unit, just in case you guys missed a beat while dozing off in detective class," Claire good-humoredly put forth.

"Funny girl," Mike bantered back.

"Very funny girl," Brenden agreed. "Remember, if—"

"—if I remember anything to give either of you a call."

"You got it."

"And you remember, if it walks like a duck, swims like a duck, and quacks like a duck, it's positively a frigging duck."

"Got it," they both responded.

"Good."

"Good-bye, Claire." Mike smiled and winked approvingly at the attractive woman and pulled the door closed behind them as the two homicide detectives stepped off the stoop, pulling up their coat collars, shielding themselves from the sudden blast of sleet and cold late morning air.

CHAPTER FOURTEEN

The parents of Veronica Severini stood against a wall within The Broken Down Valise, the bar on Pike Street, right across from the Mattituck train station, near the tracks where Janet Johnsen's bloody body had been found weeks earlier. The couple drove there for no other reason save a hopeful prospect that they might learn what happened to their 18-year-old daughter. They passed around copies of a recent graduation photo of Veronica. Had anyone seen her? Although the family lived in Jamesport, Janice and Jim Severini felt compelled to canvass specific areas between Mattituck and Greenport; namely, train stations. The Southold train station would be their next stop, followed by Greenport.

The men and women at the bar were helpful and, indeed, sympathetic. Several of them volunteered to take and make copies on their own and hang them in key locations such as supermarkets, the local Mattituck-Laurel library, and every shop and eatery along Love Lane.

"Not a problem," was the general response from patrons of the pub who took a poster with Veronica's photo, underscored by her physical characteristics and contact information.

So touched were Janice and Jim Severini by everyone's kindness that they wept as they left the bar.

Just outside the doorway, a man exited right behind them. He was holding the black and white sheet in his left hand and extending his right.

"Excuse me. My name's Tom."

Wiping his eyes on the sleeve of his coat, Jim took the man's hand into his own. "Jim," Jim said softly. "My wife, Janice."

Tom took and shook the woman's hand. "Terrible thing you're going through, I know. I'd like to ask you a couple of questions if I may."

"Certainly."

"You mentioned inside that your daughter's car was found by the police in a parking lot in Jamesport."

"Actually, *I* found her car and called the police."

"Where was it?"

"Parked in front of Lenny's Pizzeria in Jamesport, about a quarter of a mile from our home."

"On the south side of Main Road," Tom said. "Know it well."

"It was around 7:30 p.m., two weeks and two days ago," Janice Severini said and bobbed her head.

"We sent her out for a pizza, and she never came home," Jim muttered then broke down. "It's all my fault," he sobbed. "I should have gone with her or picked up the fucking pie myself. The police haven't done shit. I tried to file a police report from day one, but they said I had to wait. Wait for what? By the time they got around to doing that, two days had gone by. First, they wanted us to wait seventy-two hours before they acted. Three fucking days! She went out for a pizza and never returned," he repeated. "She wouldn't do that. She'd call if there was a problem. We haven't heard a word. The car started up just fine, so it wasn't engine trouble."

Tom looked both of them squarely in the eyes before speaking. "Has your daughter ever done anything like this before?"

Jim took a step back. "You know, you sound just like them."

Tom nodded. "I am one of them, Jim." And with that admission, Tom showed the Severinis his badge. "Southold P.D., and I want to help you."

"Riverhead Police Department dragged their feet for two days before they did anything, and they haven't got a clue. If they had acted immediately, they might have found her. And if you're a

Southold cop like you say you are, how come you don't know about my missing daughter?"

"Because Riverhead P.D. was handling the matter seeing that Jamesport is in Riverhead Township. Secondly, I just returned to Southold after being out of town for two weeks. Tomorrow's my first day back on the job."

"Well let me bring you up to speed, Tom whatever your name is. We're out here doing the job of the police. We know what happened to that man at the Medford train station. We know what happened to that woman in Riverhead by the train tracks. We know what happened to that poor woman at the Mattituck train station." Jim Severini repeatedly stabbed a pointed finger directly across the street. "The killer is making his way along the Ronkonkoma Branch Line and is working his way east, disposing of those bodies at or near Long Island Railroad Stations along the way. We're not going to sit around and do nothing. I know she's in the area. I can feel it in my heart. I know she's calling out to us, begging us to help find her. I just know she's alive. Somebody had to have seen something."

Janice Severini was bobbing her head in agreement. "Our daughter wouldn't do anything like this. She just wouldn't. Not without calling. Veronica is an honor student at Hunter College. Top of her class. She wants to go on and pursue a career as a psychologist. She just wouldn't run off like that."

Lieutenant Tom Bolton, Southold P.D., nodded in understanding. "I'm going to tell you something that I'm sure you already heard from the police, especially if you told them everything you just told me. But I want you to listen very carefully. You don't know for certain that this person has your daughter. You're assuming the worse, and I get it. I'm well aware of what happened here in Suffolk County regarding the three homicides. This is the first I'm hearing about your daughter because, like I said, I've been away two weeks. But I can assure you, and I stress the word assure, that law enforcement is on top of these cases, working relentlessly—night and day. All of us."

"Yeah, but you had time to take two weeks off you even admit," Jim sneered. "I thought that in situations like this, vacations are put on hold and manpower becomes—"

"I didn't say anything about a vacation, Jim. An example of how you jump to conclusions," Tom added and smiled sadly. "My two-week *vacation* was at Sloan Kettering in the city."

Janice Severini brought the tips of her fingers to her mouth. "Oh, I'm so sorry."

The policeman waved away her concern. "I'll be fine. I just need to take things easy for a while. One day at a time, they say. Good advice. So, like I said, tomorrow will be my first day back on the job. This afternoon, however, is a vacation day, Jim, and this is my watering hole. And I'll leave you two with this advice: Think positive. The fact that your daughter hasn't turned up in two plus weeks is ironically a good sign referencing the Train Track Killer as he's called. To be perfectly blunt, Janice and Jim, if this guy that we're all hunting for had Veronica, her body would have likely turned up by now, I'm sure. I'm speaking to you as a civilian, I'll pretend, not as a cop. Of course, I don't know what happened to your daughter. But first thing tomorrow, I'll look into it. I'll start by making some calls and get Veronica's photo and info out there." Lieutenant Tom Bolton waved the paper high above his head, turned around then headed back inside the building.

As the front door to The Broken Down Valise was closing, Janice and Jim Severini called out their thanks and appreciation.

CHAPTER FIFTEEN

It was late afternoon when the bushy-haired man entered the basement area. He walked over and unstrapped Veronica from the metal chair, removing the bindings from her feet and hands.

"Are we ready to begin our hollandaise sauce, Veronica?"

"Yes, sir."

"You know what?"

Veronica shook her pretty head.

"You don't have to call me sir, or mister, or master any longer. All right?"

"What should I call you?"

"Call me anything but late to dinner," the man joked playfully.

Veronica feigned a smile and forced a little laugh. She was not in a playful mood, having been strapped to the chair for what seemed like several hours. She stood and rubbed her arms and legs, feeling the circulation slowly returning to her limbs.

"Seriously, I've been thinking, Veronica. You can call me Cap."

Veronica paused. "Cap?"

"Yes, Cap. It's short for captor." The man giggled then absolutely roared with laughter. "It's fitting, is it not?" he added when he finally caught his breath.

Veronica said nothing.

Cap went on about the meal they would be preparing together.

"You'll prepare the hollandaise sauce this evening, right down to the roux, while I prepare the fish. I had a nice yellowfin tuna flown in from Freeport. Not Freeport, Long Island, of course, but from Freeport, Texas. That's why you and I are going to enjoy a fresh tuna steak in the middle of February, Veronica. I spared no expense. You have no idea the work involved in catching tuna this time of year. It's all about the weather and windows of opportunity. It's all about big boats: Makos, SeaCrafts, Bertrams. Yellowfin tuna is the targeted, coveted prize. Three fish per boat, per day; That's it! Something like that. Blackfin tuna, grouper, and many other species are next in line. The Gulf is where they nail them. The fish feed voraciously under the bright lights of those deep-water offshore oil-rig platforms."

"I guess you really want me to call you Cap, like a captain, because you know a lot about boats and fish," she said rather flatteringly.

Cap smiled. "Nah, I want you to call me Cap because you're still my prisoner," he reminded her again.

"But you are going to let me go as you promised. Yes?"

"One more fish dish to go, Veronica. One more. And then you're free. We won't be making as much hollandaise sauce as we did the béchamel and the velouté sauces because we won't be preparing derivative dishes like the fettuccine Alfredo, covered with clams and shrimp that we enjoyed together, or the macaroni and cheese, or transforming the béchamel into a Mornay sauce by adding, what was it? Ah, yes. Cheddar cheese. You absolutely loved my chicken Mornay casserole, too. Remember?"

"And do you remember I told you that you're making me fat?"

"Couple of pounds, maybe. You'll live."

Veronica prayed he meant that in a literal sense, prayed that he would soon release her, prayed that she would get to hug her parents, that they would take her into their loving arms, and that she'd tacitly pray for and forgive her father for having an affair, which she now believed was true. Veronica truly prayed like she had never prayed before—prayed to God that she would *live*.

"May I go to the bathroom, please?"

"Of course you may."

Veronica stiffly crossed the room, heading toward the alcove.

Moments later, she flushed the toilet, washed and dried her hands thoroughly, then exited the narrow space.

Cap inspected her hands closely. "Good girl," he said approvingly.

Toward evening, Veronica was busy at Cap's kitchen stove, melting two tablespoons of butter in a saucepan, adding an equal amount of flour in small batches, adding eggs, lemon juice, cayenne, and salt, whisking away until the mixture was free of any lumps. Yes, free. Veronica craved to be free, wishing she could vanish just as easily as those little lumps eventually disappeared. Veronica whisked the ingredients till the liquid became smooth and silky. The roux was almost ready. Veronica reduced the sauce a bit more at a low simmer. Cap stepped over to inspect.

"Looks perfect, Veronica," her captor praised his captive. Cap picked up a utensil and dipped it into the pan. "Yes, look how it clings then slowly leaves a film on the spoon. Perfect." Cap tasted the sauce. "Wonderful."

Veronica was, of course, pleased that Cap was pleased. God forbid if he wasn't.

"Now, we could have certainly embellished on the sauce if we wanted, first by chopping up a shallot and cooking it in the melted butter until tender and translucent, adding a little tarragon and/or Dijon mustard, salt and pepper to taste, finishing up with a half cup of dry white wine. Again, the possibilities are endless. But the pan-seared rare tuna we'll be enjoying momentarily already contains some of those ingredients. I've also put together a red potato and green bean salad. You'll positively flip. If it were May, I'd be doing the tuna steaks on the grill outside."

The meal was colorful and absolutely sensational. However, Veronica's appetite was curbed by her excitement, believing that she was but one more fish dish away from freedom; she ate whatever she could, solely to keep her captor happy. She had to strive to finish her meals in recent days as her only appetite was her taste and thirst for freedom.

When Cap kidnapped Veronica, she hardly ate a thing for days out of sheer unadulterated fear. Slowly, she came around, noting that he was always in a far better frame of mind whenever she consumed every morsel on her plate. The meals were always delicious.

The fact that Cap had never made sexual advances toward her, intrigued Veronica. He could have assaulted, molested, sodomized, or raped her (terms defined in her psych class at Hunter College) at a given moment, and she would be powerless to defend herself. As a psychology major, Veronica tried to psychoanalyze the man. Big mistake. Cap went wild with anger one evening. The trigger? Veronica tried to bring up Cap's early childhood with regard to his mother. Following the madman's rage, Veronica never ever brought up the subject again. So much for Psych 243 at the college.

Veronica vaguely knew about the man found murdered by the train station in Medford. Having hit closer to home, she had read about the woman murdered in Riverhead, her body discovered near train tracks. Veronica, of course, knew nothing about the woman found brutally murdered at the train station in Mattituck because Veronica had been abducted that same evening. But from the moment Veronica was grabbed from behind at the Jamesport shopping center after picking up a pizza at Lenny's for the family, the thought of the killer immediately flashed across her mind. *Could Cap be that very killer?* she wondered and worried.

When Veronica had regained consciousness on that terrifying night, she found herself on the floor before the front passenger seat of the stranger's vehicle. Her hands and legs and mouth were bound with black Gorilla duct tape; she could hardly move a muscle.

Remaining in that position for what seemed an eternity, Veronica felt the vehicle veer from a rather smooth road to a very bumpy pathway. Minutes later, she was carried from the vehicle, into the home, and down into a windowless basement apartment. The man held her clamped tightly over his shoulder within a powerful grip. In the other hand, he balanced the pizza box, carrying it as if it were a serving platter.

Once inside, he put the pizza down upon a counter and plopped Veronica onto a couch.

"Although it's only been a few minutes, Veronica, I don't think this pie's hot enough—not to my liking anyway," he had told his captive. "Ah, half sausage and half pepperoni," he declared with some surprise. "I'll just step over here and warm it up some. It'll only take a few minutes, and then we can eat. If you're good, maybe in a day or two, I'll make you my very own special pizza, and you'll see the difference. You'll never want to go back to Lenny's ever again," he swore and giggled. "But this will do in a pinch. Which do you prefer? The sausage or the pepperoni? No answer, huh? Do you even know the difference? Many people haven't a clue as to what they're eating. Pepperoni is a highly seasoned sausage that is an American variety of salami, made from both pork and beef, whereas sausage, per se, is generally pork. Actually, I prefer the crumpled sausage on my pizza instead of these slices. But beggars can't be choosers. Right, Veronica? Still no answer." The blond bushy-haired man suddenly looked down at the couch and laughed mightily before catching his breath and tapping his breast. "Oh, silly me. You really can't answer with your mouth all taped up like that, can you? Of course, you could have answered me by gesturing with your head." Her abductor had stepped over and ripped the tape from across her mouth and withdrew a rag.

Veronica remembered every detail of that one-sided conversation. Veronica remembered the sudden pain mixed with a breath of fresh air as he ripped the tape from her face, tearing part of her lower lip. Veronica remembered how he tenderly dabbed at the trickle of blood after removing the cloth from her mouth. Veronica remembered these things all too well.

CHAPTER SIXTEEN

Claire and Josh Billings entered the Iron Skillet Restaurant in Mattituck. Bob Hartz stepped out from a back room and directed the couple to a table off the kitchen. He took a seat next to them. Josh removed a bottle of wine from his neoprene bag and sat the Merlot on the table. Claire took and put the wine bag away in her purse.

"The police have been here three times already. Two detectives, twice, and a Southold cop," Bob explained.

Claire nodded. "The detectives have been to our home twice, too," she confided in a low voice, although no one else was present in the restaurant, except for Mary Ann who was busy in the kitchen.

"Yeah, twice," Josh soured. "Once when I wasn't home."

"Detectives Reilly and D'Angelo. Homicide," Bob guessed.

"Yep, that's them," Josh said with annoyance. "Mutt and Jeff. Good cop, bad cop."

"Brenden and Mike, he means," Claire clarified with a grin.

"Yeah, you'll note she's on a first name basis with them."

Bob smiled and shook his head. "Of course, they asked me who was in here that evening. Sorry for any inconvenience, guys. Anyway, they would have gotten your names from the Guest Book that you commented in and signed maybe a dozen different times. I know for a fact that they contacted at least six of my other customers;

three couples. With you guys, that now makes it four. They asked for and took the book, which they promised to return. They haven't yet."

Claire smiled in understanding and took Bob's hand. "It's all right, Bob. When we left here that evening, we were stopped at a checkpoint. The officer took our names and said that we would probably be contacted. So, they would have contacted us any ol' way."

"Yeah, because Ms. Big Mouth told him we heard the commotion shortly after we arrived here. That's why he sent the detectives. Then when they came, she tells them she remembers that she saw something."

Bob looked nonplussed. "Saw what exactly?"

"Claire said she saw a person at the back of an SUV dumping something by the train station as we were crossing the tracks to come to you. The police assumed it was a body."

"The body of the woman they found murdered," Claire made clear.

"Jesus Christ. Why didn't you call and tell me?"

"Tell you what exactly, Bob? That my wife thinks she's going to help solve a murder case out here?"

"I know what I saw, and the timing ties in perfectly. The two detectives said I was a big help."

"Tell me everything if you don't mind," Bob said with keen interest.

Claire unfolded most of the details, beginning with the first interview then launched into the second meeting.

"Again, I wasn't there," Josh reminded Bob.

When Claire concluded, she put a hand on Bob's shoulder. "What I've told you is in strict confidence."

"Of course," Bob swore.

"What did this Southold cop have to say?" Josh asked.

Bob smiled. "Cops don't *say* shit, Josh. You know that. They just ask a lot of questions and share nothing. I told him what I told the two detectives. I heard the sirens and all the commotion, went to the front door and saw beams and flashing bright lights. Thought it was probably a bad car accident. Didn't see anything besides that, I said. He asked me if I knew a Mr. and Mrs. Severini or their daughter . . . can't remember her first name, although it's plastered all over the place. Some family from Jamesport. Left a poster with me." Bob laughed. "At first I thought it was a WANTED poster by the way he handed it to me and asked if I had seen her. Turns out she's missing, not wanted. I felt like such a dope."

"Can I see it?" Claire asked, feeling a knot tightening in the pit of her stomach. "Her picture."

"Sure. He asked if I wouldn't mind posting it in a window by the front door. I told him I would after I washed the panes, that with all the rain we had, they were pretty filthy. Then I plain forgot." Bob went and got the picture. A moment later, he handed it to Claire.

Claire simply shook her head. "Never saw her. You?"

Josh took and studied the picture of Veronica Severini. "Never saw her." He carefully read the information. "Nope."

Claire took the poster back from her husband. "I have a terrible feeling, Josh."

"I know what you're thinking, Claire," Bob said. "You're thinking that that madman has her. The thought certainly crossed my mind, too. But if he had that girl, she would have turned up dead by now. Know why?"

Josh nodded. "Because she's been missing for over two weeks, and he kills his victims within several days."

"Bingo," Bob agreed.

Claire shook her head once again. "I'm not so sure."

"Here we go again," Josh chided. "The sleuth is back on the case. Why don't you call your buddies Brenden and Mikey and tell them you suddenly developed psychic powers? And get ahold of that Southold cop—what's his name, Bob?"

"Lieutenant Tom Bolton."

"Oh, a high-ranking dude. Better yet, why don't you call and make it a foursome, Claire? You, Reilly, D'Angelo, and this Bolton guy. You can discuss your insights and theories with them. Say, I have an even better idea! We have a Waterford crystal globe paperweight in the den that you could put out as a crystal ball on the coffee table, or maybe all hold hands and have a séance—"

"Just stop it!" Claire sounded sharply. "Enough."

"You want to hear something funny?" Bob thought out loud.

"Thought you just did," Josh continued needling. "Claire with a crystal ball, or at the very least, a magnifying glass."

"No, seriously. I just remembered something."

"You're getting to sound more and more like Claire, Bob."

"When Lieutenant Bolton came here, I thought that I had seen him someplace before. Couldn't recall. Now it hit me. I occasionally walk over and have a drink at The Broken Down Valise. He's pretty much a regular there."

"Your point being?"

"I never saw him in uniform. Always in civilian clothes."

"Your point being, Bob?" Josh repeated.

"He's a Southold cop, yet he frequents a bar in Mattituck. Strange."

"Maybe he lives in Mattituck, works in Southold. It's still Southold Town."

"No, he made a point of telling me he lives in Southold, right near the Peconic Bay Yacht Club. Keeps a boat there. Big fisherman. Loves to go after striped bass."

"I thought you said he didn't say much. Sounds like you two got pretty chummy," Josh jabbered away. "I'll give you two good reasons why a guy like that, who you say lives in Southold, comes to Mattituck to wet his whistle. Number one: You don't socialize in the neighborhood where you live, especially if you're a high-ranking cop. Number two: The prices of drinks at The Broken Down Valise are the cheapest than in any neighboring town. You said so yourself a hundred times. It's a cop thing; hence the civvies. The guy wishes to remain low key. Smart."

"Got an answer for everything," Bob said with a questionable grin.

"Got that right," Claire expressed behind a smirk. "Thought you knew him by now."

"Hey, we gonna order or what? I'm starving. Been so busy yakking, we haven't even touched the wine."

Bob reached across and removed two glasses from a sideboard cabinet. "There you go. Josh, you preordered the stuffed mushrooms to share as an appetizer. I just made a roasted red pepper soup to die for. Also, I unleashed a huge blue claw crab from its cage earlier. Cut it up and let it simmer lavishly in a secret seasoned liquid. You know you're getting a hearty bisque chock-full of crab meat; not just a quick walk-through a skimpy bowl of broth. Claire?"

Claire smiled. "I'll have the crab bisque, thank you."

"Excellent choice. Josh?"

"I'll go with the roasted sweet red pepper soup."

"Another excellent choice."

Josh picked up the menu and read off the list of soups. "But what if I wanted the roasted tomato with garlic, the meatless split pea, red lentil, or the creamy-chunky potato dill?"

"I'd have to tell you we're fresh out," Bob answered with a straight face.

"Just as I thought. Look who's being a comedian now."

"And Josh?"

"I'll have the pot roast with mashed potatoes and sweet glazed carrots."

"Fine."

"Claire, have you decided what you're going to have for an entrée?"

"I'm going to have the Bolognese sauce over fettuccine."

"You mean my *authentic* Bolognese sauce over fettuccine," Bob emphasized.

Claire chuckled. "That's exactly what I meant to say, Bob."

CHAPTER SEVENTEEN

Following the scandals of former Chief of Police James Burke and District Attorney Thomas Spota, the disgraced men had been replaced, initially, by Stuart Cameron (former chief of support services, then named as acting chief of police) and Timothy D. Sini (an outsider) who became interim police commissioner when Police Commissioner Edward Webber retired. Cameron went on to become chief of police, and Sini was elected district attorney. District Attorney Sini had reached out to FBI Agent Geraldine Hart, who became Suffolk County's new police commissioner.

The Suffolk County Police Department, one of the largest in the United States, was in the midst of cleaning house, attempting to restore a blemished record of corruption by top brass; namely, Thomas Spota, James Burke, and Christopher McPartland, the former chief prosecutor of the anticorruption bureau of the district attorney's office in Hauppauge.

Working closely with Suffolk County's Homicide Bureau, Detectives Brenden Reilly and Mike D'Angelo of the Suffolk County Police Department's Homicide Squad in Yaphank, coordinated efforts among the teams working the TRAIN TRACK KILLER case as dubbed by the press.

Brenden and Mike sat at their desks in the hallway, directly across from Detective Lieutenant Steve Anderson's office, the head of homicide. Their boss was sick at home with the flu.

It had been raining earlier that Thursday morning but finally stopped as Lieutenant Tom Bolton of Southold P.D. stepped out of his car and headed toward the building. Inside, he signed the register and was given a visitor's pass before being escorted upstairs by a young detective. Tom pressed and adhered the red and white pass to a lapel of his navy-blue wool suit. The department name, HOMICIDE, was neatly printed above three boxes indicating month, day, and year: 02 13 20.

Brenden and Mike greeted Tom warmly as the three shook hands.

"No coat, Tom?" Mike asked.

"Left it in the car. Finally stopped raining, but a hell of a lot better than snow. A mild winter so far, gentlemen. Now all we have to do is get through the rest of February."

"We'll use Anderson's office. Poor bastard's home sick as a dog with the flu," Brenden explained.

"It's certainly going around. We have about ten percent of the force out on a daily basis."

"About the same here, I'd say," said Mike.

"Better than that coronavirus. Fifteenth confirmed case, I just heard over the radio coming here."

Brenden sadly shook his head. "How was the drive out from Southold?"

"Fucking traffic. Hour and a quarter."

"You know, we could have done this over the phone."

"No big deal. I've got some business to attend to in the city later this morning. Anyway, better we do this face to face. Besides, I haven't seen this place in years."

The three men got themselves settled in Anderson's office.

"Coffee, Tom?"

"No thanks. Coffee'd out early this morning."

"Well, let's get started." Brenden broke out his notes.

Lieutenant Tom Bolton went over in detail the conversation he had had with Mr. and Mrs. Severini. Brenden and Mike listened without interrupting. When Tom was finished, he handed them each a poster of the missing 18-year-old, Veronica Severini.

"You think this is tied in with the Train Track victims, Tom?"

Tom shrugged. "Don't really know. This may sound like a bit of a reach, but if it is this guy who's holding her and she's still alive, it's because she majors in psychology; top of her class. Otherwise, she'd be dead by now, and we'd have found her. As you well know, he places his victims pretty much in plain sight so they'll be discovered sooner than later. Maybe she is a runaway, yet when I stand back from this, I'm really not so sure. She disappeared much like the other two women as well as the guy found in Medford—victim number one."

Mike and Brenden exchanged glances. Brenden gave Mike a nod.

"We see you've been doing your homework, Tom," Mike stated. "The time of their disappearances coincides with the time of day; early evening. He dumped the three bodies like he was putting out the garbage, and in a place where they'd be found sooner than later like you said—near railroad tracks where pedestrians walk or drive by or otherwise have an unobstructed view from a train station platform."

"We have a witness who we believe saw the Janet Johnsen woman being dumped by the tracks in Mattituck," Brenden shared.

Lieutenant Tom Bolton leaned well forward in his seat. "I'm all ears, Detectives."

Mike filled Tom in on the particulars, specifically the unsub's alleged mid-size SUV, bulky pocketed cargo pants, and the ski-like cap pulled down over his ears. "Not much of a lead to go on at the moment, but it's a start."

"Know what I'm thinking?" Tom suddenly entertained.

"Tell us," Brenden invited.

Tom pulled out and consulted a small notepad. "The Johnsen woman's body was found shortly before the Severini girl goes missing."

"Which makes us think the two cases may not be connected," Mike reasoned.

"Maybe yes, and maybe no. Another reach admittedly on my part, but hear me out."

"To use your words, Tom, we're all ears," Brenden encouraged.

"The Johnsen woman was found at approximately four-thirty p.m. as it was getting dark. The suspect is supposedly dumping a body, not grabbing another woman off the street. So, he doesn't need —at that particular moment—what is presumably in his 'bulging pants pockets' as your witness stated. Presumably a roll of duct tape, rope, probably a bottle of formaldehyde, rags, large plastic contractor's bags, et cetera. But he would need to carry and have those items handy if he's on the hunt and plans on grabbing someone later that same evening after dumping Johnsen in Mattituck, same day the woman went missing. Maybe things didn't work out the way he wanted and that's why he got rid of her that quickly. Veronica Severini went missing around five or five-thirty."

Mike and Brenden exchanged glances.

"The Mattituck train station to Lenny's pizza place in Jamesport is a fifteen-minute drive at most," Tom went on. "Maybe that was his hunting ground that evening. The time of Veronica Severini's disappearance from the parking lot of the pizzeria in Jamesport is shortly after Janet Johnsen's body was discovered in Mattituck. A kid behind the counter waited on Veronica and saw her leave. It was dark by then. Subduing and kidnapping her posed no problem since the parking area was practically empty and the restaurant is situated at the rear of the lot next to a woodlot where her car was parked."

"Interesting theory," Mike said after digesting Tom's hypothesis.

Brenden nodded.

"Well, that's all it really is at this point. A theory. Pure speculation. Conjecture," the lieutenant conceded in conclusion. "Anyhow, I made sure that every business in the Jamesport Commons shopping center as well as other key locations has her picture hanging in a window. And that includes schools and libraries and all the shops along Love Lane in Mattituck. The Severinis have her picture plastered around Southold and out to Greenport."

"The next two train stations after Mattituck," Mike acknowledged.

"Right."

"You've been a very busy guy, Tom."

"Sure has," Mike concurred. "Sure has."

"They're nice folks, gentlemen. Riverhead P.D. not surprisingly dragged their feet on this in the beginning. Their focus was on the Janet Johnsen case. I touched base with Chief Hegermiller and explained the circumstances. The Johnsen victim was and is their priority, but he assures me his people are on this Severini case, too. A little late in the game, but better late than never. They went over her car with a fine-toothed comb. Found nothing."

"I know Hegermiller," Brenden said. "Good man. By the way, you're a good man too, Tom."

Mike nodded in agreement.

"I have two ex-wives that would disagree with you guys. Anyhow, I'm married to my boat for now. Doesn't give me a lick of trouble so long as I maintain 'er in the fashion she's accustomed to. Upkeep runs about the same. Upside is I get a four-month vacation away from her each year. Thinking about changing her name, too. Gives me a chance to beat the bushes here and there."

Brenden and Mike laughed and nodded their understanding.

"Well, I guess that about wraps it up, fellas. You'll keep me in the loop?"

"You can count on it," Brenden promised.

"Say hello to your boss for me and that I wish him a speedy recovery. He's one of the good guys, too."

"Will do, Tom. You sure you can't stick around and push your appointment out a bit? Mike and I would like to treat you to lunch. Best burgers, fries, and beer in the area."

"Love to, but I can't."

Lieutenant Tom Bolton didn't want to tell them that his appointment was with an oncologist at Sloan Kettering and that he'd been instructed not to eat or drink a thing. Bad enough he had three cups of coffee that morning. He was sorry he had mentioned Sloan Kettering in front of Jim Severini and his wife, but the man had gotten under his skin. Memorial Sloan Kettering Cancer Center. It was the initial word—Memorial—with a capital M that unnerved the 51-year-old veteran cop.

The three shook hands and said their good-byes.

Mike called after Tom as he stepped from the office.

"Next time you're in the neighborhood, Lieutenant, the three of us are going out to lunch on Brenden and me."

"Got it." Tom smiled, removed the red and white visitor pass from his navy-blue lapel and waved the paper high above his head as he was being escorted downstairs by the same young detective who had accompanied him up.

"Can't be too careful these days," the detective said. "These days, they walk into a precinct and aim to take you out."

"Got that right," Tom stated flatly.

"You'll sign out like you signed in at the register over there."

"Got it. You take care, young man."

"Yes, sir."

CHAPTER EIGHTEEN

Cap was busy in the basement kitchen laying out the ingredients that Veronica would need for the hollandaise sauce, same as she had made when he prepared the yellowfin tuna dish: eggs, butter, lemon, white wine, salt and white pepper, along with a pinch of cayenne. It would go perfectly with the dish Cap was planning in celebration. Veronica would be in charge of the sauce, and Cap would be in charge of the salmon. It was to be Veronica's last meal.

"I'll be preparing asparagus and roasted potatoes Anna that I first enjoyed at the Iron Skillet Restaurant in Mattituck. Have you ever eaten there with your parents?"

"I don't think so."

"Oh, you'd remember if you had. Believe me. It's an old farmhouse just a hop, skip, and a jump from the Mattituck train station. The food there is truly fantastic. That's where I first had roasted potatoes Anna. Surprisingly, I had never ever had them before. Have you?"

"No."

Veronica prayed to God that Cap was just some lonely nutcase who got off on kidnapping women, having them listen endlessly about the history of mother sauces, cooking and cleanliness, then sharing the work involved in preparing gourmet meals before releasing his victims. And did he not promise to let her go? Yes.

"You look so deep in thought. Are you quite certain that you never had potatoes Anna before?"

"Pretty sure."

"Well, you're in store for a real treat. Not to mention the poached salmon and asparagus we'll be sharing. So, all the ingredients you'll need are set out on your side of the stove: a medium size stainless steel bowl, a whisk, and a saucepan. You know where everything is. Chop, chop."

Veronica moved quickly to a drawer and cabinet.

"I'll need a shallow pan for the potatoes, another for asparagus, which I'll drizzle with olive oil and shower with bread crumbs then place under the broiler for a couple of minutes; a cast iron skillet for pan-searing the salmon like we did the tuna; butter, shallots and olive oil for the salmon. We'll time it so that the hollandaise sauce is ready at the last moment to ladle onto the fish, finishing with a garnishing of fresh parsley. You should be a pro by now. How does that sound?"

"It sounds marvelous."

"Oh, it will be, indeed. Ah, by the way. Do you know what day it is, Veronica?"

"It's the day of the last meal we'll be preparing together. The day you promised me my freedom."

"Actually, it's the evening of the last French mother sauce we'll be preparing together, Veronica. But I asked you what day it is. Do you know?"

Veronica shook her head.

"It's Valentine's Day; Friday, February fourteenth. We've been together well over a month now. Forty-two days to be exact."

Veronica suddenly began to cry.

"Now what brought that on? Aren't you happy that you're leaving? I promised that I'd let you go."

Veronica shed tears of sheer happiness, nodding her head up and down as if it were a yo-yo on a very short string. "I'm very happy, Cap."

"But first the hollandaise sauce and a bit of history, Veronica. Hollandaise sauce was originally referred to as Dutch sauce; hence, the Holland appellation. But in spite of its name, it's generally accepted that hollandaise sauce was created in France and called

Sauce Isigny, named after Isigny-sur-Mer, a town in Normandy famous for its dairy; especially, its butter and cream. Whereas hollandaise sauce is one of the five mother sauces, béarnaise sauce is considered the 'child' of hollandaise, tangy, with the addition of vinegar, wine, shallot, cracked pepper, and tarragon. I keep telling you how closely related these sauces truly are.

"Now, you can get started with our hollandaise sauce by carefully separating the yolks from four eggs in the bowl like I showed you when we made the yellowfin tuna dish. Will you do that?"

"Yes."

"Good. After that, you'll vigorously whisk the yolks, along with a tablespoon of fresh lemon juice until it's nice and foamy and almost twice the volume. Next, you'll melt a half cup of butter in a saucepan."

"A full stick, right?"

"Right you are. Then you'll slowly drizzle the hot melted butter into the mixture while continuing to whisk away mightily until the sauce has doubled in volume once again. Finally, you'll whisk in tiny pinches of salt, white pepper, cayenne, and you're done. Cover the bowl and place it in a warm spot near the stove until I'm ready. We should finish up together. If the sauce gets a bit too thick while sitting, just add a teaspoon of dry white wine." Cap giggled with delight when suddenly the phone rang. "Excuse me a moment."

Cap crossed to the other side of the room for privacy.

Not since the evening Veronica was held captive in the basement apartment had she heard a phone or a doorbell ring. Not a single time. Cap removed his cell phone from a pant pocket.

"Yeah?"

"We've got a problem," a serious voice on the other end said to Cap.

"So, tell me."

"Not on the phone. We have to meet."

"When?"

"Now."

"Where?"

"Same place as last time."

"I'll be about thirty minutes."

"Bring the girl. Alive."

Cap ended the call and stepped back into the kitchen area. The man's disposition had changed dramatically.

"Everything all right?"

"Peachy cream," Cap replied.

Veronica knew that it wasn't. Cap was visibly upset.

"That was your ride, Veronica."

"Ride?"

"Yes, ride. You did say you wanted to go home. Correct?"

Veronica nodded unsurely. "Yes."

"I'm sorry, but we're going to have to postpone our dinner."

"Postpone?"

"I didn't mean postpone."

"What *did* you mean?"

"I meant cancel our dinner altogether. We're leaving now."

"Aren't you taking me home?"

"I'm taking you to my friend, and he's taking you home."

"Why don't *you* take me home?"

"Complicated."

"You promised to take me home."

Cap was losing patience. "What I promised was that I'd let you go free. And now I'm keeping that promise."

"Why can't you just drop me off someplace? I'll find my own way home. I promised that I wouldn't tell anyone, and I keep my promises. Always."

Cap went to get Veronica's hat and coat. "Here, put these on. It's fucking cold and windy outside." Veronica put on her coat and hat. Cap reached inside a cabinet drawer and removed several items.

"What do you need those for?"

"To keep you quiet. Turn around."

Veronica shook her head. "You're going to kill me, aren't you?"

"I'm not going to kill you, Veronica. Now turn around!"

Veronica kept shaking her head. "No, your friend is going to kill me, isn't he?"

Cap spun Veronica halfway around, grabbing her hands behind her back, locking them together with a thick cable tie. He roughly shoved a rag deeply into her gob, then with a wide band of black Gorilla duct tape, plastered it across her mouth. With a foot sweep, he sent her sprawling to the concrete floor, taping her legs tightly together before swiftly pulling Veronica to her feet.

"Honeymoon's over, honey."

CHAPTER NINETEEN

A light rain was falling as Cap and the caller met at the rear of a deli in Wading River. The two vehicles were parked next to one another, facing in opposite directions. Headlights were off. It was 6:15 p.m. Dark. Both engines were left running. The deli had been closed for several hours. The drivers' windows were sent down simultaneously.

"You have her?"

"Lying right here next to me on the floor. What's the problem?"

"The fucking problem is that a woman saw you dumping the body in Mattituck. The fucking problem is that it wasn't dark. The fucking problem is that stupid cap and those cargo pants that you're probably wearing right fucking now. Right?"

"I like this cap. Covers my ears in the cold. What else did this woman see?"

"She thinks the vehicle was a late model mid-size SUV. That your fucking pockets were bulging—like with your fucking toys."

"They're not toys; they're tools."

"Yeah, it's like walking around with a set of burglar tools on your person."

"Same as any sailor might carry around. Duct tape, rope, rags, pocket knife, et cetera."

"In the middle of fucking February?"

"You know, you say fuck a lot. Shows a limited vocabulary and an arrested development."

"Arrested is what I'm worried about. Did you hear that Spota's sentencing has been postponed again till June?"

"What else is new?"

"First it was April thirtieth, and now it's changed to the end of June."

"Like I just said, what else is new?"

"That doesn't concern you?"

"Why should it?"

"Because he knows too much. Because he could be making a deal with the devil and probably the reason for another postponement. The excuse for another delay will be the coronavirus."

"What he knows and what he suspects are two different things. He'd protect Burke if they threatened the old bastard with a hundred years in prison. He's what, practically eighty? He'll get five years and be out in four and a half. He won't say anything to undermine The Administration."

"I just hope you're right. If you want to know the truth, it's Burke who concerns me even more. He's a fucking loose cannon."

"A pothead, so what?"

"Wrong. He graduated from marijuana to coke a long time ago."

"That's only if John Ray and that female escort in her affidavit can prove it in a court of law. Partying and prostitution don't prove murder."

"What's wrong with you? Prove it or not prove it, Burke's still a crackhead and very dangerous. He even got busted in his cell for having opioids in his footlocker."

"Listen to me. He knows neither of us personally."

"He knows enough, and that's what concerns me."

"And what *we* know can bring their whole goddamn house of cards crashing down around their heads, federal investigation or no federal investigation because we hold all the cards. We, my friend, along with others in the Nassau/Suffolk area, hold a get-out-of-jail-free card. We are truly, truly untouchable. So just relax."

"All right, let's just get this show on the road. I'll back up to your front passenger door, and we'll put her in my trunk."

"You know, you owe me."

"And why is that?"

"I had a lovely dinner planned, but you screwed things up with your phone call. That's why. I was going to put her out of her misery right after dessert."

"What I think is that you'd probably keep her for an undetermined period of time is what I think. And that would prove too fucking dangerous."

"I said I was going to end it tonight."

"Then what's your fucking problem?"

"The show! The grand finale! The lowering of the curtain!"

"We're only looking out for you. Get rid of that cap, those cargo pants, and get yourself a vehicle with a trunk. It makes life and death so much easier," Cap's friend said with a wide grin, pulling away then backing up close to the SUV's front passenger door.

The two stepped out. Cap walked around and opened Veronica's door.

Veronica, of course, had heard every word of their conversation. The terror in her eyes spoke volumes although she could not utter a word with a washcloth sealed well within her mouth.

"Well, Veronica, at least I wasn't deprived of saying good-bye to you. This is not exactly what I had in mind, of course. The upside is that this gentleman is going to be far more efficient, time wise that is, before he releases you to meet your Maker."

Veronica's moans permeated the palpable cold stillness of the evening.

"Do you believe there even is a Maker, Veronica? A Maker or a Faker? I often ponder that unanswerable question. My guess is that the end is just that. The End. No afterlife. No nothing. You see, I have to believe that. Otherwise, I'd be trembling in by boots. My Muck Boots, that is. I'm surprised my friend here didn't pick on those, too. I live in them as you've probably noticed. Low-cut Mucksters in warm, dry weather, their taller ankle-high boots in nasty wet and snowy conditions, and moccasins when I'm hunting or disposing of garbage. I keep them folded right here in a pants pocket. He picks on me, but you see what he's wearing, don't you? An expensive and rather flamboyant full-length waterproof leather Outback Duster. Dresses more like a cowboy than a cop. Thinks he's the Marlboro Man without the hat, or someone like that." Cap turned to face his associate. "Might just as well put spurs on those boots, pal."

"Expensive? You ride around in a forty-thousand-dollar Subaru Outback with all the bells and whistles while I ride around in an old Chevy sedan. Talk about flamboyant. And I only wear this outfit when it's cold, raining or—" the man paused in mid-sentence, staring maniacally at the quivering woman. "What's her name?"

"Veronica."

"I only wear this outfit when it's cold, raining or when I'm taking out the garbage, Veronica."

"All right, enough nonsense. You've already ruined my evening. You're such a killjoy."

"Killjoy. Very funny."

Cap put the trembling, squirming, twisting body of Veronica Severini into the trunk of his friend's sedan then made an adjustment on the rope wrapped around the young woman's neck and between the pair of hands laced in back of her.

"You sure you got her bound right and tight? I don't need her kicking out tail lights like I saw in a Netflix movie the other night."

"The more she struggles the tighter the noose."

"You sure I won't wind up with a dead body before I get to where I'm going? You know how much I'd hate that."

"Are *you* sure there are no hidden cameras in the back of this deli. You know how much I'd hate to be caught on Candid Camera."

"You should know that I'm on top of stuff like that."

"So, where are you headed?"

The friend smiled. "You'll read all about it in the morning paper. Maybe the afternoon edition if I'm having too much fun. And by the way, forensics took tire impressions at the scenes of your crimes."

"Of course, they did. SOP." Cap looked down at Veronica. "That's short for Standard Operating Procedure in case you're wondering, Veronica. Bye." Cap slammed the trunk of the car. "I change all four tires every time I'm taking out the garbage. All right?"

"So, you figured that someone might have seen your vehicle."

"Not necessarily." Cap smiled coyly. "I just like to leave a lasting impression, just in case. They'll probably be looking for an older model SUV. You don't have well-worn tires on a late model SUV. Causes a bit of confusion. Yes?"

"Yes," the cop friend agreed and smiled. "Creating confusion is always our best cover."

Cap reached into a jacket pocket. "Here's her driver's license in case you're into souvenirs. I can't take credit for this one, I'm afraid."

Both men shook gloved hands then drove off in opposite directions.

CHAPTER TWENTY

Lieutenant Tom Bolton of Southold P.D., dressed in uniform, rang the doorbell at the Severini residence. The man stood on the doorstep, waiting, tears welling up in his eyes. Tom rang the bell again.

Janice and Jim Severini came and opened the door. One look told them all they needed to know. Janice ran upstairs and slammed shut the bedroom door. Jim stepped back from the door and wept as he walked over to the couch and sat. Tom closed the door and went over to a chair beside him.

"May I sit down?" Tom asked politely.

Jim pointed to the chair.

"I thought it best if I came and told you and your wife before you heard it elsewhere."

"Did she suffer?" was Jim's initial question.

Tom's silence answered the question for the grieving man.

"Is it the same person who murdered those two other women and that man from Medford?"

"We're not sure."

"How could you not be sure? Was she found near train tracks or not?"

"It's not that simple."

Janice opened the bedroom door and came to the top of the

stairs. "The meaning of Janice is 'God is gracious,'" she called down. "GOD IS NOT KIND," she screamed. "God is a fucking joke! Working in mysterious ways, my ass." Janice turned and abruptly returned to the room, slamming the door anew. A mournful muffled cry filled the upstairs. The preternatural wailing permeated the door and walls.

"I'm going to make you a promise, Jim. A promise I will keep. I am going to find your daughter's killer. It's not going to bring Veronica back, but it might bring a bit of comfort to you and your wife. Forget about the word closure, Jimmy. You and your wife will never have closure. Police have closure when they close a case. Families that are close are left with the remnants of grief for the rest of their natural lives. You'll bury your daughter, but no matter how hard you try, you will never completely bury the anguish, the sorrow, the pain. It's a package all wrapped up into one. But I will offer a bit of comfort, Jim, and hope that it will suffice. I will find the killer," he repeated.

"Where is she now?"

"With a Suffolk County medical examiner in Hauppauge. I'm leaving you with a name and number to call."

When the lieutenant left their home, Jim had a long talk with his conscience, deciding that he was being punished by God for cheating on his wife. Period. End of story. He considered suicide rather than go upstairs to console his grieving wife.

CHAPTER TWENTY-ONE

Detectives Brenden Reilly and Mike D'Angelo sat in their unmarked car, marking time, mulling over the murderous event. The mutilated body of Veronica Severini had been found last evening behind the Village & Beverage Market along Wading River Manor Road, not far from the long-abandoned Wading River train station, dating back to the late thirties.

"I never saw anything like that in my life," Brenden declared. "A beheading, yes. But nothing ever like that."

The first two syllables of Severini's surname were not lost on the two detectives.

"I couldn't imagine anything like that if I lived to be a hundred."

"Bizarre."

"An understatement."

"What do you think?"

"I think we got two killers on our hands."

"One vicious, yet skillful with a knife."

"The other, savage, too, but sloppy, and with a flair for the dramatic."

"Symbolizing Valentine's Day, Saint's Day."

"Her heart wrapped and sealed in clear plastic and pinned to the sleeve of her coat."

97

"Wearing one's heart on one's sleeve as the expression goes."

"Openly displaying one's feelings and emotions rather than keeping things bottled up inside, is what he's telling us."

Brenden nodded in agreement. "Both clever and sick to be sure."

"He'll be the easier of the two to track."

"Speaking of tracks, there are none this time out. What do you make of that?"

"I think he disposed and posed her body knowing it was a safe secluded area, yet still conveying the idea of train tracks, abandoned or not, still having us believe we're dealing with a single killer."

"You think they're working in concert?"

"I do."

"Not a copycat killer?"

Mike slowly shook his head. "The body was posed. Both the Endicott and Johnsen women were not. Their bodies lay exactly where he dumped them, like garbage."

"I think we're both on the same page."

"Several things keep bothering me, though."

"Spit it out."

"The Gilgo Beach/Manorville murders. The body of Shannan Gilbert. Very different, of course, from the Train Track murders. I keep going back to what Claire Billings said and believes. That there's more than one or two serial killers running around. From what we're learning, there may be four, or maybe more. We're the police, but we might have our blinders on. You know what I'm saying?"

"That a savvy outsider looking in sees more clearly because we're too close to this whole business."

"None of us wanting to believe that a cop or cops are somehow involved."

Brenden nodded in understanding. "I'll tell you something, good buddy. I believe that better than half our guys believe something along those very lines. Yet we keep it to ourselves. Nevertheless, we keep our eyes and ears open to the possibility."

"I think you're right on target."

"Getting back to our Valentine's Day killer, assuming there are two serial killers, why would one seemingly change his M.O. if he really wants us to believe there's only one?"

"To cause confusion and have us second-guess ourselves like

98

we're doing right now, coming to the conclusion that there's only one."

Brenden smiled. "That's the craziest reasoning I ever heard."

"That's why it makes perfect sense."

"Are you sure about all this?"

"Absolutely not."

Brenden laughed and shook his head. "That's exactly what I thought."

"In all seriousness, if we adhere to the cliché of 'just follow the evidence,' it'll lead us to where *they* want to lead us. And that's astray. That's been part of the problem all along."

"What do you wanna do?"

"Go back to the scene where the one killer posed Veronica's body."

"Veronica, huh?"

"Victim sounds so cold and impersonal. I'm taking this case very personally, Brenden, like Tom."

"What do you expect to find that forensics hasn't already uncovered?"

"I just want to see the place again in broad daylight."

"Amazing that anyone even found her body that quickly last night."

"Not so amazing when you're told exactly where to look. The anonymous caller was probably one of the killers. No one's out walking their dog at that hour in the freezing cold and in that isolated area."

"All right, we're off and running with another one of your hunches."

"That's what we do, good buddy. Hunches are the intuitive side of our male brain. And who has better intuition in this gender game?"

"Women."

"More specifically?"

"Claire Billings."

"Bingo. And that's why we're going to stay in constant contact with that lady. She's got a sixth sense, I'm telling you. She may remember something further down along the line. I take that woman very seriously, Brenden."

"Well, I don't know what her sixth sense or the intuitive side of your male brain has to do with us going back to the crime scene, but I'll tell you what. If we find anything of interest out there besides empty soda cans and/or beer bottles, I'll spring for dinner tonight. But if you're sending us on a wild goose chase and we find nothing, you spring for dinner. Whattaya say?"

"I say that I only bet on a sure thing."

"How about I give you an incentive. Ten-to-one odds. Dollars to doughnuts. A sawbuck against one jelly doughnut sometime tomorrow morning when we're having our coffee."

"You know, I think I'm going to sign you up for Gambler's Anonymous."

Brenden smiled. "Been there, done that, partner. I only made it to step two of their twelve-step program."

"Got that beat, good buddy. I went to one AA meeting and told everyone there that it's extremely easy to give up drinking. Told 'em all that I've done it hundreds of times."

Brenden laughed and Mike headed their vehicle toward the Village Beverage & Market on Wading River Manor Road in Wading River.

CHAPTER TWENTY-TWO

It was the middle of February. Jim and Janice Severini sat quietly in the front row at the De Friest-Grattan Funeral Home in Cutchogue. Janet Johnsen's body had also been brought to the same funeral home. The parents of Charlotte Endicott along with Jeffery Johnsen sat to either side of them in a show of solidarity. Endicott's body had been taken to Tuthill-Mangano Funeral Home in Riverhead in the beginning of January. The five folks were seated in the front row to the left of the closed casket of Veronica Severini. Families and several friends of Veronica from Hunter College were seated right behind them.

Law enforcement personnel in civilian clothing roamed the property, the parking area, and the funeral parlor, looking for anything out of the ordinary or anyone who would fit a certain pattern of behavior. The team included two women, several men, and a young fellow who looked and dressed like a teenager but was in his early twenties. Nothing unusual would escape them.

Cooperation among police, the victims' families, and the funeral director extended services a day longer than what the Severinis really wanted, but they understood the need to leave more of a time frame should a suspicion or a suspect suddenly surface. The police had very little to go on, so it was certainly worth a shot.

A cadaver dog dressed in a silly outfit made its way with its female handler while the woman pretended to look for her car keys in and around vehicles within the parking area. Had a body recently been in the trunk of someone's vehicle, the canine would have alerted the handler.

All efforts there and elsewhere netted no positive results, including Detectives Brenden Reilly and Mike D'Angelo's recent revisit to the crime scene in Wading River.

The police were stymied. Frustration was at an all-time high. Pressure from the public was mounting by the minute. The killer or killers were lying low.

CHAPTER TWENTY-THREE

In the upstairs kitchen, which was hardly ever occupied, Cap sat across from a stick figure representation of his mother. Its head was a hand-picked gourd in the shape of a human skull wedged within a broken rung of a high-back wooden chair. Its matted gray-like appearance of hair was an inverted damp mop, propped up to encompass the back and sides of a human face.

"I've got to lie low for a while, Mother. The police are looking everywhere. I know because my cop friend keeps me abreast of such matters. If I didn't have him in my corner, I'd be apprehended in a heartbeat. That's the beauty of our operation. We're a club. A very unique and specialized club. Truly a bunch of party animals.

"Well, enough about me for the moment. The reason why I'm even bothering with you is that I had one more fish dish to prepare and finish off with a hollandaise sauce, Mother dear, before I was rudely interrupted by this friend of mine. Yes, a hollandaise sauce. That was one of your favorites, I'm sure you recall. Of course, I embellished on the recipe over the years—just a tad. Remember how you used to hate that? Everything had to be done your way. You wouldn't ever let me deviate from the norm. You thwarted my creativity from the start. You were a stupid, stubborn old woman. I really did you a big favor by putting you out of your misery. From

103

that day on . . . correction. From that *moment* on, I was free. Free of you forever. And you were free of me. See how neatly things worked out?

"Your case is what's referred to as a cold case, meaning a case that has never been solved but remains open in a cold case file. The evidence referencing your case is locked away in a property room in a police station in another country. The fact that you're not my natural mother helped confound matters. Adoption records destroyed ensured my anonymity. No fingerprints to be sure because I made sure of that. However, DNA *is* a twenty-first century fingerprint, chemistry that can link a suspect to a particular crime. Murder being of particular interest to the police. But unless they have a suspect to match such genetic information, it's proved useless. Except for the fact that the police have gotten very, very clever, having received permission in some states to trace filial connections, narrowing an investigation down to even a distant family member. In other words, if my DNA were found on a victim, even though they have no suspect, a sophisticated database could pick up a hit from say a distant cousin. Although that cousin is not the culprit, the suspect pool is now narrowed down to perhaps several family members. The rest becomes routine police work in pinpointing the actual murderer.

"Anyhow, I was smart enough to cover my tracks, disappearing like a ghost. Poof! There one moment then gone for good. But enough about the past. Tonight, you're going to help me recreate *your* original hollandaise sauce. I will allow it, Mother. I was all set to do my very own version with the help of a lovely young lady whom I'm sure you would have approved of—when you were in your right frame of mind, that is—when I was rudely interrupted by a phone call from my friend as I mentioned a moment ago. Why are staring at me like that, Mother? Did I say something to offend?"

CHAPTER TWENTY-FOUR

Cap was done touting his five mother sauces while offering brief histories of each. No one really appreciated his efforts, he realized. He needed a respite from the tedium. Moreover, he had frozen enough Espagnole sauce to last at least the rest of the year. The other four sauces were a cinch for him to prepare, so he'd whisk them up as needed. From this point forward, his recipes would be somewhat simpler yet spectacular. Perhaps he had overwhelmed his *students* with too much information, he considered. Possibly playing too much the pedantic. Yes. He'd tone things down a bit. Maybe then he would win them over he reasoned as he washed then shucked a dozen top necks, placing each fleshy morsel back in half its shell. KISS, Keep IT SIMPLE STUPID would be his new mantra. He didn't need an apprentice to share the labor of his love. He'd simply explain the procedure, assign the work (if one could even call it that), divvy up the dish, then bring the evening to a close. What could be more rewarding?

Why he had spent so much time with Veronica was beyond him. Did she really believe that he would let her go in the end?

"I guess she did!" he exclaimed then laughed heartily. "I guess she did."

Cap was so sorry he had been interrupted by his friend's call. It would have been a glorious evening, followed by dessert. But his associate in The Administration—as well as the other members—truly had his best interest at heart, he knew. Things would be different from here on out, for he finally realized that he was putting others in jeopardy. The line drawn between selfishness and stupidity was a thin one. He should never have kept Veronica Severini for a full six weeks. Foolish. Very foolish. Yes. Things would be very different with his new guest.

Then again, after instructing his guests on how to prepare at least one of the five mother sauces, Cap had so wanted to follow up with several lessons and expand on four of the basic taste receptors: bitter, sour, salty, and sweet—a metaphor for life's experiences, he posited rather sadly.

"You were a very bitter person, Mother . . . leaving me with a sour taste in my mouth for sixteen long years . . . followed by the salty flavor of sweat upon my tongue as I carried your pate by its head of hair to the toilet bowl after slicing your throat from ear to ear . . . savoring the sweetness of life ever since.

"I was saving the fifth taste receptor for a very special guest. Yes! Veronica Severini would have had the privilege of being that veritable soul, I now realize. So, my friend had been right all along. I would have kept Veronica indefinitely, for I truly wanted her to experience the taste sensation of umami, the fifth receptor unfamiliar to most Westerners—but with my very own secret combination of nine special ingredients. Secret, I said! So, if Veronica were to have asked me to name them all, I'd have told her that I'd have to kill her, Mother," Cap concluded then laughed hysterically for a full minute until he finally caught his breath.

"Would that not have proven to be a bittersweet experience, Mother? And then I'd be right back to playing the role of scholarly instructor, explaining the discovery of umami by Japanese chemist Kikunae Ikeda, the molecular mechanism of nucleotides, glutamic acids, and the misinformation concerning MSG. But not this time, Mother. No! This time out I'm going to keep things very simple."

Cap went down the basement stairs and entered the spacious basement apartment.

"So, Sarah. Are you ready to assist me in preparing the best clams casino you ever had?"

106

Although it was a comfortable temperature in the basement apartment, Sarah Townsend sat shivering in the metal chair bolted solidly to the concrete floor. The tall black-haired, big-eyed woman shook convulsively.

"I'll take that as a yes." Cap stepped over from the kitchen area and unstrapped the 21-year old, first from the waist, then her legs, and finally her hands. "If you'll just step over to the kitchen area, we'll get started."

Sarah did as she was told, eyeing the many knives held fast by a magnetic strip fixed high above the counter.

"You can see that I cut open each clam, separating it from the muscles then placing it back in its shell. You'll note the ingredients we'll need on the counter next to you: spinach, cloves of garlic, dried basil, dried oregano, crushed red pepper, onion, a red bell pepper, a green one, flat-leaf Italian parsley, butter, bacon, gorgonzola cheese, lemon juice, extra virgin olive oil, dry white wine, and some breadcrumbs."

"I want to g-go home," Sarah pleaded. "Please."

"You'll go home when I say you can go home. Now, I want you to begin by cutting and finely chopping up two cloves of garlic, half an onion, then cut about a quarter of each red and green bell pepper. But be careful because my knives are very, very sharp." Cap removed a paring knife from the magnetic holder, carefully handing it over to her by its handle.

"I'm scared."

"I'm a bit scared, too, Sarah. You have no idea what I've been through the last several days. I had a friend warning and telling me how to better cover my tracks." Cap giggled. "I had to get rid of my favorite hat, pants, and footwear. He's teaching me how to better blend in with my surroundings. Oh, I don't mean like camouflage. I mean my appearing to look like most everyone else. Normal. Now that in itself is a trick." Cap guffawed maniacally. "I was never, ever flamboyant, Sarah. I simply selected my outfits based on practicality: a cap that snugly covered my ears when it was cold, cargo pants with several pockets in which to carry important items to have at the ready, rubber boots of different sizes when first exploring a potential area along a set of railroad tracks, and finally a pair of moccasins, no matter the weather, whenever I would dispose of garbage."

"You're not going to let me go, are you?"

"Not if you don't cooperate and learn."

"I'll do anything you say."

"That's what I want to hear, Sarah."

"I'll do anything you ask," she repeated.

"Good girl. Do you remember what I just told you about cutting and chopping the vegetables?"

"Slice and chop the two cloves of garlic, half an onion, and one quarter each of red and green pepper."

"Excellent. Excellent. I don't think I'd remember my name if I were in your shoes. But I just want you to try and relax. Do as your told, and I'll let you go."

"When?"

"Shortly. Right after we enjoy our clams casino. How's that?"

"Promise?"

"Sarah, I always keep my word."

Sarah knew that she was in the hands of a serial killer. Of this there was no doubt. She had watched the news, listened to the radio, read the newspapers religiously: the local *Riverhead News-Review*, *Newsday*, *The New York Times*. The stories were everywhere. *Why would he ever let her go?* she questioned. *Why?*

As if the madman could read Sarah's mind, Cap answered her.

"You've only heard or read stories about those murdered women, Sarah. You haven't heard about the women I let go. They promised not to tell a soul, and I believed them. And so, they're free," he lied.

"I swear on my grandmother's soul I will not tell anyone," Sarah promised. She had nothing to lose but her life. Sarah smiled inwardly at the irony, glancing at the many larger knives hanging from the middle of the magnetic strip.

"Truth is eternal," Cap stated evenly.

"I always tell the truth." Sarah fought to keep her eyes from returning to the largest of the chef knives in the middle of the magnetic strip.

"Then we'll get started. And remember what I told you about those knives," Cap added uncannily, as if once again reading her mind.

"That they're very sharp."

"Actually, they're scary sharp, Sarah."

"I promise to be very careful."

"I wouldn't want you to cut yourself," Cap said and smiled benignly. "Ready?"

Sarah nodded.

"I'm going to place these clams onto a cookie sheet lined with foil so we don't have a mess at the end. Then I'll slice some very thin slivers—ah, redundant; slivers *are* thin," Cap clarified and giggled. "Then again, I did say *very* thin slivers, did I not? Yes, very thin slivers of gorgonzola cheese. Pats of butter, and one-inch strips of bacon. When you're done cutting up the vegetables, we'll put all the ingredients together in a given order."

Sarah had finished cutting and chopping the vegetables. Cap stepped over to inspect. Sarah was standing next to him with the paring knife in her right hand. Had it been a longer blade, she would have plunged it into his throat. She believed she had the courage to do exactly that. Sarah would bide her time, hoping, no praying, that she'd have the opportunity to reach for and wield the far larger kitchen knife.

"Good job, Sarah. What we'll do now is fill, not stuff, the clam shells because we're not making baked clams. Actually, the clams we're preparing are a combination Clams Casino/Rockefeller that I perfected."

Cap had sautéed the spinach, cut the strips of bacon, and worked with the other ingredients while Sarah watched intently. He showed her how to fill the shells, starting with the condiments and ending with a one-inch piece of bacon sprinkled with bread crumbs.

"The secret to cooking the bacon is that when it's golden brown under the broiler, you turn the piece over, sprinkle it again with bread crumbs, close the broiler and wait until that side turns golden brown also. It'll take less than half a minute, and the clams will be done to a turn."

At the end of the meal, served with garlic bread and a tossed salad, Cap strapped Sarah back into the metal chair, tightly binding her waist, her hands, her feet.

"You're hurting me."

Cap ignored the complaint.

"I said you're hurting me."

"In just a few minutes, you won't feel a thing. Promise. But first dessert." Cap crossed over to a counter drawer, pulled it open and withdrew a double-ended melon baller, selecting the smaller size with which to work. Walking back over, he roughly grabbed and pulled Sarah's long black head of hair rearward then scooped the metal rim in and around the fleshy spherical organ. Cap had to shout above her bloody screaming in order to be heard.

"You see, I mean with your good eye," Cap clarified and giggled, "you really have to bear down hard and twist this tool around in order to obtain a perfectly round shape. At least it's true of melons because if you don't dig deeply into the flesh, you come away with one flat end. Of course, I'm orbiting within a boney cavity within your skull and not a melon rind. Ah, here we go." Cap dropped the eyeball into a porcelain ramekin. "And now for the other." The madman scooped out Sarah's other eye with indisputable aplomb.

Afterward, he sharpened the tool's rounded edges and deftly removed her eyebrows.

Sarah went into shock before Cap sliced her throat with the large kitchen knife she'd been eyeing earlier.

CHAPTER TWENTY-FIVE

Detectives Brenden Reilly and Mike D'Angelo as well as other members of Suffolk County's Homicide Unit surrounded the body of Sarah Townsend. The victim had been dumped alongside the railroad tracks near the Speonk train station on the Montauk Branch of the Long Island Rail Road. It was 7 p.m.

"Who found her?" Brenden asked a uniformed officer.

"Woman inside," the officer said, pointing to the waiting room inside the building.

"She see or speak to anyone?"

"Negative," he responded, shaking his head slowly from side to side.

"Out walking her dog, right?" Mike said.

The officer smiled. "Out walking her cat when she spotted something shiny." He pointed to the body.

Mike bent down for a closer look, noting the woman's missing eyebrows and the empty sockets that had earlier beheld her eyes. He carefully studied her mouth. A vertical row of four needle-like pins with alternating rounded loops at one end had been pushed through her lips. "They look like stainless-steel pins."

The officer flipped open his notepad. "The woman said they're poultry lacers, used to close up a bird like a chicken or a turkey. She said, and I quote, 'They're generally used with trussing twine laced alternately between each pin.' She went on to say that most cooks prefer a single trussing needle and some twine, like sewing."

"You find any string or twine around?" Brenden questioned.

"Nope, area and the body are just like you see now."

"Did anyone touch anything?" another detective from the team inquired.

"Not since I arrived. I kept everyone back."

Brenden took Mike aside. "You know what they're going to find in her mouth, don't you?"

"You don't have to be Sherlock to know the answer to that one."

Brenden and Mike stared down at the bloody eyeless corpse.

Brenden glanced inside the building before turning his attention back to the police officer. "We'd like to have a word with the woman. She up to it? I see that's she's lying down."

"Your show. She's been very cooperative in spite of the shock of finding the woman like that. Take it nice and easy, and she'll answer all your questions. She's a very sharp woman. The trauma of the discovery is just now sinking in. Just be careful of her cat, though. None too friendly." The officer smiled and flipped closed his notepad.

"You're a good cop, Sergeant," Brenden commented. "Thorough."

"Ditto that," Mike seconded.

"I appreciate that, Detectives."

Brenden noted the sergeant's name and badge number.

Mike marched over to one of the senior women on the forensic team. "I want her body brought in and autopsied tonight."

"Tonight?"

"Did I just stutter?"

"Yes, sir. I mean no, sir."

"Get it done. My partner and I will be there by ten for a report."

"Ten o'clock tonight?"

"Are you dense?"

"It's pronounced Denise, Detective."

Detective Mike D'Angelo bit his bottom lip to stop from smiling. "Denise. This is extremely important. I just got off the phone with the police commissioner," he lied. "She insisted that you people move on this, now. Do I need to make another call?"

"All right," she said, nodding her pretty head.

"Who'll be on tonight?"

"Sheffield."

"Tell Sheffield that the commissioner will consider it a personal favor if he moves his ass at breakneck speed."

"I'll do just that," she stated solemnly.

"Great, Denise."

CHAPTER TWENTY-SIX

That evening, Suffolk County Homicide caught a break that surprised even Deputy Medical Examiner Sheffield. Alan Sheffield told Detectives Reilly and D'Angelo that a macroscopic examination referencing the stomach contents of 21-year-old Sarah Townsend had revealed undigested food consisting of whole clam and inch-long pieces of bacon. Additionally, the liquid pulpy matter was believed to contain pieces of bell pepper, cheese, and spinach.

"A microscopic analysis will, of course, take a bit more time," Sheffield told the detectives, "and might not tell us anything further. Interestingly, the victim did not chew her food; she swallowed her meal whole. If I had to make an educated guess, she had clams casino, less the pair of eyeballs," he added with an attempt at gallows humor that was anything but lost on the detectives. "There's nothing wrong with her teeth for masticating. I initially had this sneaking suspicion that she was deliberately speaking to us from the grave, or more accurately, right here in Hauppauge.

"As you well know, a pathologist generally concerns him or herself with stomach contents in order to estimate time of death, being that the digestive organ stops functioning at that point," Sheffield went on. "A couple of slices of pizza can turn to a liquid pulp in less than four hours, though digestion can vary from person to person. A meal is generally digested six hours after ingesting. I'm glad you fellas pushed the envelope. Had she chewed her food thoroughly in lieu of swallowing her meal whole, it could be difficult to tell precisely what she had to eat."

Mike and Brenden had hoped for this kind of a break, discovering a clue as to what the victim might have eaten, had she eaten anything at all. Sheffield's report proved to be a breakthrough. They thanked the pathologist profusely, especially for going the extra mile at that late hour. They were about to leave.

"But I'm not through, gentlemen. I've saved the best for last."

The detectives looked at one another then back at Sheffield. The man was smiling excitedly.

"Well, we're listening, Alan," Brenden coaxed.

"This is what I found in the first section of her duodenum." The pathologist reached over and with forceps lifted a soggy 2¼ x 3-inch red and white vinyl-backed barcode label from a metal tray. "It's taken from the packaging of a five-pound bag of littleneck clams."

Mike and Brenden leaned forward and studied the label. The red Signature KIRKLAND name appeared in the upper right-hand corner of the label, signifying the Costco chain warehouse club. The closest Costco to the murder scene was in Riverhead.

The medical examiner continued with his findings. "Below the duodenum, between the small and large intestine is the ileocaecal junction. This is what I found next." Alan Sheffield put down the first label and picked up a second. "This label was taken from a rack of Australian lamb rib. KIRKLAND Frenched Lamb Rack from Costco. Normally what would happen if someone accidentally ingested plastic from the packaging of these items is that it would pass through the alimentary canal and be excreted as feces. While I initially suspected that this woman was speaking to us from the grave, so to speak, I am now certain that this is, indeed, the case. These labels were not forced into her mouth by her killer to be chewed and then swallowed as some sort of sadistic act." Alan Sheffield was shaking his head emphatically. "No. These labels with their plastic backing were intentionally swallowed whole by the victim as were those clams and bacon. What he does with his victims, gentlemen, is to feed them well, very well, before he murders them. So, on a very serious note, Nurse Sarah Townsend, with her knowledge of surgical anatomy, is clearly speaking to us. She wanted us to find those blockages in her gastrointestinal tract."

It was a *major* breakthrough.

It all fits," Brenden said. "The killer probably kept records of the meat and fish and such he bought at Costco, and maybe other stores as well. Look how evenly the packaging labels are cut."

Mike was nodding in agreement. "Sarah Townsend somehow got ahold of a couple of them."

"Do you have any further questions," Dr. Sheffield asked.

"Just one," Mike said. "Do you happen to know Denise's last name and phone number?" he joked around in his excitement.

Alan shook his head and smiled. "Happily married."

"I was once, too."

Alan withdrew his smile. "She happens to be my niece."

"Nice. Nepotism does have its benefits, Doctor."

"How to win friends and influence people," Brenden said, grabbing his partner around the shoulders and leading him from the room. "I take him on these outings with me often, but then I have to take him back to apologize," he called from the doorway. "We'll see you soon, Alan."

"Make it later than sooner," Dr. Alan Sheffield replied good-naturedly.

Sitting in their Ford Taurus with the engine running, Brenden and Mike ruminated over the possibilities taking shape regarding the Train Track murders.

"I think our guy, or at least one of them, is a true foodie," Mike seriously entertained. "Pathology reports referencing the other victims tend to point a finger in that direction, too, although the contents of their stomachs were degraded to a large degree because of the time element as the doc explained. But this time around, we got the mother lode, Brenden. Literally."

Brenden nodded. "Sarah Townsend knew she was going to die and left us the only clue she could."

"Like Sheffield said, this guy feeds them well before he kills them, like it's going to be their last meal, which, indeed, it was."

"Yeah, not porridge or oatmeal or some cheap crappy cereal shit like that to keep them going, but rather substantial food like beef and

116

maybe chicken and fish."

"Nothing substantial in the Johnsen woman's stomach."

"Because she was saving her appetite for dinner with her mom that evening. She hadn't eaten all day before he grabbed her. And like I told you back then, and I'm telling you again, she didn't last but several hours because of her temperament. She was a fighter. The longer they stay in line, the longer they live."

Brenden nodded in agreement. "Sheffield found what he believed to be meat in the Medford victim's stomach as well as the Endicott woman. Probably steak."

"And exactly why Josh Billings had been our *prime* suspect for so long. Get it?" Mike punned in a rather giddy mood. "We were all so focused on steak, steak, and more steak. Not to mention other food stains in their hair and on their clothing."

"When I saw those pins sticking through Townsend's lips, and the woman at the train station went on about trussing needles and poultry lacers, I got this gut feeling he's definitely connected with food; like a chef or somebody at a fancy restaurant."

"Or the pins could simply symbolize two sets of train tracks."

"Or a gate or railing to keep her mouth shut because she pissed him off."

"Or we could just be pissing in the wind altogether."

"You think?"

"I think this fucker fancies himself some sort of gourmet. At least we know he shops at Costco."

"I think we should take a closer look at Sarah Townsend's career as a surgical nurse practitioner is what I think."

"I think we should take a closer look at that sous-chef at Michelangelo's Restaurant in Riverhead," Mike funned.

"Christ, are you still harping on that?

"Yes."

"Why, because he didn't give you a dozen littlenecks last time out?"

"No, because he also fucked up my order between Clams Oreganata and Clams Luciana, I must have told you at least a hundred times."

"I think you got clams on the brain."

"You could be right."

"I think we're getting punchy."

Both men laughed sillily as Brenden peeled out of the parking area reserved for Suffolk County Medical Examiner personnel, heading east along Veterans Memorial Highway.

CHAPTER TWENTY-SEVEN

Cap and his friend entered a busy coffee shop in Greenport. It was a Friday evening. The two men took a table in the corner.

"I'm glad you listened to my advice and changed your hat and pants," the friend said solemnly.

"Oh, and what about these sensible shoes?" Cap questioned and joked in a forced effeminate manner.

The friend glanced down. "Better. You're beginning to blend, my friend."

"I must say that was quite a spectacle. A rather impressive display. I really think you got to the heart of the matter."

"*Your* performance, on the other hand, lacked eye appeal."

The pair guffawed, drawing a bit of attention to themselves.

"I so wanted it to be a bit more public," Cap expressed in *sotto voce*, "figuring that I had found the perfect spot earlier when suddenly this old woman and her darn cat appear from out of nowhere. So I, too, pussyfooted around the area until the two were gone. And then I dumped the garbage."

The friend sat in dead silence before he spoke. "But I thought she found the garbage and called for pick up," the man replied, couching his cryptic wording carefully.

"She had, but that was after her return with puss and boots," Cap

119

explained with a giggle. "How in hell was I supposed to know she's a back-and-forth commuter?"

"What the fuck are you talking about?"

Cap leaned in closer to his friend. "The old woman gets on the train in Speonk, rides the rails east to Westhampton, which is six minutes away, exactly three point four miles, then apparently gets off the train there and walks back to Speonk. I guess for the exercise."

Cap's friend looked at him as though he had two heads. "Are you nuts?"

"What?"

"A person walks approximately four miles an hour. So, it would take twice that time if she's walking a fucking cat. But let's say she's carrying it back. That's just under an hour. You mean to tell me you were milling around there for a fucking hour before dumping garbage?"

"I mean to tell you that I'm learning to blend, friend," Cap retorted with a smirk.

"I think you're losing it."

"Listen, I saw her returning in the distance. She's an old lady and couldn't see shit from several hundred yards away. I was out of there before she and her cat arrived back at the Speonk station. Besides, it was getting dark."

"Seems to me you cut things rather close."

Cap reached inside a jacket pocket and withdrew a train schedule. "Let's just say I pay attention to timetables and leave it at that. No one was at the station when I dumped the garbage."

"Trains don't always run on time, my friend."

"Tell me something I don't know."

"All right, let's change the subject."

"Fine by me."

"I've got a party planned for mid-March. Saint Patrick's Day."

"The 17th."

"Always is."

"Falls on a Tuesday this year. You free?"

Cap laughed. "Unless they nail my ass. No, I have no plans. Where're you throwing it?"

"Gilgo Beach," the friend said straightaway and with a straight face, waiting for a response.

Cap hesitated before breaking into a queer grin. "Seriously?"

"Yep. And I might have a big surprise for you."

"Is she Irish?" Cap half joked.

"As a matter of fact, she is."

"Should I bring my shillelagh?"

"Only if you plan on *cudgeling* up with her."

Cap and his crony cried out with peals of laughter.

"You're a rip," Cap concluded.

Cap's friend continued laughing, nodding in agreement. "If you say so, so long as that doesn't translate to mean **Rest In Peace**."

CHAPTER TWENTY-EIGHT

Lieutenant Tom Bolton of the Southold Police Department paid a visit to Mrs. Brenda Featherston of Speonk. The two were seated in the kitchen as the upholstered living room furniture was covered with cat hair.

"Sorry, Lieutenant, but if we sat down out there, you would be blanketed with Tabitha's fur," the woman explained. "She knows that the kitchen is off limits. I love her dearly, but I don't want her fluff flying through the air around food. The parlor and the lavatory are otherwise her domain."

"What kind is she?"

"She's a Cymric, a long-haired breed. Tabitha is my 'watch-cat' that will actually growl like a dog when someone comes to the door, and she's been known to attack if she feels threatened. Of course, I had her declawed and spayed when I first got her. I knew you were coming, so I put her in the lavatory."

"Very thoughtful, Mrs. Featherston."

"Please call me Brenda. Would you like a cup of tea?"

"No thank you, Brenda. As I mentioned on the phone, I'd like to ask you a few questions about the other evening."

"And as I said to you then, the police thrice asked me a dozen questions, both at the train station and here at home," the woman stated politely. "First the Southampton Town Police, and then those two detectives. However, you were very persistent but mannerly, and so here you are."

"Yes, ma'am."

"Brenda."

"Brenda. The two detectives that you spoke with earlier that evening said that you neither saw nor heard anything strange that evening, that you were just out walking with Tabitha—"

"Neither of them addressed her as Tabitha; they just called her 'the cat.'"

Tom Bolton smiled. "Brenda."

"Lieutenant."

"Please call me Tom."

"Oh, my! That sounds so disrespectful."

"Not at all."

"All right then, Tom."

"The two detectives said that you neither saw nor heard anything strange that evening," Tom repeated, "that you and Tabitha came across the body and called 911."

"Well, to be very accurate, Tom, it was Tabitha that happened across the body of that poor woman. When Tabitha has her mind fixed on something, that's it. She was busy fussing with something. I looked down and saw something shiny. When I looked closer . . . it was so grotesque. My heart was pounding, and I could hardly catch my breath. That's when I called 911."

Tom nodded his understanding. "Brenda, how long would you say you were out there walking Tabitha?"

"How do you mean?"

"Well, from the time you walked from your home to the train station, till the time Tabitha and you discovered the body."

"Sometimes I carry her. So which time do you mean?"

"Excuse me?"

"Do you mean the first time when I walked Tabitha down to the station, or the second time when I carried her most of the way back before setting her down, or do you mean all total?"

"I beg your pardon? I really don't understand, Brenda."

"Well, then I'll give you the whole nine yards, and then you can take your pick. The first time was about fifteen minutes because I like to get to the station a little bit early in case Tabitha has to do her thing. And I always pick up after her, you can be rest assured. Not like some of those scoundrels I could go on and on about. The train pulled in at six twenty-three p.m. sharp."

Tom had his notepad out and was jotting down the information.

"The second time doesn't count I guess because Tabitha and I were not walking."

"You weren't walking."

"No, of course not."

"What were you doing?"

"Sitting down and cuddling Tabitha. She absolutely loves the train."

"You were on the train?"

"Yes, of course."

"And where was this train headed, Brenda?"

"Westhampton is the next stop, and that's where we got off."

"Got off." Tom's words were not framed as a question. "And where did you and Tabitha go after you got off the train in Westhampton, Brenda?"

"Back home, of course."

"And you and Tabitha walked back home to Speonk from the Westhampton train station."

"Well, like I said a moment ago. I had to carry her most of the way. She gets very lazy after dinner."

"And may I ask you why you boarded a train in Speonk, rode one stop to Westhampton, got off and walked back home?"

"Because Tabitha loves the train, and I enjoy the exercise, Lieutenant. I mean, Tom. I'm seventy-eight-years young and in pretty good shape for a person my age."

"Do you do this often?"

"Twice a week."

"And how long does it normally take you from the time you leave here, walk to the station, board the train in Speonk, travel to Westhampton, get off and walk back to the station with Tabitha?"

"Door to door takes about an hour and a quarter. That is, if Tabitha doesn't dillydally. It's only a six-minute ride to Westhampton."

"And you do this walking back in the dark?"

124

"This time of year, yes; but it's getting lighter earlier as the days go by, Tom."

"And you didn't see or hear anything strange in that hour and a quarter period of time?"

Mrs. Featherston raised her chin in contemplation. "No, not on the way back, other than Tabitha and I seeing that poor woman."

Tom Bolton was truly blessed that he had been born with patience. "How about when you first walked from your home here, down to the Speonk train station? Did you see or hear anything strange or suspicious?"

"Well, really not suspicious, but perhaps a bit odd."

"And what was that—and odd in what way?"

"Odd in the sense that you don't usually see someone picking up soda cans and bottles and putting them in a trash receptacle instead of carting them off in a bicycle basket or some jalopy for return deposits. Odd in the sense that you don't see someone policing the area, picking up papers and other debris with one of those trash grabbers with a handle. I was going to get one for picking up after Tabitha if I could find one with a scooper on the end rather than that claw. Although I'm in pretty good shape, like I said, it is getting tougher to bend down as I get older."

"Brenda. Can you describe this person you saw?"

"Oh, sure. The station is pretty well lit. Around five ten. Big shoulders. Wearing one of those construction helmets and a matching yellow safety vest with that gray reflective tape running down and across it."

"Anything else you remember about him?"

Brenda lifted her head high, staring at the ceiling as if the image of the man was hovering right above her.

Tom helped her along. "Young, old, black, white."

"Definitely Caucasian. Late twenties or early thirties."

"His clothing, aside from the vest?"

"Dark trousers. Black or brown. I'm not sure."

"Any distinguishing features: color of his eyes, shape or appearance of his nose, mouth, cheeks or chin?"

"His mouth."

"Go on, please."

"He was wearing a big, bright smile."

125

"Anything else?"

Brenda was shaking her head.

"Maybe a scar?'

"It was getting a wee bit dark, Tom. I don't see like I used to."

"Do you think you would recognize him if you saw him again?"

"Oh, absolutely."

"Did you happen to notice if he had a vehicle? A truck? A van? A car?"

"Oh, it was definitely an SUV. That's why I found it odd at first that he didn't put the cans and soda bottles he collected into his vehicle for deposit return but instead threw them in the trash container."

"Why is that, Brenda?"

"Because if you're driving a shiny late model SUV, you wouldn't necessarily go around picking up soda cans and bottles and policing the area unless you were working for sanitation or something like that, now would you? And if you were working for sanitation, you'd probably have a company vehicle with a decal showing that. I simply sized him up as a good Samaritan is all."

"Can you recall the color of the SUV?"

"Definitely gray. That I can tell you."

"Shade?"

"Dark gray."

"Do you have any idea of the make or model?"

"Oh, that's easy. It was a Subaru Outback. A midsize vehicle."

"Midsize?"

"Yes, midsize, because Subaru makes a larger family-size vehicle for seven to eight passengers called the Ascent."

"Did you happen to see the license plate? Numbers or letters? New York plate? Out of state? Maybe a bumper sticker?"

"No, I didn't take notice of anything like that."

"Tell me exactly where it was parked."

"In the lot to the left as soon as you would drive into the station."

"Brenda."

"Tom."

"Why didn't you tell the detectives what you're telling me?"

"Why? Because they asked if I had seen or heard anything strange at the time Tabitha and I found the body of that poor woman.

126

I hadn't. That's why. Nor did they even ask how Tabitha was faring. She was very, very upset as was I. At least you showed some interest in my little darling the moment you arrived here."

Lieutenant Tom Bolton nodded his understanding and did his best to repress a broadening smile. "One final question, Brenda."

"But of course."

"I'm curious about your knowledge concerning makes and models of cars."

"Oh, I love cats and cars, Tom. I can't afford the latter; at least not the car I would want to drive today. Anyhow, Tabitha loves the train and that's just fine by me."

"A word of advice before I leave, Brenda."

"The best thing to do with advice, Tom, is to pass it along. Oscar Wilde. I'm paraphrasing, but that's the gist. Ever read him?"

"No, I haven't."

"You would enjoy his wit. Anyhow, as you were saying?"

"It's too dangerous out there for you to be walking alone after dark."

"You forget that I have my watch-cat, Tom. She'll look after me."

Tom smiled, shrugged his shoulders, and stood. "I've really got to be going. It's been a real pleasure, Brenda."

"Likewise. I hope that I've been some help to you."

"You certainly have, my good lady. You certainly have."

"Are you sure you don't have time for a cup of tea?"

"Perhaps another time. If you remember anything more, especially about that fellow with the SUV, please don't hesitate to give either me or Detectives Reilly and D'Angelo a call. All right? You have their cards and mine."

"You would be the first person I'd call, Tom."

Brenda got up from the table, and the two shook hands.

"And please lock the door behind me."

"I will do that, Tom."

CHAPTER TWENTY-NINE

Josh and Claire Billings were finishing up a lovely dinner at the Iron Skillet when two customers entered the restaurant. Bob Hartz came out of the kitchen and greeted the pair. There were now four patrons present. Bob preferred limited seating. No more than a dozen folks in an evening and with staggered hours and required reservations. Josh and Claire would soon be leaving, and the two men would be enjoying a quiet evening alone as there were no further reservations scheduled for that night.

"We're a little early, I know," one of the men apologized.

"Not a problem," Bob said, directing the two to a corner table. "Take a seat, and I'll be with you in a moment. I just need to bring these folks their coffee while it's piping hot."

The taller of the two, dressed in a long black leather-caped coat and matching high leather boots, placed a bottle of wine in the center of the table, removed his coat, draped it over an adjacent chair, then sat.

His friend sat, too.

"You just gonna leave your hat and coat on?"

"Until I warm up, I am."

After several minutes, the man removed his baseball cap and hung it off the ear of the ladder-back chair. Removing his jacket without getting up, he let it hang off the back of his chair.

Claire studied the two with interest.

The shorter big-shouldered bushy blond-haired man was leaning forward, drumming his fingers impatiently upon the table.

Bob came out with two cups of steaming hot coffee and set them down carefully. "Very hot," he cautioned. "Just the way you like it."

"Thanks, Bob," Josh replied.

"Thank you, Bob," Claire responded by way of rote, her attention fixed on the two arrivals.

Bob reached inside a sideboard, removing two wine glasses along with menus and a corkscrew, carrying the items over to the men's table. "May I open that for you?"

"You bet," the taller of the two responded.

"First time here, I believe?" Bob inquired.

"Yes, first time."

His friend said nothing.

"When you made the reservation, I explained that the special-order items needed to be preordered. Correct?"

"You did. We understand; we'll be ordering from the regular menu."

"Fine." Bob opened the bottle of wine. "Might I interest you in any of the soups we have tonight?" Bob went on to explain the selections and what had been prepared, fresh as fresh could be, earlier in the day.

Josh canted his head toward Claire's. "Did anyone ever tell you that it's impolite to stare?" he whispered with a grin.

"Was I staring?"

"You haven't stopped staring since the moment they came in."

Claire lowered her eyes to her cup of coffee. "You finished?"

"With my coffee or my complaining?"

"Both."

"Yup."

"Then ask Bob for the check when he comes back out."

As if on cue, Bob exited the kitchen with a check. "I trust everything was fine this evening."

"Better than fine, Bob," Josh said sincerely. "Everything was fantastic as always."

"Fabulous," Claire rejoined.

"Great. That's what Mary Ann and I want to hear."

"Say hello for us." Josh pulled out Claire's chair and helped her on with her coat.

"Certainly will."

Josh and Bob shook hands. Claire received a warm hug and a kiss upon the cheek.

Once outside, the couple headed straight ahead toward the parking lot.

"Creepy guys," Claire adamantly declared.

Josh hit the remote twice, and the doors unlocked. Claire broke stride and suddenly stopped in her tracks.

"What?" Josh questioned.

She was standing behind an SUV. "Go warm up the car. I'll just be a minute."

"What do you want to do, steal this one because it's a later model than ours?" he kidded.

"And much cleaner, too. Go."

"If you're thinking of a newer model, Claire, you can just forget it."

"I'm thinking you should go warm up the car."

Josh just shook his head and walked ahead toward their SUV. Once Claire had something in her head, there was no letting go. Except for the owners' cars, there were only two SUVs in the lot: the Billings' and the SUV belonging to the two men in the restaurant.

Claire walked around the vehicle, studying it carefully. She repeated the license plate number to herself, over and over again so that she wouldn't forget it, immediately heading toward her husband and the running engine.

"What the hell was that all about?"

"Shut up and drive." Claire opened and quickly reached inside the glove compartment for a pen and piece of paper, scribbling down the plate number on a napkin.

"Will you tell me, please, what's going on?"

"It's very strange."

"You're strange. What's up?"

"That SUV."

"I figured that much. What about it? What are you driving at?"

"*You're* driving. Now, be quiet and listen."

130

Josh pulled out of the parking lot and headed north. "I'm not supposed to be driving. You're the designated driver. Remember? I'm the one who drank most of the wine. Last time here you made a big stink. But you were right. I don't need to get pulled over."

"Then pull over there, and I'll drive. What I have to say will sober you up."

Josh pulled the vehicle to the side of the road; he and Claire switched seats. When the two were settled, Claire started telling Josh what she believed.

"One of the men back there . . . there's something funny about him."

"I'm listening."

"You're going to say that I'm nuts, but I think that's the same man who I saw pulling the carpet out from the back of the SUV by the train station weeks ago. The carpet that hid that woman's body. The SUV that's sitting in Bob's parking lot right now."

"You're right. You're nuts. First off, you couldn't even describe the man except for the fact that he was what? Silhouetted against the sky? A shadowy figure in bulging cargo pants? Give me a break. That detective filled your head with that crap."

"No, Josh. He did not."

"You couldn't even describe the vehicle either, expect to say it was something like ours. An SUV. What makes you so certain now that's the same SUV? Huh?"

"It's a late model Subaru Outback. Its body is clean as a whistle. But the tires are worn and very dirty all around. One of the rims is dented and rusted, yet the hubcaps are shiny and new. Who would put old tires on a virtually new vehicle?"

"I see what's happening here. You sized up those two guys as unsavory characters. Saw that they drove an SUV, and your imagination is getting the best of you."

"You're not listening to me."

"I'm listening and hearing a lot of nonsense. Once again, you couldn't even describe the man better than a month ago. But now you're sure it's him. Get real."

"There's something else."

"Always is."

"It's the way he was leaning forward, pulling the carpet from the

131

vehicle before straightening up that evening. There was something that I just couldn't quite put my finger on until tonight, when I saw him leaning forward, drumming his fingers on the table."

"And what pray tell is that?"

"Posture."

"Posture?"

"Yes, posture. His carriage. Hunched slightly forward as he came through the door with his friend. Taking off his hat and coat and hanging them off the back of his chair. Like when the man straightened up after pulling the carpet from the vehicle and dumping the body. He was slightly hunched over. Like tonight when he sat forward in his seat."

"And what are you going to do with this suspicion of yours?"

"I'm going to call Brenden and Mike and tell them what I saw and firmly believe."

Josh sent his seat back and reclined. "You'll call them in the morning, not tonight. I don't need them showing up at six something in the morning like they did the first time around. Hear?"

"Yes, dear," Claire answered subserviently, securing the napkin deep within her coat pocket. "I'm glad I took my wallet and left my pocketbook at home."

"And why is that?"

"Because I'd hit you with it. That's why."

"Let me hear how you're going to begin your conversation with the police. Maybe you could start out with something like this: 'Yes, this is Claire Billings. Listen, I have some solid information on the serial killer case. Well, actually it's a hunch about a hunched over guy with a dirty set of wheels.' That ought to grab their attention."

"Shut up and go to sleep. I'll wake you when we're home."

When Claire and Josh got home, the couple undressed, brushed their teeth, and climbed into bed. As soon as Josh fell asleep, Claire got up, tiptoed into another room, and phoned the police.

CHAPTER THIRTY

Based on Claire Billings' discussion with Detectives Reilly and D'Angelo, Lieutenant Thomas Bolton sat across from Brenda Featherston in the kitchen of the widow's one-bedroom Speonk apartment, conducting his second interview with the woman. A mini-cassette tape recorder was on and running.

"Brenda."

"Tom?"

The lieutenant smiled and decided to forego explaining the prescribed procedure of keeping things rather formal for the recorded interview.

"I want you to think carefully back to that late afternoon when you saw the man policing the area, collecting soda cans and bottles, picking up paper and such with that clamping tool."

"Like it was yesterday, Tom."

"Good. Now, I want you to concentrate on the man's posture."

"Posture?"

"The way he carried himself when he walked."

"I know what posture is, Tom. I'm just not sure what you're getting at exactly."

Tom Bolton did not want to put words into the woman's mouth, but it was difficult to explain what he was looking for without being more specific. "Was he hunched over when he walked? I mean even ever so slightly."

"Well, of course he was hunched over, and a bit more than slightly like you say because the man was stooping in order to pick up those cans and bottles."

Tom smiled and shook his head in mild frustration. "That's not what I mean, Brenda."

"Then say what you mean, Tom."

"I mean when he was finished collecting those cans and bottles and picking up papers and candy wrappers or whatever. I mean when he stood up straight."

"Well why didn't you say so, Tom? You're beginning to confuse the issue like those two detectives, Reilly and D'Angelo, asking me if I saw or heard anything strange when Tabitha and I came across the body of that poor woman instead of an hour and a quarter earlier before I got on the train in Speonk, en route to Westhampton."

"Brenda, please answer the question."

"Yes, he did have a slightly crooked posture when he stood and walked, now that you mention it. But I mean ever so slightly. Hardly noticeable. Didn't give it a second thought because when you're picking up stuff, even with that grabber-like tool of his, after you straighten up, you're still hunched over for a moment or so. You know what I mean?"

Tom nodded a yes. "Brenda, I'm going to show you several drivers' license photos, and I'd like you to tell me if you recognize anyone. All right?"

"All right."

Tom displayed six photos in a row across the kitchen table.

Brenda smiled. "Is this what you call an in-house or house call police lineup, Tom?" she couldn't help but tease.

"Do you recognize anyone, Brenda?"

Brenda put on her eyeglasses and without hesitation pointed to and touched the photo I.D. of Mathew Hansen.

"Are you certain, Brenda?"

Brenda nodded in the affirmative.

"I need a verbal response."

"Does an unspayed female feline go into heat?"

"I need a verbal yes or no, Brenda," Tom said patiently.

"Most assuredly, a yes."

Lieutenant Tom Bolton turned off the tape recorder and reached for his cell phone to call Detectives Brenden Reilly and Mike D'Angelo.

CHAPTER THIRTY-ONE

By 10 a.m. that morning, detectives from the Suffolk County Homicide Unit in Yaphank, the Suffolk County Sheriff's Department in Riverhead, the State Police Department (Troop L) in Riverhead, the Riverhead Police Department, and the Southold Police Department were all on high alert. The event had been precipitated hours earlier from information provided by Claire Billings of Riverhead, referencing a suspected serial killer, or possibly killers, in the East End vicinity of Long Island. An expedited search via the Department of Motor Vehicles had furnished law enforcement with a photo I.D. of Mathew Hansen of Laurel, a hamlet with a population of 1,394. An all-points bulletin was issued for a dark gray, late model Subaru Outback, license plate number KNG 9023. The broadcast was generated to Suffolk and Nassau County law enforcement. All parties concerned were instructed not to engage but to keep the suspect under surveillance until a green light was given by Police Commissioner Geraldine Hart. An arrest and search warrant would be issued based on a positive I.D. made by 78-year-old Brenda Featherston of Speonk.

Within an hour, law enforcement authorities were given the green light. Arrest as well as search warrants had been issued for Mathew W. Hansen, his vehicle, home, and premises. If there had been a 'see something, say something' award given to the tipster of the decade, it would have gone to Claire Billings. If there had been an eyewitness for the month of March award, it would have gone to Brenda Featherston.

Set several hundred yards back off a tertiary road, the police converged upon the Laurel address and surrounded the single-story home, garage, workshop and storage shed. With handguns drawn and serious firepower as backup, the team announced themselves. There was no response. The front door of the house was easily opened with a 30-inch, 13-pound Halligan bar. Working in teams of two, eight men cleared the four rooms. The thick steel-framed door leading down to the windowless basement had to be struck multiple times with a battering ram before it gave. Hansen was not to be found inside the home or anywhere on the property. The garage showed no signs of the SUV. What the workshop revealed were four sets of worn but functional tires on rims, a Daytona long-reach 3-ton hydraulic floor jack, along with jack stands, wheel chocks, cases of engine oil, oil and air filters, spark plugs, and other sundry items relating to the vehicle in question. The storage shed held garden and lawn equipment.

"I'll bet you dollars to doughnuts at least one of those frigging tires matches the impressions forensics took at the Severini scene," Detective Brenden Reilly swore.

"Guy's certainly good at covering his tracks," Detective Mike D'Angelo punned.

"Is that supposed to be funny?"

"Funnier than your analogy of 'dollars to doughnuts,' partner."

"The comparison wasn't supposed to be funny."

"Comparisons relating to doughnuts, coffee, and cops are always funny, especially to civilians looking at us from the outside in."

"Josh Billings didn't find it so funny when we popped in on him and Claire at five a.m. this morning."

"No, he certainly did not. Not after Claire woke him up and told him to get dressed and that we were on our way over."

"Then telling him to put up a big pot of coffee and to serve the assorted doughnuts she had picked up even earlier at Dunkin' Doughnuts, open twenty-four/seven."

"He must have been up half the night."

"Guy looked like death warmed over, sitting there in his PJ's. with jelly from a doughnut clinging to his chin."

"That the doughnut shop on 58, combined with a Baskin-Robbins?"

"That's the one."

"Haven't been there in years."

"Used to be pretty good. When you were in the kitchen with Josh, Claire said it's gone way downhill. Customers wait forever for their fancy coffees; kids behind the counter rarely get the orders right. She says she just picks up doughnuts there and heads for home."

As the two were jabbering away, a forensic investigator from the Trace Evidence section walked over and sighed: "This has got to be one of the most sterile scenes I've ever worked. Guy's meticulous."

"Well, unless he Roto-Rooters those drainage pipes on a regular basis," Brenden was pointing to the six-inch wide hole-filled plates in the concrete floor, "you're bound to find something to keep your team busy, Harold."

"That I would not doubt for a second, so move your butts out of the way and we'll get started."

"And Harold, please go over that uncomfortable looking metal throne with your proverbial fine-toothed comb."

Detective Mike D'Angelo was, of course, referring to the stark metal chair bolted solidly to the concrete floor, the centerpiece situated in the core area of the basement apartment. The chair boasted coal-black webbing restraints fashioned from seat-belt material and fitted for a person's hands, waist, and feet.

"Oh, and I was just going to sit in it and have my coffee since I love being the center of attention," the forensic fellow bantered back.

"Maybe we could take a picture of you in it and send it to the *Post*, headlined **Forensic Foibles at Their Finest**," Mike kibitzed.

"Hey, that's pretty good. Highly alliterative and rather catchy. But I have a better one. How about **Dork Detectives Botch Interview with Initial Witness – Delay & Derail Investigation**. Yeah, I heard about that fuckup."

"Whoa, Harold. That's hitting way below the belt," Mike barked.

"Oh, yeah? I walk over here to chat with you guys, and the first thing out of your mouths is to tell me how to do my job."

"I wasn't telling you how to do your job, Harold," Brenden countered. "All I said was that you're bound to find something of interest in those drainage pipes."

"You don't think I know that? I've been doing this job for thirty-one years. And Mike here tells me I'd better go over that chair with a fine-toothed comb."

"Harold, I was just funning with you, fella, when you got all uppity and told us to move our big butts out of the way; you started it."

"I didn't say big; I said move your butts so that me and my team can get started."

"It's '*my* team and *I*,' not 'me and my team'," Mike tormented the man.

"Oh, you're one to talk about grammar, with your dis, dat, dem, dere, dese and dose."

"It's not my grammar, Harold. It's my accent. I have a very distinctive style of enunciating."

"What say you let me get to work, gentlemen?"

"Gentlemen? Now, that's much better, Harold. And when you're done cleaning out dems shitholes and finish up with your analysis, be sure to give Brenden and *I*, or is it *me*, a fucking shout."

"It's *me*."

"Yes, I know it's you, you moron," Mike barked.

Harold waved away the insult and walked off in a huff.

Brenden smiled. "How to win friends and influence folks."

Mike and Brenden stepped aside as the forensic team set up lighting equipment in key areas of the rather large basement apartment. A pair of crime scene photographers had done an initial walk-through, taking both stills and video of the apartment and its contents. Later, the two moved from floor drain to floor drain, one person setting up a tripod and camera while the other positioned a ruler across the diameter of each steel plate to depict scale. The drains, particularly one directly beneath the seat of the metal chair situated in the middle of the room, became the main focal points. The drain covers were then removed, and special tools were used to scrape and collect the contents from the interior of the pipes.

Another detective from the homicide unit stood in fascination before the numerous number of shiny, vertically displayed kitchen knives and cleavers in several sizes, held in place along a lengthy magnetic strip: pairing knives, utility knives, boning knives, bread knives, chef knives, santoku knives, carving knives, slicing knives, fillet knives, and a set of steak knives.

Mike and Brenden walked over to the young detective.

"Quite a collection, yes?" Brenden asked rhetorically.

"I'll say," the detective agreed. "He either raided a high-end restaurant or a knife manufacturing company. He's gotta be some kind of gourmet guru. These knives are worth a small fortune."

"Along with those knife-sharpening systems," Mike agreed, pointing to a large corner table showcasing several expensive manually-operated, angle-guided, precision sharpeners, one model touted as the finest knife-sharpening system in the world: Wicked Edge, with a wide assortment of diamond honing stones ranging from 400 to 2200 grit so as to put a scary-sharp edge on most any blade.

"Not to mention the number of folding knives he has lined up in those cabinets," Brenden added to the mix.

"Yeah, and if Denise wasn't so thorough in recording every single item on that list of hers, a couple of those beauties might not make it back to the evidence room," Detective Chad Kelly half-kidded.

"One thing I'm certain of now," Mike put forth. "We're definitely dealing with more than one killer."

"How do you figure?" Chad questioned.

"Because our guy here is a perfectionist. He didn't butcher the Severini girl. No way. No how. He cleanly cut the throat of that Gilmore guy back in Medford. He cleanly cut the earlobes off the Endicott woman before breaking her neck with a single snap. Next, he carved up the Johnsen woman as one would carve a turkey—with surgical precision. The Townsend woman he neatly slit her throat after adroitly removing both her eyes and eyebrows. But Veronica Severini was murdered by a butcher. Not a killer with surgical skills. I'm telling you there are at least two serial killers that we're dealing with here, Chad," Mike concluded.

Detective Chad Kelly shrugged his shoulders undecidedly, excusing himself and walking over to Denise who was down on her knees, busy recording information into an inventory log.

"I think he went over to check and see if she forgot to record one of those folding knives on her list," Brenden joked.

"I think he went over to check out her fine ass," Mike said quite decidedly.

"On a more serious note, good buddy, I think someone tipped off this Mathew Hansen maggot that his ass is grass and that we're on the cutting edge of bagging his butt."

"Hey, I like that a lot. Pretty fancy way of putting it. Can I use that line?"

"Feel free. Listen, why don't you go over and see what's going on with Harold, and at the same time apologize for your bad behavior."

"Nah, but maybe I'll check with Denise, soon as Chad's finished chatting her up."

"Not to change the subject or your one-track mind, but I think we got a mole in our midst, Mike."

"No bout a doubt it, partner. No bout a doubt it."

"I'll see if Tom can pop in on the Billings with the photo array, and I'll send him a fax of last night's phone interview with Claire. She'll likely I.D. Hansen like Brenda Featherston did, and we'll go from there. Maybe we'll learn something new about Hansen's friend that could be useful."

"Sounds like a plan. Better Tom Bolton than us if Josh Billings is home and answers the door," Mike said and smiled mischievously.

Brenden smiled, too. "Got that right, partner."

141

CHAPTER THIRTY-TWO

Lieutenant Tom Bolton stood at the threshold of the Billings' waterfront residence in Riverhead. The cop wore civilian clothing and had his credentials at the ready as Josh opened the front door. Claire couldn't have been more cordial or considerate, taking the man's overcoat and inviting the Southold police officer into the living room, having him take a corner seat on the couch that overlooked the Peconic River. Josh, on the other hand, came across as being quite irritated and made his feelings known as Tom began the conversation.

"I really appreciate you both seeing me on the spur of the moment, Mr. and Mrs. Billings."

"At least it's not five or six in the morning like some of you guys show up."

"I'm sure it's been an inconvenience, but I'm also sure you know how important this matter is, sir."

Josh said nothing in reply.

"May I offer you a cup of coffee, Lieutenant? Freshly made."

"No thank you, ma'am."

"Claire. Please call me Claire."

"Claire, I know you've gone over this with Detectives Reilly and D'Angelo on the speaker phone last evening. You're to be commended for coming forward with your information."

The Long Island Serial Killer Murders ~ Gilgo Beach and Beyond

"Were you able to do anything with it, Lieutenant?"

"Can't comment," was the lieutenant's succinct reply.

"I see," Claire said rather sadly, "but I understand."

"What I can say is that Detectives Reilly and D'Angelo are very busy at the moment, otherwise they'd be here. They asked me to come by and speak with both of you and to show you some photos. All right?"

"Of course."

Tom Bolton reached inside his suit jacket and took out an envelope containing several photos, leaning forward and spreading six pictures across the coffee table. Josh and Claire took a seat on the L-shaped sectional next to Tom.

"Do either of you recognize anyone in these photos?"

Josh noted that the picture of each individual had presumably been copied from a driver's license. All printed information above and to the right of the photo as well as where a person's signature normally belonged, just below the photograph, had been deleted.

Claire carefully studied the array then pointed to a photo in the middle. "That's the man I saw sitting with the other one at a corner table in the Iron Skillet last evening."

"You're sure?"

"Positive."

Tom nodded his satisfaction. He set his eyes on Josh. "Mr. Billings?"

"Kind of looks like him, but I can't really say for sure because I was enjoying my dinner and not looking around. But Claire, here, facing in their direction, had her eyes locked like radar on those two guys."

"Do you recognize anyone from the photos?"

Josh simply shook his head.

Tom looked squarely into Claire's bright brown eyes. "Claire, I know that you went over this with the detectives last night on the phone, but I'd like you to tell me everything you can about this other fellow sitting with the man in the restaurant who you pointed out here. Everything. Will you do that for me?"

"Certainly, Lieutenant."

"Call me Tom, Claire."

Josh stood up and stretched. "Do you need me, Lieutenant? Or

143

may I call you Tom, too," he snipped and smirked. "I have work to do. I'll be in my office." Josh didn't wait for a response, heading right around the corner to the next room.

Claire looked down at the carpet and shook her head. "I apologize for my husband's behavior, Tom. He's been under a strain at work and with what's going on with all this other business."

"There's no need to apologize. It's probably better that he stepped away. You'll be able to concentrate. And don't just limit your observations to this man you pointed out. I'd like to hear about any interaction between the two of them, even if you think it's trivial, silly, or not worth mentioning. All right?"

"All right, Tom. I'll start at the beginning from the time that they both walked into the restaurant."

"Good."

Claire's attention to detail was remarkable and one of the reasons why Brenden and Mike had asked Lieutenant Tom Bolton to personally interview the woman as soon as possible. The earlier the better because a witness's recollection tends to wane as time elapses. Nevertheless, Tom had the distinct feeling that if Claire Billings were asked to recount an event that happened a decade ago, she'd be spot-on.

Besides the positive I.D., the lieutenant came away with a powerful piece of information concerning Mathew Hansen's friend that hit Tom like a brick. It wasn't that the information faxed to him hours earlier had been omitted from Brenden and Mike's report. It was there. It wasn't that Claire had missed a beat in describing what the man was wearing that evening. She hadn't. It was there in her statement and in Mike and Brenden's faxed report that Tom was now holding in his hand: a description of the man's coal-black, full-length leather coat. Tom realized where he had seen such a garment most recently—a wool-lined Australian-style Duster coat.

Tom thanked Claire and apologized for having to rush off.

Outside the home, Tom immediately phoned Brenden.

"Yeah, Tom?"

"What's the status with Hansen?"

"Hansen and his vehicle's in the wind, Tom."

"I figured as much. Listen, we've got to meet immediately if not

144

sooner. Is Mike there?"

Brenden heard the urgency in Tom's voice. "He's standing right next to me. Did Claire identify the guy as Hansen?"

"Yes. But I believe I've got something just as important. Where are you guys?"

"Leaving Mathew Hansen's residence now," Brenden replied.

"You know Sunny's Riverhead Diner."

"Yeah, on Main Street."

"Can you meet me there ASAP? I'll be sitting at a back table."

"Be there in ten minutes."

"Listen to me carefully. Don't tell a goddamn soul we're meeting. You, Mike, and me, and that's it."

"Can you give us a hint what this is all about?"

"Not on the phone." And with that remark, Tom terminated the call.

CHAPTER THIRTY-THREE

Lieutenant Bolton was seated at a booth in the rear section of Sunny's Riverhead Diner & Grill when Detectives Reilly and D'Angelo walked in. The pair slid and settled into the seat opposite Tom. They listened with rapt attention as he began explaining in detail what had transpired during his interview with Josh and Claire Billings. He recounted Claire's positive photo I.D. of Mathew Hansen. He reiterated Claire's clear description of Hansen's friend's coal-black, full-length, bright wool-lined caped leather coat.

"That's all there in your report along with the notes I took of the interview. Then it hit me where I've last seen a coat like that. It was on the morning of Thursday, February thirteenth when I first met with you guys at headquarters in Yaphank. It had been raining earlier but then it stopped. I signed in downstairs, and one of your young detectives escorted me up. I noticed a long black garment hanging on a coat rack in the hallway. What first caught my attention were the water droplets and how they clung to the waterproof leather material. The way the coat was hanging there, with its bright plaid wool lining folded back a bit, I was thinking what a warm and practical coat that is."

Mike and Brenden exchanged uncomfortable glances.

"Listen, I know exactly what you guys are thinking, but hear me

146

out. The coat's a lengthy classic-style Australian Outback coat, commonly referred to as a Duster or a Drover, sometimes made from waxed canvas, oilskin, or waterproof leather." Tom showed them a picture of such a garment on his smartphone. "Caped storm flap across the back of the shoulders. Button-up collar. The way Claire went on to describe the black leather coat with a bright plaid lining, it looked very much like the coat hanging on the rack that morning in your department. And the way that she described the guy wearing it, walking into the Iron Skillet Restaurant last evening, fits the description of one of your young detectives to a T—the same detective who escorted me upstairs when I first arrived at Yaphank headquarters.

"He was seated at your desk, Brenden, directly across the hallway from us in your boss's office that morning; the office we took over while Anderson was home sick with the flu, I'm sure you recall. The door to the office was left open. The detective had his eyes cast down, perusing some paperwork, but he had his ears tuned into our conversation. You couldn't see him directly because Mike was blocking the view from where you were seated behind Anderson's desk. Mike, you had your back to the detective. But I had a view of him and can tell you that for a person supposedly so involved in the pile of paperwork before him, I don't believe he picked up a single sheet.

"Now, I know you know you got a mole in your midst because someone had to have told Hansen that we're on to him. With all the manpower we have out there looking for him and his vehicle, we'd have heard something by now if he hadn't been tipped off. I won't say that I hope I'm wrong about all this because if I'm right, you have your mole. That young detective.

"And before I finish, I realize that from where you're sitting this all may sound a bit crazy: a long shot, an Australian-style long black leather coat with a bright lining that hundreds, maybe thousands of people wear; not unlike a late model, mid-size Subaru Outback that an untold number of drivers could operate. But a clean, late model, mid-size Subaru Outback vehicle with a set of dirty well-worn tires? My point, fellas, is that Claire Billings' observations are keen as ever I've seen. She carefully studied the photos and pointed to Mathew Hansen. And before all that, she gave you guys a rather sketchy, vague description of that man and his vehicle. And now she spoon-feeds you a most accurate description of the man seated with Hansen last evening in the Iron Skillet Restaurant. A man whose description uncannily matches that of your young detective."

Brenden and Mike sat in stone-cold silence, mulling over every detail Tom had put forth. A good half minute went by before Brenden spoke.

"We'll bring a recent photograph of the detective to Claire Billings for identification ASAP, but we won't do this through normal channels. This has to be handled rather delicately."

"I agree," Mike said.

"I'm noting that neither of you gentlemen are volunteering the young detective's name."

Brenden and Mike glanced at one another uncomfortably.

"Come on, fellas. The three of us are on the same team and page, and until we close this chapter, I suggest that's how it remains. Let's work together. We have no idea how deep this matter goes."

Mike and Brenden had a very good idea of just how deeply 'this matter' could possibly run.

"Chad Kelly is the detective's name," Mike confided.

"He's a fine detective," Brenden said.

"Know where he is now?" Tom questioned.

"When we left, he was still at the crime scene. Hansen's orderly house of horrors, or more specifically his basement apartment."

"What are you going to do, guys?" Tom questioned, knowing the next move was theirs.

Brenden lowered his eyes to the table and shook his head in wonderment. He couldn't believe what Chad Kelly was suspected of.

"Well, I have an idea," Tom suggested.

Brenden lifted his head. "I'm fresh out of them. So, let's hear what you have to say."

Tom unfolded an ostensibly preposterous plan, but a plan that just might work. The trio would have to coordinate and work together clandestinely, but first, confirmation of Chad Kelly's connection to Mathew Hansen had to be established. It wouldn't prove conclusively that the pair was working in concert, but it would be the building blocks for a circumstantial case that could lead to a conviction.

It was agreed that Tom Bolton would pay the Billings another visit with a recent photo of Chad Kelly.

"The Billings could be in danger," Brenden pointed out.

"I already took care of that," Tom said. "After I called you, I made arrangements for twenty-four/seven protection. Men are on the job as we speak. Surveillance front and rear of their riverfront home along the Peconic River."

"Wait a minute," Mike interjected. "I thought we're all in agreement that others could somehow be involved. 'That we have no idea how deep this matter might go,' quote, unquote, Tom. That the three of us are working surreptitiously. And now you have your Southold police officers covering the Billings' home?"

"Who said anything about police?"

"I don't follow you, Tom."

Tom smiled. "I have a team of highly trained professionals watching that residence in three around-the-clock shifts. If Claire or Josh leave the house, they're on them like seagull shit at a shipyard. They're protected."

"And you simply put this team together from the time you left the Billings?"

"I had this in the works for some time because I had a hunch where things were headed. Let's leave it like that."

"And who's paying for all this, can I ask? No one works for nothing with the kind of hours involved."

"Let's just say I'll probably be paying for many, many drinks at The Broken Down Valise in Mattituck, until the day I die."

"Why are you doing this, Tom?" Mike asked.

"Why? A self-imposed obligation. I promised one of the victims' families that *I* would find their daughter's killer. But I now realize I can't go it alone. I don't have unlimited resources."

"Which victim are you referring to, Tom?" Brenden questioned.

"Does it really matter?" Tom answered straightaway.

Brenden sat there in deadpan.

Mike shook his head slowly back and forth, either agreeing with Tom that it really didn't matter, or in response to the man's premeditated action. "Do the Billings know that they're being protected around the clock?"

"Wouldn't be prudent."

"And why is that?"

"I just get a bad feeling about the husband is all. Not really sure."

"We had him checked out very early, Tom," Brenden stated. "He's eliminated as a suspect. He's just a big royal pain in the ass."

Tom shrugged off Brenden's explanation.

Mike looked squarely at his partner. "When are we going to put Tom's crazy but crafty plot into play?"

"Sooner than later." Brenden fixed his eyes on Tom. "Tom, if you come away with a positive I.D. from Claire Billings as Detective Chad Kelly being the man who was with Mathew Hansen last night in the Iron Skillet Restaurant, which would break my heart, we'll move immediately. Again, it won't prove anything beyond a relationship, of course, but we'll have to play this one close to the vest and hope for the best."

Tom knew and understood Brenden and Mike's dilemma all too well: a suspected accomplice of Mathew Hansen, entrenched within their ranks. A mole. Perhaps a serial killer, too—working in concert with one another. Needless to say, the prospect would not bode well with either the new police commissioner or the new district attorney, whose objective it was to repair a blemished record, to 'create a culture of excellence, professionalism and ethical conduct' among its hierarchy as well within its rank and file.

CHAPTER THIRTY-FOUR

In a second interview and with a new array of photographs, Lieutenant Tom Bolton came away from the Billings' residence with Claire's positive photo I.D. of the man she had seen with his friend last evening at the Iron Skillet Restaurant in Mattituck. The photo was of Detective Chad Kelly, Suffolk County Homicide's youngest detective ever to have been brought into the ranks. The Billings, of course, did not know the names or status of either individual at that point. One man was unquestionably a serial killer at large; the other, a homicide detective currently under suspicion of working in concert with Mathew Hansen.

Josh had concerns that the matter was coming to a head and worried for Claire's and his own safety—the police having conducted four interviews over the last two months; two of those interviews in the past two days.

Claire believed in her heart of hearts that she had identified two men either directly or indirectly responsible for the murders of at least one man and five women. What she did not know was that a seventh victim was about to be reported in short order.

Across the hallway from Detective Lieutenant Steve Anderson's office, Detectives Reilly and D'Angelo were seated at their desks.

The phone rang in Anderson's office, and the head of homicide answered it, listening carefully, shaking his head in sheer disgust.

"When?" Anderson snapped.

A virtually one-sided conversation continued for a full minute as the person on the other end of the line filled the commander of the unit in on the details. Anderson was jotting down notes, repeating the location and waving Brenden and Mike into his office.

Chad Kelly got up from his desk and placed some paperwork on Brenden's desk, pausing momentarily.

Mike and Brenden stood before their boss.

"We got another Track Murder. Southold. Youngs Avenue and Traveler Street, just east of the train station. Bolton's boss just called and asked if you guys would meet Tom out there and have a look. I told him you're on your way."

"We're on our way, Lieutenant," Brenden said solemnly.

The two did an about-face, grabbed their coats, went down the stairwell, out the building, and headed toward their car.

CHAPTER THIRTY-FIVE

It was late morning when Brenden and Mike arrived at the crime scene in Southold. Town folk had been milling about for the better part of an hour, observing the drama from a distance. Two reporters and camerawomen from the *Suffolk Times* and *Newsday* were on hand to cover the story. Dressed in uniform, Lieutenant Tom Bolton explained to the two detectives that a father and his teenage son had been tossing a football back and forth when the boy stumbled across the body of a young woman partially covered in burlap, her long strawberry blonde hair and face exposed, hands bound behind her, feet drawn up tight with ¼-inch nylon rope to meet the small of her back, a noose-like loop wound around her neck, similar to the posed body of the sixth victim found in Wading River—Veronica Severini.

Tom pointed to and explained that the woman's body had been brought over to the coroner's blue and white vehicle parked along Youngs Avenue, which was well cordoned off from gawking spectators and reporters. Folks were stretching their necks like cranes for a better view, trying desperately to get a glimpse as personnel lifted the lifeless-like form onto a gurney. The contorted figure was wheeled off then slid into the back of the van, presumably to be transported to the office of the Suffolk County medical examiner in Hauppauge. The team was finishing up their task.

A moment later, Brenden and Mike stepped over to the spot where Tom was now standing and pointing down at the ground. "That's where the boy and his father found her, not four feet from the railroad tracks."

Mike stooped down and surveyed the area in all directions, indicating the distance from the train station to where the three were now gathered.

Brenden was busy taking notes.

Moments later, Tom, Brenden and Mike headed toward the coroner's van. At the apex of the narrowing barricaded intersection, Tom paused just long enough to be sure that one of the reporters overheard the reasoning for the forensic team's unprecedented inaction of not undoing the rope that bound the woman's body in that bizarre position.

"Forensics has a specialist waiting in Hauppauge to untie and examine the knots," Tom explained. "I'm going to follow the van with my car. I'd like both of you to meet me there and hear what this guy has to say. All right?"

"Not a problem, Tom."

"Ditto. We'll be there."

Tom signaled for the van to leave and then headed toward his cruiser. Brenden and Mike headed for their car.

As the coroner's van made a U-turn and the barricades were removed, the vehicle turned north on Youngs Avenue then headed west along Route 48. The man seated on a bench beside the woman lying on the gurney reached down and untied the rope at her back, freeing her feet and hands then unwound the loop of line from around her neck.

"A really first-rate performance, Donna, he assured the 22-year-old. "Truly quite a show."

The strawberry blonde stretched and rolled onto her back, staring in relief at the vehicle's ceiling. "I'm sure as hell glad that's over with," she sighed. "I don't know why in hell you couldn't untie me an hour ago."

"Nosy people, like the press. That's why. They know no boundaries. You want to give someone a heart attack if you suddenly moved after a death scene like that?"

154

"You know, Jamie and his father didn't have to play it that close. One of them almost hit me in the face with that fucking football."

"Comes with the territory, Donna. Besides, a little more blood on your body would have brightened up the scene. Don't you think?"

"Very funny. And I just want you to know that I thought Uncle Tommy was going to first drown me with all that corn syrup and red and blue food coloring crap. A virtual bloodbath."

"Well, he did a first-rate job, and a wonderful job of keeping everyone back, including his own people. Amazing."

"I couldn't see a thing after he covered my eyes with that burlap and told me not to move a muscle, but I certainly heard him loud and clear. 'No one goes near that body till the team arrives.' Where did he get them, and have them play their roles so well?"

"Hand-picked members of the Mattituck Gun Club in Cutchogue, who watch a lot of crime drama, I'm told."

"You know, he must have taken me there a million times, and I never thought to ask why it's called the Mattituck Gun Club if it's in Cutchogue?"

"Beats me. I only shoot bow and arrow."

"And where did he get this vehicle, I mean a coroner's vehicle?"

"Would you have preferred a hearse?"

"No, I'm serious."

"Borrowed."

"Borrowed?"

"You know, you're asking way too many questions."

"The star of the show is allowed to ask questions. And who's driving this van, anyhow?"

"Your father."

Donna Carter shook her head in disbelief.

"We had to play this thing as real as real could be. No law enforcement other than Tommy's inner circle of trusted friends."

"So, who were those two he was waiting for, delaying the show a good half hour while my body ached in pain and my legs went numb?"

"Two detectives from homicide who Tommy's working with."

"Do you think this will all work out the way they want?"

"Hope so, Donna. I truly hope so."

"What are they actually trying to accomplish with this charade?"

Donna's stepbrother shook his head. "I'm just a good soldier on a need-to-know basis, sis. I know better than to ask too many questions."

"Well, the one thing I'll say about Uncle Tommy is that he pretty much keeps it all in the family."

"Amen to that."

CHAPTER THIRTY-SIX

Detective Chad Kelly knew that it was the Billings woman who had positively identified Mathew Hansen from a photo array referencing the two of them at the Iron Skillet Restaurant in Mattituck two nights ago. However, the young detective had no idea that Tom Bolton had gone back to the residence with a second set of photographs, one of which included a photo of the young detective. Chad believed that even if Claire or Josh Billings could describe him, inclusive of the outfit he was wearing that evening, there was no way in the world either of them could identify him as a Suffolk County homicide detective unless the couple came into police headquarters in Yaphank and recognized him, which was unlikely. Chad had no distinguishable features, no scars, no bushy hair like his accomplice, just a clean-cut, nice-looking chap was he. And even if they or anyone could prove a connection between Hansen and himself, so what? It wouldn't prove anything. It would all be supposition. Besides, he knew he was protected from within. He truly believed he was untouchable, that he had a get-out-of-jail-free card if push ever came to shove.

Chad was positive he was not under any cloud of suspicion. He knew, of course, that his colleagues believed they had a mole within their ranks who had tipped off Hansen as to his imminent arrest.

Chad figured that between the elderly Brenda Featherston woman and the Billings couple, those witnesses had pretty much sealed Hansen's fate. Hansen was getting sloppy if not downright stupid. How could he have gone off halfcocked and disposed of that Southold woman in broad daylight? he questioned a hundred times. It had to have happened well after 6 a.m., for he had left Hansen shortly after making arrangements to dispose of Hansen's Subaru Outback and arranging refuge for him.

Chad phoned Mathew in the late afternoon after confirming that the Southold woman's body had been taken to the Suffolk County medical examiner in Hauppauge, the woman apparently having succumbed to multiple stab wounds.

"What's wrong with you?" Chad questioned angrily.

"What's wrong with me? Now that you found me a safe haven for the moment, not a goddamn thing. Why do you ask?"

"You dumped her body in broad daylight? Are you a moron?"

"What are you talking about?"

"The woman from Southold who you stabbed thirty-three times then dumped her body by the tracks near the Southold train station. That's who I'm talking about. I got the full report."

"And just how the hell was I supposed to do that? You took the car and had it disposed of, you told me. I'm stuck here in a dilapidated farmhouse with a stupid swing set and a tricycle in the backyard, and nothing to eat until you move me to permanent digs, you said."

"You're adaptable. Probably stole a fucking car and killed the cunt."

"I got all of Suffolk and Nassau County hunting for my ass, probably all five boroughs, too, by now, and you think I'm off dumping some bitch's body by some railroad tracks. And in broad daylight. Are *you* nuts?"

"You've done this before. That's why you were seen. Two witnesses saw you. You know that. That's why you're in this fucking mess."

"Listen to me carefully. I never dumped trash in broad daylight. That would be suicide. I dump garbage just as it's getting dark so as to avoid suspicion."

158

Chad chuckled. "Avoid suspicion?"

"Yes, avoid suspicion. Set out garbage after dark, and the eyes of night will note suspicion. Set out garbage in the evening as it's turning dark, and you avoid suspicion because you blend into the background naturally. It's worked well for me for ninety-nine pieces of garbage. It would have been a hundred, but you took Veronica Severini away from me that night. Sarah Townsend was the last piece of garbage I deposited—in Speonk. An even hundred! You're either being played like a fiddle, or there's a copycat who's entered our game—uninvited."

Chad said nothing for several seconds, considering the possibilities before speaking. "Gotta go."

"Why? I got more to say."

"Pings and things. You should know that. Drown that burner phone, leave the trike inside where it is now, and stay fucking put. I'll see you shortly."

Mathew Hansen ended the call then continued with his game of solitaire. He hadn't felt so alone in a long time. On top of that, he was losing the card game—badly. Not a good sign.

CHAPTER THIRTY-SEVEN

Cell tower location would have proved invaluable had Mathew Hansen used his cell phone. However, this proved not to be the case. Mathew Hansen was out there in the wind, and Detective Chad Kelly was not at his desk. Tracking, tracing, and triangulation were not in the cards from the moment Hansen disappeared off the grid. Had Detective Kelly warned Hansen about using his cell phone now that the man was homicide's number one suspect? Was Detective Chad Kelly truly suspect number two, or was this all some sort of remarkable coincidence involving a case of mistaken identity on behalf of Claire Billings? Considering Brenda Featherston as a witness in identifying the individual seen picking up bottles, cans, and trash at the Speonk train station, it could be argued in a court of law that the woman was elderly, wore glasses, and was somewhat of an eccentric. However, Lieutenant Tom Bolton later learned that Brenda only needed glasses for reading, not distance, and could see grass growing while preening her cat's whiskers if asked to demonstrate the latter. The exaggeration set aside, Tom Bolton knew he had a reliable eyewitness in Brenda Featherston, just as confidently as Detectives Brenden Reilly and Mike D'Angelo would have bet dollars to Dunkin' doughnuts on Claire Billings' eyewitness accounts.

Mike was getting out of his own vehicle in the parking lot outside police headquarters when Brenden phoned him.

"He's not up here, Mike."

"I just pulled in. His car's not here.

"He was just at his desk a moment ago."

"Must have pulled out shortly before I drove up."

"Maybe I should call him."

"And say what? Want to join us for coffee, Chad old chap?"

"I just hope he's not following up on this Southold business. I don't know how long Sheffield can keep this ruse going."

"It's not Chad's case and would only cast suspicion. He's not stupid. Besides, it wouldn't be the first time Alan lost a body."

Brenden couldn't help but laugh. "You mean misplaced; there's a difference."

"We just have to sit tight and wait for Kelly to make a mistake."

"You mean, hope he makes a mistake."

"Oh, he'll make one. That's why we're playing it like this. Okay, partner?"

"I think I might have made a mistake by not having my eyes on him from the moment he walked in this morning."

"You can't be standing over his shoulder, otherwise he'd get suspicious. You didn't know he'd be in this early. Hardly ever is on his rotation."

"Yeah, I also didn't know he'd be leaving a half hour after he got here."

"Just relax. If we don't have eyes on him by this afternoon, we'll have eyes on him by tomorrow morning."

The following morning, Detective Chad Kelly called in sick with the flu.

CHAPTER THIRTY-EIGHT

Detective Chad Kelly drove his black 2010 Chevy Malibu off a paved road and toward an overlook, parking on the narrow strip of pebbly surface. He sent down his window and glassed the back of a dwelling in the distance, checking to see that the tricycle was back inside the farmhouse. Had the trike remained outside, it would have signaled that Hansen was in a world of trouble and that the safe house was anything but safe. Satisfied, Chad set the binoculars on the seat next to him and continued along, circling 180 degrees before turning into a gravel driveway leading to an old farmhouse. The morning was sunny, with temperatures climbing into the high fifties.

Chad got out and walked to the back of the house.

Mathew was standing at the back door and let Chad in.

"You sure you weren't followed?"

"I left the house at five in the morning, drove around for a fucking hour just to be sure, called in sick with the flu so I wouldn't be bothered today, and you're asking me if I was followed. I've been at this game awhile. All right? How about a fucking cup of coffee?"

Mathew pointed to the sink and the counter next to it. "You left me with a hotplate and an empty container of coffee. I got running water and electricity but not a stitch of food. Yeah, you've been at this for a while. You're a young whippersnapper who's still wet behind the ears. They brought you along a bit too quickly if you ask me. Just like Spota brought Burke along too quickly."

"No one's asking you."

"And you're a bit too cocky to boot."

"How about I give you a boot in the ass?"

"How about getting me out of this dump ASAP?"

"And here I thought you were going to make me one of your gourmet meals like you made for all your guests."

Mathew laughed bitterly. "You see this shithole I have to stay in? You have any idea what I'm leaving behind?"

"Yeah, I know exactly what you're leaving behind. I got the cook's tour of your lovely basement apartment. You never even made me a present of one of those many folding knives I saw."

"Tell you what. When I set up good housekeeping again, wherever the hell they're sending me, I'll send you one. All right? You just can't order one through a company without leaving a paper trail. And I know you'd never bother to travel to a blade or gun show and pick one up for yourself."

"Got that right. ATF guys and gals are everywhere. Wouldn't take the chance."

"I purchase my weapons of choice at several trade shows; cash on the barrelhead. No paperwork. No trace. Which one would you like me to send you, Mr. Paranoid?"

"Without question, CRKT's Seismic, with its new Deadbolt Lock design"

"With or without Veff serrations?"

"Serrations."

"Good choice. Satin finish blade or black?"

"Black."

"But of course."

"Great. I'd appreciate that."

"And you'll be sure to let me know in coded details its performance?"

"I will, indeed."

Both men smiled their understanding.

"I'll share something with you. When I finished off that Townsend woman, I used that very knife. You'll love the feel of it in your hand. It's masculine. Not necessarily for everyday carry, but I

163

love it. You will, too."

"Is that what you used to pluck her eye out?"

"No, I used a double-ended melon baller that removes fruit from a rind."

Mathew thought that Chad would die right there from a fit of sheer laughter. "A melon baller!" the young detective pealed. "You scooped out her fucking eyeballs with a melon baller?" he went on for a full minute. "Now, ain't that rich," Chad concluded, collecting and calming himself after several deep breaths. "Now, ain't that fucking rich."

"But that was before I sharpened its edges with dowels and sandpaper."

"Elaborate. I find this positively fascinating."

"Well, the periphery of the scoop of course is rounded, unlike the straight edge of a blade."

Hansen went on to explain how he had cut and glued strips of 400, 600, 800, and 1,000 grit wet/dry automotive sandpaper onto four 4-inch lengths of 5/8-inch wooden dowels, using contact cement, working those homemade sharpeners in proper sequence until the interior of the rounded edges could and did shave a pair of eyebrows off a brow without any effort.

"I'm sure Detectives Reilly and D'Angelo were appalled by, yet appreciated, my handiwork. When you sharpen the serrations of the Seismic that I'll be sending you, you can use the same method."

Hansen elaborated in further detail how he cut wooden dowels in sizes 3/8, 1/2, and 5/8 inch, covering the range of Veff serrations, named after Tom Veff, found on several other blade designs. "Three designers to keep in mind are Ken Onion, Flavio Ikoma, and Eric Ochs. Do your research."

"I'll keep them in mind. Oh, and by the way. I loved that touch with the placement of pins through the Townsend woman's lips. Symbolizing train tracks, or just holding in her eyeballs so they didn't fall out of her mouth?"

"The latter. Huh! Train tracks, though." Mathew grinned mischievously. "Never occurred to me. If I were remaining here on the Island, I might consider it my very own signature next time out. Only this time I'd leave the body at the Yaphank train station, which, as you know, is literally two minutes away from police headquarters.

Right under your noses. That ought to give your guys a start," he chaffed.

"Forget it."

"Then will you please tell me when I'll be leaving here and where exactly they'll be sending me?"

"You'll be leaving the country and living the good life in Monaco. Lavish hotels, the French Rivera, fine French restaurants. You'll be very happy there."

"When?"

Shortly after our Saint Patrick's Day party in Gilgo Beach. It will be the perfect time for you to leave."

Mathew Hansen nodded his approval. "You know something, Chad? You and I are very much alike."

"Let me stop you right there. We are not at all alike. You seemingly love the company of women. You love to feed and entertain and torment, giving them last-minute hope before you slice, dice and display them openly. I, on the other hand, get right to the point. I give them zero hope. They know they are going to die from the moment I snatch them from the cradle of the world. So complacent they all were in their tiny bubble without a care or clue as to what awaited them until I came along. Their very own bogeyman. As real as real can be. I know who and what I am. I am a true misogynist; a hater of all women. You, however, have ambivalent feelings toward women in that you crave their attention and affection, something you feel that your mother was supposed to provide but didn't. So, you seek the potential of their dying devotion yet at the same time realize the naked truth that it is all for naught, knowing full-well that they can't wait to get away from you, both in life and on the threshold of their death. You're in a constant state of conflict, Mathew Hansen. If I could feel empathy for you, which you know I can't, I'd tell you how sorry I am for you."

"Boy, I see that I really hit a nerve." Mathew Hansen smiled. "You see, in that regard we *are* very much alike. No empathy. No remorse. Yes?"

"In that respect, yes."

"We are complicated individuals, Chad."

"We are indeed unique."

"Which is why we have a network."

"Throughout the world."

"And why we must protect one another."

"And why I must remind you once again. You screwed up."

"I know."

"This is the very first time I'm hearing you admit that."

"I know that, too," Mathew acknowledged.

"I won't belabor the point, but when I killed several of those women and dumped their bodies along Ocean Parkway, I didn't leave them on display for the public to see. I pulled them into the brush under the cover of darkness, and they remained there for eons until Shannan Gilbert came along. You may have killed many more women in a far shorter period of time, but look where it got you. You were going for some sort of a record. You're dealing with high risk victims. Very foolish. I'm dealing with low risk prostitutes that wouldn't likely be missed."

"Did you kill Shannan Gilbert, Chad?"

"No."

"Do you know who killed her?"

Detective Chadwick C. Kelly did not answer the question.

"Did Burke or Bissett kill Gilbert?" Mathew pressed.

"Unlike you, I'm concerned about Burke," Kelly answered evasively. "Like I said earlier, he's a loose cannon."

"But protected, too, so I wouldn't concern myself like I said when we last had this conversation."

"We'll see what happens at Spota's and McPartland's sentencing, or the period in-between."

"Yes, we'll see."

"You'll be taken care of like I said. But there won't be another chance. Witnesses saw you, Mathew: The Billings woman re the Johnsen victim— Mattituck train station. The Featherston woman re the Townsend woman—Speonk train station. I've already arranged to have those two taken care of. But I need to know one thing right now, and I won't ask you again. Did you kill that woman in Southold? If you did, apparently no one said they saw you. But I need to know."

"Like I told you. We've either got a copycat, or someone's playing you."

"All right, let's consider those assumptions. If it was a copycat, we'd likely know that by now."

166

"Not if he or she happens to be a late bloomer. Or say a trucker delivering from the Midwest happened to read the headlines and decided to ply his trade, so to speak, here in Suffolk County before heading back home. We wouldn't know squat, now would we?"

"All right. Both reasonable explanations. Let's consider the other possibility you posited earlier. How are we being played, and to what avail?"

"As to the first part of your question, I'm not sure *how*. As to the second question, a logical reason as to *why* would be to throw us off guard, create confusion, get us buzzing and moving about like we're doing right now, hoping we make a mistake . . . something along those lines."

Chad considered the possibilities for a long moment before speaking. "Back to your point of not being *sure* as to the possibility of being played. Any speculation whatsoever as to the *how*? Take a stab, so to speak." Chad smiled.

Similarly, Mathew weighed Chad's question carefully before answering. "Did you physically see the Southold woman's body?"

"No, but like I told you earlier on the phone, I read the autopsy report. What are you driving at?"

"It just seems strange to me that a body winds up in Southold where that Tom Bolton cop happens to be headquartered and working with homicide in Yaphank."

"Nothing really strange about it when you figure that two of your earlier victims wound up near the tracks in Riverhead and the train station in Mattituck. Southold's obviously next along the LIRR Ronkonkoma Branch before Greenport. If you think they staged a murder to get us buzzing and moving about like busy bees, well, that's just plain crazy. Besides, they had a host of personnel out there covering the scene: forensics, coroner, both Southold town police and my cohorts from homicide. If there had been anything duplicitous going on, I'd have known about it."

"Just seems odd is all."

"All right. I'll look into this further."

"Just *you* be careful, or this could be *your* first mistake."

"And while we're sharing war stories, I'm curious about that guy in Medford."

"Wilbur Gilmore, the accountant."

"Yes, why a guy?"

"He got in the way is all. Collateral damage, you might say. Nice enough fellow. Promised me he'd do my taxes free for a decade if I let him go. I told him I don't pay taxes. He didn't know what to say. I showed him my entire knife collection, fixed blade and flipper types, and asked him if I could receive any kind of a write-off if I reported it. He told me I'd first have to show some sort of income. He actually said that. I don't know who was humoring who. I fed him and sliced his throat quickly, figuring I'd cut my losses."

Chad smiled, changing the subject. "Did you drown that cell phone like I asked you to do?"

"Yeah, do you think I could write it off as a loss?"

Chad laughed and shook his head. "You know, you are a little bit crazy."

"Thank you."

"You're welcome."

"I wonder if they have knife and gun shows in Monaco, you think?"

"Just remember to put the tricycle outside if you sense trouble."

The day was warming up nicely. Detective Chad Kelly started the engine then sent down his window, tires sounding crunchily along the gravel driveway as he drove off and onto the paved road. Chad headed home, stopping along the way to pick up over-the-counter medicines and chicken soup to give the appearance that he was fighting off the flu should a colleague drop by to see how he was faring. Of course, he'd have to put on a quite a dog-and-pony show as he looked to be and was the picture of perfect health.

CHAPTER THIRTY-NINE

The hours passed by slowly for the man sitting in his vehicle, having observed the arrival and departure of Detective Chad Kelly earlier that morning, likewise surveilling the area from the overlook, glassing the old farmhouse. As dusk approached, the figure drove to within several hundred yards of the dwelling, parked the vehicle in a spot where it could not be seen from the overlook or any direction for that matter. The man got out and walked toward the structure, keeping to the edge of a tree line. He waited a good half hour before he closed and crossed the open distance between himself and the building. Dusk had evolved into a foggy darkness. A dim light shown in one of the back windows of the farmhouse.

The figure withdrew his Colt Python .357 revolver and approached the back door. He tried the doorknob. The door was locked. What to do? The man turned around and could barely make out the set of swings. Stealthily, he made his way over and slammed one wooden seat against the metal frame then quickly took cover behind a woodpile.

Mathew Hansen appeared at the lighted window then moved to the back door of the building, opening it and stepping a foot outside. He could hear the swing in motion, lilting from side to side in a rhythmic rusty cadence before coming to a silent stop.

169

"Goddamn deer," Mathew mumbled, about to step back inside.

"No deer, Hansen. Move a muscle, and I'll drop you in your tracks."

"Oh dear," the serial killer calmly replied, noting the pinpoint of laser light on the center of his chest.

The figure moved toward Hansen and ushered him inside.

"I guess you didn't see the no trespassing sign," Mathew mocked.

"Too dark out there to see a hand in front of your face," the man said. "But you did see that red line of reckoning. Now, sit yourself down in that chair."

Mathew Hansen did as he was told. "How did you find me, whoever you are?"

"Let's just say that I *tracked* you down."

"What do you want?"

"Oh, just justice. Justice for all those people you killed."

"Who the hell are you?"

"Lieutenant Bolton, Southold P.D."

"Tom Bolton! Jesus Christ."

"You're going to meet him shortly."

"No such person. Not in the sense that you conceive Him or His mythical Father."

"God will be the judge of that. Here, lean forward." Tom Bolton handed Mathew Hansen a pair of handcuffs. "One cuff on, then both arms in back of you."

Again, Hansen complied.

Bolton grabbed an arm and snapped a cuff on Hansen's other wrist, tightening the pair till it gripped and securely locked skin to bone.

"When is your friend returning?" the cop questioned.

"What friend?"

"Detective Chad Kelly who was here earlier."

"I don't know who or what you're talking about."

Tom cracked the butt of his handgun hard against the side of Hansen's skull. "That jog your memory some?"

Hansen winced. "Do you recall what happened when Chief of Police Burke beat a handcuffed prisoner shackled to the floor at the police station in Smithtown?"

"We're not at a police station, and you do not have the benefit of witnesses who will later attest to any beating—or anything for that matter." Tom Bolton knocked Hansen out of his chair and dragged him over to the old-fashioned cast iron stove standing in the corner. Holstering his weapon, he removed a section of rope from a jacket pocket, then hogtied Hansen's legs to his cuffed wrists before looping the line around his neck, lashing the killer to a leg of the heavy antique green and cream-colored wood burning stove. "Now, I'll ask you once again. When is your friend Detective Chad Kelly returning?"

"He didn't tell me. He said I have to wait. I don't know for how long."

Tom Bolton withdrew his weapon and smacked the butt of the handgun across Hansen's mouth. Blood fell freely onto the linoleum kitchen floor.

"I'm going to ask you again. And then again, and again, and again."

"I DON'T KNOW!" Hansen screamed in pain.

Tom took a step back and almost tripped over the tricycle. "What the hell is this rusty piece of shit doing in here?"

Hansen said nothing.

Tom went over and opened a cupboard. Next, he examined the contents of an icebox in lieu of any refrigerator to be found. He walked over and opened the two faucets at the kitchen sink then closed them before heading toward the other rooms with his weapon at the ready.

"Be right back, Mathew. Struggle and you'll let me know by choking if I tied those knots just right."

Tom went through the rooms and returned to the kitchen, pondering the single oddity. The dirty, rusty tricycle sitting adjacent to the kitchen door.

"You're a pretty sloppy temporary tenant, Mathew Hansen. Didn't even make your bed, I see. Detectives Reilly and D'Angelo told me how neat and clean you kept your Laurel home. But I guess that's what happens when you're staying in someone else's place. You've got running water, electricity, but no food in the pantry. Nothing in the icebox except containers of antifreeze for winterizing the place, jumper cables, and a bunch of rags and some duct tape. A hotplate over there on the counter and an empty coffee container. I'd say from the look of things, someone is coming for you soon. What do you say?"

"No one told me how long I'd be here. I swear."

"Well, we'll just have to wait and see, won't we?"

"I don't expect you to understand, but Detective Kelly and I have get-out-jail-free cards. You can't touch either of us."

"Huh. Get-out-of-jail-free cards. Really? But I imagine they would only be good if you could use them. And I'm not going to allow that to happen, Mathew Hansen."

Mathew Hansen knew that so long as the tricycle remained in the kitchen, he didn't have a chance of surviving since Detective Chad Kelly, or whoever it might be coming by to collect him, would presumably believe that the coast was clear. Hansen knew he had to figure a way to have Tom Bolton move the tricycle outside the back door, seemingly of his own accord, without creating any suspicion. But how was the big question. The killer realized he had been right all along in assuming that Chad had been set up, that the alleged murder out in Southold had been staged to create confusion in order to force their hand to take immediate action. A fatal mistake he feared, knowing now that Chad had been followed to the farmhouse and would soon return when Tom Bolton would take him down, too.

CHAPTER FORTY

Detective Chad Kelly had decided not to go home should a concerned colleague or someone else come by the apartment. Chad Kelly called in sick again, saying that he was staying with a friend and was to be checked out the following day for coronavirus. That would nip it in the bud, giving him time to move Mathew to a rental home in Gilgo Beach, near where a Saint Patrick's Day party had been planned for weeks. It would be a send-off party for Mathew Hansen as well. Packed in a cooler in the trunk of his car, the chicken soup Chad had picked up earlier at a deli would not be wasted, for he knew Hansen would be starving by the time the detective arrived back at the farmhouse.

Mathew Hansen lay whimpering in a corner of the kitchen, still tied to the leg of the heavy cast iron stove. He mumbled incoherently in a panic through the wad of rag stuffed firmly in his mouth and secured in place with duct tape.

"What are you trying to tell me, Mathew?" Tom Bolton asked, awakened from a catnap as he'd been awake for many hours surveilling the farmhouse, the property, as well as Detective Chad Kelly's arrival and departure. "Telling me that you have to go to the bathroom badly or you'll piss and shit in your pants? Is that what you're trying to say?"

Hansen tried desperately to communicate an urgency.

Tom got up from a chair, went over to the killer, reached down and ripped the tape from his mouth. "You have something to say? Spit it out."

Mathew forced the wadded rag from his mouth with his tongue. "Put the tricycle outside the door. It's a signal. If the tricycle is upright, it means that the coast is clear. If it's on its on its side, it signals danger," Mathew made up on the spot and was nodding in earnest.

"And what if I just leave it the way it is, here inside the way I found it?"

"It doesn't mean anything. It has to be placed outside upright, not down on its side."

"And how come you didn't do that before I came by to say hello to you?"

"I was just about do that."

"You were just about to do that." It wasn't framed as a question.

"Yes."

"Do you realize you had hours to do just that after Detective Kelly left? Hours, Mathew."

"I have a lot on my mind," was Hansen's lame excuse. "I was going to do that before I turned in."

"Huh."

"I don't want to die, please. If whoever's coming by and doesn't see that tricycle in the upright position outside, they'll know that's something wrong and they'll leave me here to die," Mathew lied. "Put the trike just outside the door in an upright position, and whoever is coming will feel safe and come to the back door."

"Tell me what will happen if I stand the tricycle upright in the front yard. Will it much matter?" Tom toyed, figuring he knew the answer, figuring that Mathew Hansen desperately wanted that tricycle out in the backyard.

"I don't know. He told me to put it out back. Upright."

"Detective Chad Kelly told you that."

"Yes."

"Tell you what. I think we're going to leave the tricycle right where it is."

Mathew Hansen shook his head and sighed mournfully. "I have to go to the bathroom."

"All right. Tell you how this is going to work. I'm going to untie you and take you to the bathroom, but the cuffs stay on. Door stays open. You'll work your pants down, take a piss or a shit, whatever. If you have to wipe your ass, there's a short-handled mop in a caddy used to clean the toilet. I suggest you use it." Tom smiled. "Wipe your ass, flush, wash the mop out in the toilet, flush till it's relatively clean, pull up you pants, and then I'm bringing you back here, retying you to the stove, muffling your mouth, and then we'll wait to see who comes by to collect you."

"Why are you doing all this? Why don't you just arrest me?"

"Because I know that you have friends in high places. That's why. This business ends here."

Tom led Mathew to the bathroom.

"I need help with my pants."

Tom unbuttoned the man's trousers and yanked the belt through its loops. "You won't be needing this unless you want to hang yourself. If you had shoelaces, I'd—"

In a sudden movement, Mathew's powerful shoulder smashed into Tom's side, pinning the cop against the wall. The killer tried in vain to grab Tom's holstered weapon. Tom recovered quickly and, with a foot sweep, sent Mathew sprawling to the floor. Raising Hansen's head by its bushy blond hair, Tom slammed the killer's skull thrice against the porcelain bowl.

"Let me know when you finished, Mathew. I've got to use the can myself. So, please don't leave a fucking mess."

"You're not going to get away with this, you fuck."

"I just did. Oh, you mean my killing you. Well, we'll have to wait and see. Won't we?"

CHAPTER FORTY-ONE

Moving Mathew Hansen back into the kitchen, Tom Bolton again secured the serial killer to the stove and muffled his mouth, drawing the man's legs tight against the back of his body, the loop of rope wrapped securely around his neck. Only this time he positioned Hansen so that he couldn't move one way or the other, for Hansen was literally lashed to the side of the heavy cast iron stove. Tom checked then rechecked the knots and handcuffs, making little adjustments to ensure that the man's slightest movement would cause asphyxiation, resulting in unconsciousness or death.

"Comfy?" Tom went over and pulled the curtains closed.

Hansen did not make a sound or move a muscle. Tom knew the man was in pain.

"This is but a taste of what you put your victims through. I want you to dwell on that while we wait for your savior, or who you think will come to save you. When whoever comes for you, oh and I do hope it's Detective Chad Kelly, I want to see his face. You see, I believe he hasn't a clue that we're on to him. And if he does, I know he truly believes he can get away with what he's done because he's protected.

"What I think I'm going to do first off is to secure him to the other side from you, then start a small fire in the wood stove. I'm sure that woodpile outside is nice and seasoned. Cast iron heats up nice and evenly as I'm sure you know. Really retains the heat. Oh, and I'll be sure to pull the wad of rags from your mouth because I do want to hear your screams. I wonder who will scream the loudest. We could make it a contest. Whoever screams the loudest gets another log placed closer to their side of the firewall. You see, I'm just warming up with bright ideas."

Tom went on for a good half hour before he let his eyes close then went to sleep in the chair several feet away from his captive.

Tom was suddenly awoken by the sound of tires traveling slowly over gravel. He didn't know how long he had slept until he glanced at his watch.

"Jesus."

Daylight was pressing up against the curtains. Tom looked down at the killer. The man was enveloped in a ball of sweat but otherwise appeared alive. Both heard the car door close. Footsteps followed. Tom stepped over to the doorway, his Colt .357 Python revolver held chest high as he unlocked the door, opening it ajar.

"I brought you—

In a flash, the barrel of Tom's handgun was leveled at Detective Chad Kelly's chest.

"Inside, now!" Tom ordered.

Chad stared at the .357 magnum. "Aren't you going to say something like 'Go ahead, make my day'?" he chided behind an evil sneer.

"I say you're as dead as a doornail in the next second if you don't step in and close the door." Tom took two steps back.

Chad Kelly stepped inside the doorway. "Wouldn't it make more sense to say 'dead as a coffin nail' instead of a doornail, Lieutenant Bolton?"

"I said close the door; put that package on the counter."

Chad closed the door, stared down at Mathew, then addressed Tom Bolton. "I'm going to tell you but once. You won't get away with this. You are making the biggest mistake of your fucking life. Mark my words, motherfucker."

Tom smiled. "Of course I'm going to get away with this. And just so that there's no mistake, I'm talking about a double homicide.

Yours and his. Now put that package down."

Chad set the package on the counter. "You pull that trigger and neighbors will hear the shots, asshole. It will be reported."

"Neighbors are a good distance from here as you're well aware. Besides, any shots they hear they'll think came from a hunter taking a deer or two out of season. Happens all the time. And whether or not it's reported, I'll be long gone from here."

Chad moved toward the stove and stooped to loosen the rope from around Mathew's neck.

"Leave him be."

Chad ignored the order and started to remove the duct tape from around Mathew's head and mouth.

Tom pointed the barrel of his handgun directly at Kelly's head. "You don't listen very well, do you? Touch him again, and you're dead."

"He's suffocating."

"Fuck 'im. Now, let's see what you have here in this package." Tom started to unpack the items. "Ah, soup, crackers, sandwich, pickle, and coffee. I'm starving. I haven't had a thing to eat since I left Southold. I guess you ate; otherwise, you'd have brought something for yourself and Mathew to share. At least you'll die with something in your stomach besides lead."

It was as Chad Kelly stood, his eyes filled with hatred, that Tom lowered the barrel of his weapon and aimed it at the detective's stomach.

"I can make you a deal that will set you up for life. Just hear me out. You want to kill him? Fine. We were going to move him because he became a liability here. He'd be set for life. You could take his place. Look at it sort of like being in the witness protection program. We protect our people."

"And what kind of people are they, Kelly? A clan of killers? A clan of serial killers, of which I believe you're one."

"Doesn't matter what you think. It's what you can prove, and you can't prove a fucking thing. Hansen here is another story. He's now expendable. I and my people can set you up for life. How much do you make a year, Lieutenant Tom Bolton? A little over a hundred thousand plus perks? I can see to it that you enjoy a hundred thousand a month. Live a lavish lifestyle, vacation at the fanciest resorts, and enjoy the finest restaurants in the world."

Tom was smiling and shaking his head while taking a big bite out of the tuna fish sandwich on rye. "I guess you've forgotten. Country after country are on their way to limiting all those pleasures. Coronavirus. Anyhow, you see, my life is just about over. Pancreatic cancer, stage four. Doctors give me about a month, no more than two. I know folks who have been in my situation who swore they would take revenge on someone who wronged them in their life. Kill him or her before they die. After all, they haven't really very much to lose. It's just all talk, though. They never did anything about it because life is too precious, right up to the moment of their own death. Me, I'm under an obligation. I promised a victim's parents that I would find their daughter's killer. I have. I also made myself a promise that I would avenge that woman's brutal murder. I will."

Mathew Hansen struggled with all his might against the restraint that held him tight. A single rope, the pair of handcuffs notwithstanding. The man's face was turning blue, or a shade thereof. Chad Kelly watched his so-called friend about to succumb to asphyxiation.

"You see, Chad. That's what we call an assisted suicide. Now, I'll make *you* a deal. Give me the names of those in the Nassau and Suffolk County Police Departments who form the so-called Administration. I mean besides Spota, Burke, McParkland, and yourself, of course, and I'll let you live."

The young detective arrogantly shook his head. "Believe me, you'll pay dearly for this."

Tom sadly shook his head. "I guess I'll take that as a no."

"You think that this ends with us? You have no idea who's waiting in the wings, asshole. No fucking clue."

Tom lowered his weapon to the detective's abdomen and watched Chad Kelly go to pieces before his very eyes—before the man suddenly lunged at him.

"You're not faster than a speeding bullet, Chad," Tom said after pulling the trigger of his untraceable lethal 1978 .357 Python magnum handgun, hitting the man squarely midsection. The expression on Chad's face was one of awe.

Tom watched Chad bleed out and Mathew asphyxiate.

The feeling throughout Tom's whole being was one of . . .

exhilaration. To ensure that the two were surely dead, Tom fired a hollow point bullet at point blank range into each of their temples. He removed the rope and handcuffs from Mathew's bloody body and put them into the paper bag that the detective had brought then stuck it in his field jacket pocket. Still hungry, he thoroughly washed his hands and finished his sandwich, bringing the container of chicken soup over to the hotplate. He found a pot under the sink and a spoon in a kitchen drawer, washed them, then unhurriedly went about heating up the broth.

He'd leave the Montauk farmhouse under the cover of darkness, the same way he came in last evening. Then he'd call his people who would come by later to deal with the two bodies. Next, he'd pay a visit to the parents of Veronica Severini and tell them that he had kept his promise. Lastly, he'd contact Detectives Brenden Reilly and Mike D'Angelo. He wasn't quite sure exactly what he'd tell them, except to say that there wouldn't be any more serial killings at the hands of Mathew Hansen. Maybe he'd tell them, too, that the mole in their midst had been eliminated. He wouldn't use the word exterminated.

CHAPTER FORTY-TWO

It was Tuesday evening, March 17th, Saint Patrick's Day. The rain had stopped and the sun was trying to break through the clouds. The turnout for the scheduled party at a rental home in Gilgo Beach proved somewhat disappointing. People were more than practicing social distancing, maintaining at least a three-foot space between one another as first advised by the state. Folks were canceling appointments, dinner engagements, conferences, travel plans, and sporting events. Bars and eateries had initially been told to limit capacity to 50 patrons. Shortly after, it had been announced that by Monday 8 p.m., all restaurants would be closed, except for takeout. Schools in New York City had already been closed. Movie theaters were shutting down. The situation was deteriorating exponentially. Things would be getting worse before they would, hopefully, get better. The economy was severely being impacted. Financial institutions were in a state of flux. Investors were being blindsided by the state of confusion.

But today was Saint Paddy's Day, and despite the fact that the annual Saint Patrick's Day parade had been canceled, then postponed, then decidedly/undecidedly declared on-again–off-again, a small parade of people managed to make their way to the oceanfront Gilgo Beach house party. Ice-filled coolers containing bottles of beer lined a table along one wall: lager (Harp), stout (Guinness), and red ale (Smithwicks) were the mainstays in the beer lineup. Marijuana (Gorilla Glue Strain), cocaine (Snow Coke), and heroin (China White) were the drugs of choice in the get-me-up-to-speed game and on full display in one of the upstairs bedrooms. Sex and money were on the minds of the men and women at the party, respectively.

A redhead who just walked into the home was a knockout. A Nassau detective had his eye on her from the moment she paraded through the front door. In fact, most everyone did. Although the weather was still cool, the 22-year-old wore a thin strappy red bralette, matching culottes, and red suede pumps.

The host immediately walked up to her.

"Lady in red. I'd like to make your acquaintance before someone else sweeps you off your feet."

Sharon Walsh stopped abruptly and gazed around the room, taking in the casually dressed men in polo shirts and jeans, some in cardigans and slacks, the older stuffed shirts in business suits and ties, and a small number of young women in an assortment of attire. She returned her attention to the man standing before her, addressing his silly comment. "I don't think there's a soul here who could do that; that is, sweep me off my feet."

"Pretty lame come-on, huh?"

"If that's what that was, Mr.—"

"Detective Ramìrez, Ms.—"

"Walsh. Sharon Walsh."

Detective Diego Ramírez curled his lips into a sad frown. "Yes, indeed, it was lame. Please let me start over, pretty lady in red. I'd like to make your acquaintance before someone else comes up to you and makes a complete fool of themselves, too."

Sharon Walsh smiled warmly and laughed. "That's much better, Detective Ramírez."

"Diego, please."

"Where do you work out of, Diego?"

"Mineola. Homicide/Robbery."

"Wow!"

"Not as impressive as it may sound."

"And why is that?"

"Several detectives are actually requesting to turn in their shields and go back to patrol duty."

"You're kidding."

"I kid you not."

"Why?"

"Well, the way things stand now, the benefits and pay are actually better to remain a police officer than to apply for a promotion to detective."

"And why is that?"

"Because the pay increases for detectives are not enough of an incentive for police officers to look for a promotion and upgrade to detective. And because of that, we have quite a shortage of good detectives."

"How does something like that happen?"

"It's because of all the bullshit politics involved in collective bargaining. It's complicated, but the bottom line is that salaries, benefits such as workers' compensation, and working conditions suffer greatly. Just a couple of years ago, we had seven detectives handling over three hundred gang related cases involving the Bloods, the Crips, MS-13, and the 18th Street gang."

"I certainly know a bit about the Bloods, the Crips and MS-13, but I never heard of the 18th Street gang."

"They started in L.A. Been active since the sixties, right up to the present. Mainly Salvadoran, Guatemalan, and Honduran, but they also have members from other parts of Central America. Just as violent as the rest of the scum. Enough of this nonsense and me. Tell me about yourself."

Sharon cupped her hands behind her back and set her bright blue eyes on the high ceilings. "Let's see. I'm twenty-two going on thirty. Very smart in many ways. Stupid in others. That's why I'm here this evening at this Saint Paddy's Day party. Second year of a four-year program at Touro Law Center. I drink beer and booze." Sharon narrowed her eyes to a couple sitting on a couch in a corner of the commodious room who was obviously stoned. "I do not do drugs."

"Well, no hard liquor to be had here. Just beer and food; that is, downstairs. Upstairs is another story, I'm afraid. So, don't go there and you'll be fine."

Robert Banfelder

"Thanks for the heads-up. Oh, and by the way, I have an acquaintance who's a homicide detective, too. Suffolk County."

"What's his name?"

"Detective Chad Kelly."

"I know Chad very well. We're pretty good friends. Very bright, young detective. Rose through the ranks rather quickly. As a matter of fact, he's supposed to be here tonight."

"Yes, I know."

Sharon watched as a man came down the staircase, wide-eyed and stone-faced, a smidgen of white powder visible beneath his nostrils.

"I'm supposed to meet him here." Sharon looked at her watch. "Unless he's upstairs doing something stupid, I'd say he's late. Late, I do not like."

"Well, I can assure you he's not upstairs. So, I guess he is late."

"Then I guess I'm going to have to make him terribly jealous when he comes waltzing through that door."

"I didn't know he was a dancer."

Sharon smiled sweetly. "Well, that's a bit better than that 'sweep me off my feet' line of yours."

"I'm trying, Sharon. How long have you known Chad?"

"Just a couple of weeks. We met at a bar and made a date to get together for dinner. He had to break that date because he was working on an important case. I guess they're all important. Anyhow, he apologized and invited me to this party tonight. He said that from the party he was taking me to a very special place. A big surprise. But two strikes and you're out; I don't take to three, Diego."

Detective Diego Ramírez loved the sound of his given name trailing off her lovely rose-colored lips.

"Did Chad happen to mention me?" the detective asked casually. "I ask only because we crossed paths a couple of weeks ago working the same case."

"I'll tell you something about your friend and guys in general. Guy's love to talk about themselves. But I had to pull information from Chad. After sitting in a bar with him for two hours, I realized that he was a cop of some sort because when he loosened his tie and opened his jacket, I saw the gold shield. Up until that point, he led me to believe he was in public relations, working for the city. I found

184

that evasiveness and laconism rather refreshing."

"Laconism? Wow! A three-syllable word that's thrown me for a loop. Please don't use any multisyllables on me, or I'm really going to be at a loss. Listen, from here on out, I'm going to tell you as little about myself as possible. How's that? Then maybe you'll find that as refreshing as Chad's, ah, laconism. No such word as laconacy?"

"Nope. The noun is laconism; laconic is the adjective; laconically is the adverb."

Diego smiled. "Maybe you should become a linguist instead of a lawyer."

"Linguistics is fun. Lawyering is a language that will pay the bills."

Detective Diego Ramírez studied Sharon Walsh carefully. "You know Sharon, you're going to make a great lawyer."

"I know that, thank you."

"You just have to work on building up your confidence," he teased. "You're too shy. And I'll tell you something else you might not know."

"Please do."

"You don't find Detective Chad Kelly refreshing because of his evasiveness and laconism."

"No?"

"No. You find Detective Chad Kelly refreshing because he's tall and good looking, has an athletic build, and a charming disposition. That's what you find appealing."

"Diego."

"Sharon."

"Do you know what we have to do with you?"

Detective Diego Ramírez shook his head.

"We have to work on building up your self-esteem."

"You think?"

"I know."

"You know, I hope Chad doesn't show up."

"Doesn't matter."

"And why is that?"

"Because I'm with you tonight."

Diego smiled seductively. "What say we get out of here, and I buy you a proper drink, lady in red?"

"Absolutely."

"What do you drink besides beer? You mentioned booze."

"Absolut."

"Got it. You said Chad had a special surprise for you."

"He did."

"Well, since there's no Saint Patrick's Day parade today—"

"Very, very sad. They even canceled the parade in Ireland, so you know how serious this coronavirus situation is."

"As I started to say—"

"Sorry."

Diego smiled and shook his head. "Are you always like this?"

"Just when I'm nervous."

"Why are you nervous?"

"Oh, for a couple of reasons, I guess."

"Like?"

"Well, for one, with the coronavirus going around, we're supposed to be limited to groups of ten, and here we are at a party with at least twice that. And that's not even counting those I hear upstairs."

"Fifty people were invited to this party, Sharon. Not including their guests, but many canceled at the last moment. Now, what's the other reason that's making you nervous?"

"You."

"Me?"

"Yes, you."

"And why am I making you nervous?"

"Because when I drink too much vodka, I do things I might be sorry for later."

"Then I'll just have to limit you to double shots of Cîroc Ten Vodka. Forget about Absolut."

"You're kidding."

"Would I kid a kid?"

"You just happen to have a two-hundred-dollar bottle of Cîroc Ten vodka lying around?"

"Oh, I see you know good Vodka."

"Yes, indeed. So, what are we doing here?"

"Exposing ourselves to many more people than we should. Mind if we sneak away in your car?"

"No, but why?"

"Because I'm hosting this party. People will wonder where I vanished off to. It would be very rude of me. But if they see that my car is still here, they'll figure I went for a walk on the beach and got lost or whatever. I'll drive us back here, and it's like we never left the party. You leave through the front, and I'll go out the back and meet you in your car in about ten minutes. What are you driving?"

"2019 Audi R8."

"Color?"

"Red."

"But of course."

"Can't miss it."

One of the stuffed shirts came down the staircase on his way to the expansive hot and cold buffet tables, practically tripping over a thick busy blue printed carpet. "Hi, Diego. Nice party. Where's Chad?"

"Don't know."

"You going to introduce me to this lovely lady?"

"No."

Sharon giggled.

"Oh, well then. Please excuse me while I make my way to the chow line."

"Plenty of food, Colonel."

"I can see."

"Enjoy."

The man marched smartly up to one of the tables and started piling his plate.

"Colonel, huh?" Sharon said, apparently impressed. "I thought most of the men here would be law enforcement or politicians. He looks mighty military to me."

"He is. Retired army colonel. Most of the others are law enforcement. A few from other districts. If everyone came who was invited, it would have been your Who's Who of the elite from Nassau and Suffolk Counties."

"Really?"

"Really and truly. Several of their guests in the past were celebrated actresses, super models, and notable businesswomen."

"And you're hosting this party?"

"Yep."

"I am impressed."

"Impressed? Wait till you see what I have in store for you. You like red? I'm going to shower you with your favorite color."

"I can hardly wait." Sharon quietly left through the front entrance. Ten minutes later, Diego exited through the back.

CHAPTER FORTY-THREE

Detectives Brenden Reilly and Mike D'Angelo were sitting at their desks in the hallway at police headquarters in Yaphank when Lieutenant Tom Bolton was escorted upstairs by a uniformed officer. The look on the detectives' faces displayed a composite of confusion and displeasure. Tom looked past them and into the empty office of Detective Lieutenant Steve Anderson.

"He's out today," Brenden volunteered without being asked.

Tom smirked. "Out with the flu?"

"Party last night, he said. Hungover, would be my guess."

"Can we use his office, with the door closed this time?"

Mike put his hand out, palm up, inviting Tom across the narrow hallway. "After you."

The two detectives followed Tom into Anderson's office. Mike closed the door.

Tom took a seat against a wall. Brenden went and sat behind his boss's desk. Mike stepped past Tom and sat adjacent to his partner.

"Where the hell have you been?" Brenden began.

Tom smiled. "You all pissed off because you didn't have a Saint Paddy's Day parade followed by festivities, Brenden?"

Mike had to laugh and in return received a stern look from his partner. "Gotta admit that was pretty funny, Brenden. No? Guess not.

189

Sorry, I need something to tickle my funny bone these days," he added with a sigh.

"Let me begin again," Brenden snapped. "Where the hell have you been, Tom? We're supposed to be a team. The Three Musketeers. That's what we three agreed on. Kelly gave us the slip. Left here without telling anyone. Called in sick two days in a row and not answering his phone. He's not at home and supposedly staying with a friend, so we no longer have him under surveillance. Hansen's still out there in the wind. And you disappear without a word then show up downstairs without even calling. What fucking gives?"

"Been very busy, fellas."

"That's all you have to say, Tom?" Mike asked, turning very serious.

Tom turned his head and glanced at the door. No one was milling around or passing by.

"We're all alone here, Tom," Mike said, noting the cop's apprehension.

Tom pulled his chair closer to the desk. "There's an appropriate line from *The Godfather* where Sonny asks Clemenza where Paulie is. And Clemenza responds, 'Oh Paulie. Won't see him no more.' You don't have to worry about Mathew Hansen and Detecti—I won't even denigrate that title. Chad Kelly. You don't have to worry about him either," Lieutenant Tom Bolton stated resolutely. "They're gone."

Mike and Brenden looked at one another in shock.

"Gone where?" Brenden asked.

"How?" was Mike's follow-up question.

Tom looked down at the floor then back up at the two detectives. "It will be as cold a case as ever there was. That's all I'll say on the matter for the moment."

"That's all you'll say on the matter for the moment."

Lieutenant Tom Bolton ignored Brenden's anger. "I don't think the three of us really know how deep this matter goes. But I'm beginning to believe that it goes deeper than any of us could ever imagine," Tom put forth bluntly. "Way deeper."

"Did you kill or have them killed, Tom?" Mike asked directly.

Tom rose from his chair. "What I suggest for now is that you just let this matter rest and concentrate on what's ahead."

"And what's that?" Mike pressed.

"More of the same but with different players I'm afraid."

"Jesus Christ, Tom!" Brenden exclaimed.

Tom smiled sadly. "That's twice His name's come up in the last two days. Let me leave you to ponder over this, my friends. And by the way, you are my friends. Mathew Hansen and Chad Kelly got what was coming to them. If they hadn't, they'd somehow have escaped the full punishment of the law they each deserve, euphemistically referred to as justice."

Brenden slowly and sadly shook his head. "Tom. Mathew Hansen wasn't going anywhere. We have him cold. He had a safe deposit box in Maryland, under an alias. With a court order, the box was opened and authorities uncovered the driver's licenses belonging to ninety-five women throughout the United States."

"And, of course Wilbur Gilmore, Charlotte Endicott, Janet Johnsen, and Sarah Townsend's driver's licenses were not among them because he hadn't made a visit down there recently," Mike added.

"Team Three found those four licenses hidden in an upstairs hall closet," Brenden elaborated.

"But not Veronica Severini's," Tom guessed.

"There's no question that Hansen had her in his basement apartment, Harold tells us," Mike said. "But we're sure someone else killed her."

"I'm figuring Kelly," Tom said.

"Probably," Brenden agreed, "but proving it is another thing."

"Brenden's not finished, Tom."

"No, go ahead, you tell him."

"I'm all ears," Tom said.

"One of the driver's licenses belonged to Hansen's adoptive mother who lived in Norway. Police there had been looking for the boy for years."

"Why am I not surprised?"

"So, you see, Tom," Brenden repeated, "Mathew Hansen isn't, or should I say wasn't, going anywhere. And you know we would have found him. If you are in any way involved in Hansen's and/or Kelly's disappearance or demise, which it appears you are, you're in a world of shit, my friend."

"Not to worry, guys."

"And why is that, Tom?" Mike questioned.

"Because I have—not a get-out-of-jail-free card—but rather, a *keep*-out-of-jail-free card," Tom assured them with a saddened smile.

"And where might that come from?"

"Memorial Sloan Kettering in Manhattan. You'll soon have a full report of what I learned and what happened with Hansen and Kelly. And please don't tell me not to leave town or any kind of crap like that. All right?"

And with that remark, Tom opened the door and walked out of the office. The same police officer who had just escorted Tom upstairs escorted him back down.

"Have a sparkling day, sir," the officer said as Tom stepped out of the building.

"You, too." Tom paused. "Can I to ask you a question?

"Certainly," the cop answered.

"How long you been on the job?"

"Twenty-nine years and counting the months. Out in thirty and retiring with the missus down to the Keys."

"Got a boat in mind?"

"Along with some serious fishing rods and reels."

"It's a good life. God bless."

"Amen to that."

CHAPTER FORTY-FOUR

The parents of 22-year-old Sharon Walsh reported their daughter missing to a desk sergeant at the Quogue Village Police Department on Friday March 20th, three days after Saint Patrick's Day. It was not unusual for Sharon to disappear for a few days at a time. What was very unusual was for their daughter not to call after a day or two to let them know that she was all right. The sergeant passed the information on to his lieutenant, who in turn notified the chief of police. The chief wasted no time in contacting then interviewing Phil and Dorothy Walsh as a personal favor to William Walsh, chief operating officer of Bank of America (one of several large banking concerns in the Baltimore area), and the brother of Phil Walsh. In weighing the seriousness of two ongoing situations, William Walsh had Donald Trump's Treasury Secretary Steven Mnuchin's phone call put on hold while William advised his younger brother how to proceed with the local police concerning Sharon's disappearance.

"Phil, I'm in the midst of meetings and phone calls with the White House regarding this pandemic situation. I have the secretary of the United States Department of the Treasury on hold while I'm trying to explain to you how to handle this matter. So, please don't tell me that I'm avoiding your phone calls. When I get off the phone,

I'll once again call the chief of police in Quogue, personally. Meanwhile, I want you and Dorothy to make a nuisance of yourselves by going to the police station and demanding an updated report . . . . Yes, I know you went down there initially to file a missing persons report. I'm talking about going back there today and every day until they find her . . . . Of course, she's your only daughter, and I'm her only fucking uncle. Finding my niece is as important to me as it is helping the White House . . . . Phil, you're not listening to me. I don't give a flying fuck about them telling you they're short staffed and that twenty-five percent of their people are out sick with the flu, flu-like symptoms, tested positive for coronavirus, or even if they dropped dead from the disease. They've got seven police officers, three sergeants, one detective, one lieutenant, and one chief of police who comprise their department. By this afternoon, every swinging dick will be on this case. Whoever is out sick will be replaced by others from another jurisdiction. I'll see to that. Otherwise, the chief of police will wish he had joined the fire department instead of the police department. Now you and Dorothy do like I said and show your faces and a little gumption. I spoke with Touro's president earlier, and just like you're practicing social distancing, Touro Law Center is practicing distance-learning. All on-campus classes are canceled. Sharon will be doing remote-learning either online or video transmitted. You know she's a free spirit, Phil. Probably feels she can take a day or two off from her studies while the college is setting things in motion. So, you and Dorothy just try and relax . . . . You're welcome, Phil."

William Walsh depressed the hold button. "Mr. Mnuchin, I am so sorry. I had to take that call. It was an emergency, sir. Not that this isn't. My niece has—"

"Please call me Steve, William. No need to explain. It's a very stressful time for all of us. What we need to do immediately is further discuss this COVID-19 stimulus plan. I'm calling on several of you guys in the area. I have a car waiting for you downstairs. Despite traffic, you'll be here at the White House within an hour."

William J. Walsh got up from behind his desk. "I'm leaving the office now, Steve."

"Geoffrey will be standing outside the front entrance of your building holding a sign with your name on it."

"Got it."

"See you shortly."

CHAPTER FORTY-FIVE

Detective Diego Ramírez sat on a corner of the king size bed with a black baseball bat gripped in both hands. Twenty-two-year-old Sharon Walsh lay on her side in the center of the bed, her naked body wrapped and sealed in two clear plastic six mil thick construction trash bags. Both arms were tightly bound behind her with thick plastic cable ties, legs folded back and secured with rope. A clothesline connected Sharon's wrists to her ankles then snaked firmly around her neck and throat. Three red ratchet tie-down straps secured her body firmly to the bed: along the side of her neck, across her waist, and below her knees. Sharon could barely move a muscle, but she could and would scream and plead for her life.

"This bat that I'm holding, Sharon, is called a Cold Steel Brooklyn Smasher. It's not made of steel at all but rather polypropylene, constructed of the same material as police batons. I picked this one up in 2006 when they first came out. Hasn't failed me yet. Before that, I actually broke two wooden bats: initially on the knees of a young girl; another on the skull of a woman. But I will admit I went a little wild. Oh, and aluminum is way too light. With this bat, however, I never had a problem, and believe me when I tell you that I put it through its paces with some serious punishment. It has a pretty heavy end, but it's not at all uncomfortable to swing.

They make a mini model called the Basher, but I much prefer this twenty-nine-inch Smasher."

Sharon was begging for her life.

"Some folks carry it around for protection," the detective rambled on. "As I watched some of the advertising videos, I tried it out on a watermelon, a big block of ice, a large—and I do mean large —cow bone straddling two cement blocks, then shattered those cement blocks into pieces."

"Please just let me go I beg of you. I'll do anything you ask. Anything. Please," Sharon pleaded and sobbed. "Please."

"I'm sorry, but you'll have to speak up a little louder as those two six-mil plastic material bags you're cocooned within pretty much muffle what you're trying to tell me, although I do get the gist of what you're saying, Sharon," Diego responded behind a sneer. "Actually though, you're really not cocooned as it were because you're in a pair of ninety-five gallon, extra heavy, puncture and tear resistant contractor's bags. Of course, you're not a two-bagger at all, Sharon. Get it?" Diego laughed at his chauvinistic joke. "I had to tuck you in a bit here and there to prevent you from wiggling around; hence, those restraints. It won't be too much longer before you run out of air to breathe I would imagine, which would deprive me of so much fun. But I never let it get that far. I also have to be careful how I deliver each blow because bone could perforate those bags. That's why you're double bagged and with an absorbent rubber-back liner beneath them in case I have a mess."

Sharon fought with all her strength to free herself, trying in vain to turn her head to bite a hole in the plastic for air.

"Please," she mouthed and wept bitterly. "Please."

"Do you remember before we left the party that I said I would shower you in red, Sharon? No? No that you don't remember or no that you're sorry for the way things turned out? But I do want you to know that I enjoyed our time together even though it was short lived."

With Diego's final comment, he lifted and wielded the bat, first shattering the side of Sharon's right knee. The next powerful blow clearly broke a hip. The final blows—and there were many of them— bashed, crushed, and shattered Sharon's skull. Blood showered her entire body. Although Diego was certain the girl was dead, he spoke to her as if she were surely alive.

"Confession time, Sharon. You probably don't even know the name Shannan Gilbert unless some professor cited the Gilgo Beach serial killer murders in one of your John Jay College of Criminal Justice courses before you went to Touro. Well, that was me. I strangled her, but that was well before I took up batting practice. A bit sketchy, but it was ruled an accidental death by drowning. You see, we protect one another. I have what's considered a get-out-of-jail-free card. Myself and several other close friends. We're bigger than the three who initially formed The Administration: Thomas Spota, James Burke, and Christopher McPartland. You probably don't know those names either. Anyhow, we're bigger than G.M. In fact, today, we're bigger than Tesla. Oh, and speaking of car companies, no one will ever see that Audi of yours." Diego laughed lightly. "At least not in the same shape I left it. I think it wound up in a chop shop. I'm really not sure. I don't ask questions. The important thing is that authorities never find it. If you lived in Nassau instead of Suffolk County, my partner and I might have been assigned to the case. Wouldn't that be a rip? I'd be looking for your killer and the car." Diego laughed hysterically and didn't stop laughing for a full minute. "If it had turned out that only the car went missing instead of both you and the Audi, I'm sure dear old Uncle William Walsh would have bought you this year's model. You think?" Diego patiently waited for an answer, prodding her with the handle of the bat.

CHAPTER FORTY-SIX

A poster of missing 22-year-old Sharon Walsh was disseminated around Quogue, East Quogue, and Quiogue. The Suffolk County resident was recognized in less than 24 hours as having briefly attended a Saint Patrick's Day party in Nassau County. On the condition of anonymity, a young businesswoman spoke with homicide Detectives Brenden Reilly and Mike D'Angelo in an interview room at police headquarters in Yaphank. A man introduced to her as a consultant sat in on the conversation. The woman gave a description of the outfit Sharon was wearing that evening: a thin strappy red bralette, matching culottes, and red mid-high block heel suede pumps.

"Did you see what this young lady was driving?" Brenden questioned.

The woman shook her head. "No, I did not."

"Please tell us in detail exactly what you saw and heard that evening," Mike said. "Take your time, and like Detective Reilly said earlier, this conversation is completely confidential. Off the record. No audio or video recording other than the notes that Detective Reilly is taking."

"And I want to say, how brave of you to come forward; how difficult this is for you I'm sure," Brenden added.

Tom Bolton nodded his head in agreement but said nothing.

"Before we begin," Mike said, "I want to be clear that it was your brother who lives in Quogue who pointed out the poster of the missing woman when you were visiting the area. Is that correct?"

"Yes. I recognized her picture immediately. And that's when I called."

"And your brother is waiting for you outside, you told the sergeant downstairs."

"That's right. He's waiting in the parking lot. I didn't want to take my car."

"You live alone in Queens, yes?"

"Yes."

"All right, Ms. Fraser. Let's start. Please tell us everything you saw and heard. All right?"

The woman nodded nervously. "Well, this gorgeous creature comes sashaying through the front door like she owns the place." The woman pointed down at the poster of Sharon Walsh. "I don't mean to seem judgmental; that's just the way it was."

Mike nodded his understanding. "Go on please."

"It wasn't thirty seconds that passed when one of the men at the party approached her. They struck up quite a conversation." The woman paused.

"Can you tell us anything that you overheard?" Mike asked.

The woman shook her head. "No, not a word. But from their body language, which spoke volumes, they were obviously enamored with one another. And then she suddenly left the party. Just like that."

"Did this man leave with her?"

"That's what's strange and how I carefully have to answer you. No, he did not leave with her. He remained at the party and went around to all of us downstairs, reminding us that the food was ready and that the spread was sensational and to get up off our asses and enjoy. Then he disappeared upstairs, I guess to tell the rest of the people at the party. I didn't see him again until about an hour later. If I had to guess, he hooked up with that striking redhead."

"I had asked you earlier on the phone if you could describe this individual, and you hesitated. But from what you're telling us now, it seems that you could give us a very good description. Yes?"

The woman stared down at the floor before looking up and

setting her eyes on Mike, then Brenden, and finally the man who was introduced to her as a consultant. "I can do more than describe him to you. I can tell you who he is. But that's the reason why I'm insisting on anonymity, and why I want it in writing like I said earlier, and you agreed."

Tom Bolton leaned forward and handed the woman an official looking document. "As promised, Ms. Fraser."

The woman took the single page document and read it carefully, noting who had signed it. "And who is this person who signed this?"

"My commander," Lieutenant Tom Bolton truthfully declared.

But Betty Fraser was shaking her head. "I need this signed by the governor or someone like that, sir."

Tom smiled benignly. "We're offering you anonymity, not amnesty, Ms. Fraser. You haven't done anything to warrant that kind of authorization."

Again, Betty Fraser shook her head doubtfully. "With all due respect, gentlemen, I want to run this by my lawyer."

Mike pulled his chair closer to the woman. "May I call you Betty?"

Betty nodded nervously. "Yes, Detective."

"And I want you to call me Mike. Okay?"

"Mike, I really need to run this by—"

"Betty, please listen to me. Your lawyer is basically a tax lawyer, and who I'm sure has your best interest at heart. But this person who you say was at the party and who you can identify was probably one of the last people to see Sharon Walsh alive. I'm sure you entertained that thought or you wouldn't be speaking to us now. We need to talk to him, Betty. Your name is not going to come up. That's a promise. You're going to remain anonymous. We're not going to reveal where we got this lead. But the more time we waste here, the less chance we have of finding that girl. With your help, we'll likely be speaking to others who were at that party as well. But again, your name will not surface. Who is this person, Betty, that you indicated earlier, seemed to know everyone there?"

"He hosted the party like he does every year." Betty was shaking from fear. "Every year I see the same faces of the regulars. Invited guests of the regulars. I'm talking about those very young girls who I never see again. I only thought about it when I saw this young

201

woman." Betty was pointing to Sharon Walsh's picture anew. "She came and then left the party so quickly."

"And you go to this Saint Patrick's Day party every year, Betty?"

Betty was shivering and shaking her head. "Not every year, but most years."

"How many parties would you say?"

"Maybe seven or eight."

"Over how many years?"

"Maybe eleven or twelve."

"You've been going to these parties for over a decade?"

"Ever since I was fifteen."

Mike glanced down at a paper before him. "You're thirty now; is that correct?"

"Yes."

"And were these parties held at the same place every year? Places that you're reluctant to tell us until you had that piece of paper in your hand."

Betty Fraser was staring back at the floor.

"Well, now you have that piece of paper along with our solemn word that you will remain nameless—but not blameless if you continue to keep from us what might help find that girl. Where were these parties held, Betty?"

"Oak Beach and Gilgo Beach. This year's Saint Patrick's Day party was held at an oceanfront home on Gilgo Beach."

"And the person's name who hosted the party?"

Betty was trembling. "Detective Diego Ramírez, Nassau County Police Department, Homicide Squad, Hempstead."

The three men stared fixedly at Betty Fraser.

Tom Bolton asked for the address of the home on Gilgo Beach.

Betty gave the address. Brenden jotted it down and read it back. "Is that correct?"

"Yes," Betty answered, picking away anxiously at her cuticles with a thumbnail.

"Okay. Let's go over the other people that you know who were at this last party. The regulars as you refer to them. Tell us everything you can about them."

Betty Fraser spent the next 45 minutes unfolding information about the oceanfront home and the regulars at the party—especially a

Colonel Oliver Davis from East Islip—while answering scores of questions about them and their guests who were present at the Saint Patrick's Day party on the afternoon of Tuesday, March 17th.

When Mike finished the interview, asking Brenden and Tom if they had further questions of Betty Fraser, which they did not, Mike sincerely thanked the black woman for coming forward with her vital information.

"I'm scared," Betty trembled.

"You tell no one, and we mean no one, about this meeting—excepting of course your brother who is waiting for you—and you have nothing to worry about. And you tell him the same. All right?"

Betty Fraser nodded in the affirmative and was escorted out of the building to where her brother Terence was waiting to drive her back to his apartment in Quogue, where she would take her own car and head back home to Queens.

The three men sat in silence, each considering the best way to proceed from this point.

"We could simply go through proper channels and—"

"Which we won't," Brenden flatly stated. "Tom, any ideas?"

"I think I should question this colonel chap myself. Seems to be the oldest of the lot. Hopefully not the wisest. The way Betty Fraser explained it, he was rebuffed when he approached Ramírez and the girl. I'll introduce myself as a private investigator representing the Walsh family, specifically William Walsh. I'll tell the colonel that this is all on the q.t. This way, if Phil Walsh or anyone gets wind of it, it would be understandable that his brother William would deny hiring anyone. And it leaves out the element of police. This time out, we don't need to stage an event to get someone talking or have them on the move. Hansen's and Kelly's disappearance will be enough to shake their tree. All I need is someone to quietly point us in the right direction. If Ramírez has the girl, or knows where she is, I'll secure that information."

"The problem with that approach is whoever is involved is going to remain as quiet as a clam. No one is going to be talking."

"Betty Fraser just talked," Tom reminded Mike. "You know as well as I, that in most cases, we solve these types of cases through informants. And if not through an informant, then hopefully the perpetrator will make a mistake."

"You know you're preaching to the choir, Tom," Brenden rebuked. "We're all part of the same ensemble."

"Then you should hear my song loud and clear. Sharon Walsh is going to turn up dead either in the short or long run. You know that, and I know that. Someone has had her too long. We're dealing with I don't know how many serial killers. Two have been eliminated."

"Be careful what you say to us, Tom," Mike interjected.

Tom ignored the comment. "Unless either of you have a better way to proceed, I say we stop wasting time. I'll go see this Colonel Davis character."'

Brenden and Mike looked at one another for a long moment.

Brenden fixed his eyes on Tom. "You're looking tired, my friend. Go talk to this colonel, and this time tell us sooner than later what's going on."

Tom got up and was about to exit the conference room.

"A question before you go, Tom. What exactly was in that document you handed to Ms. Fraser?" Brenden asked.

Tom smiled. "Exactly what I said was in it. A declaration of anonymity signed by my commander."

Brenden laughed. "That paper doesn't mean crap because if push ever came to shove, I'd drag her butt into court to testify. That's a given, Tom. Meantime, it's our word that counts."

"*Now* who's preaching to the choir, Brenden," Tom gibed. "Yeah, your word. Like a young successful black woman from Queens is going to believe the words coming out of our white mouths whether they're true or not true. She wanted it in writing, and that's what she got. I had to humor her or she wasn't to tell you—to use your word—crap."

"So why did she come here in the first place?"

"To help us find a killer and hoping that one of us would have that letter offering her anonymity. That's why. Any more questions?"

"I have one," Mike said, scratching his head in puzzlement.

"You always do."

"He's getting a bit testy lately," Brenden bantered. "Don't you think?"

Mike nodded in agreement. "So, why would she put down her Queens address as Addisleigh Park, when it's really St. Albans?"

"For the same reason you put down your Queens address as Fresh Meadows when it's really part of Flushing, before you got transferred. Addisleigh Park is a section of St. Albans, an enclave of predominately upscale African-Americans like Betty Fraser. She just wants you to know that she lives in a better part of town, just like you wanted people to know that you lived in a better part of town before transferring and moving out here to Suffolk."

"You been checking up on me, I see."

"Actually, the both of you. If I were going to be working with you guys, it behooved me to learn everything there is to know about you."

"Anything else we should know, Tom?"

"Yeah, you both passed muster. Oh, and if it turns out that Detective Diego Ramírez is responsible for Sharon Walsh's abduction and/or possible demise, Betty Fraser might not have to worry about any sort of threat from that man."

"Once again, Tom. Be very careful what you're implying."

"I don't know what you're inferring, Brenden. I was speaking hypothetically, alluding to the man contracting a very serious case of coronavirus."

"Go on, get out of here."

"Rude, very rude." Tom smiled and left the conference room.

CHAPTER FORTY-SEVEN

Tom Bolton had no problem locating United States Army Colonel Oliver Davis. Everyone in the town of East Islip knew him. For those folks old enough to remember the British cartoon character Colonel Blimp, Colonel Oliver Davis was the spitting image of the man: elderly, obese, walrus mustache, pompous, ultraconservative—both in terms of his politics and religion.

Tom found Colonel Davis alone in his 92-year-old, six room Georgian Colonial waterfront home in East Islip. After introducing himself as a private investigator representing the Walsh family, referencing the disappearance of Sharon Walsh, the colonel invited him into his spacious living room.

"Have a seat," Davis gestured, "over there," he directed, pointing to an overstuffed Gurdon armchair. "Can't be too careful with this virus crap going around. I've been practicing social distancing going on fifty years, but they just keep coming around," he said, taking up a matching chair spaced a good six feet away.

"Who's they?" Tom asked out of politeness rather than any sort of curiosity.

"Every fucking body with their goddamn hand out. That's who."

"Mr. Davis, I'd like to ask—"

"Colonel, call me Colonel. Everybody does."

206

"Colonel, I'd like to ask you about the Saint Patrick's Day party that you attended at Gilgo Beach."

"Would you now? When you came to the door, you said this was about a missing girl."

"A girl who went missing from that party."

"And who told you I was at any party?"

"Colonel, do you know Detective Diego Ramírez?"

The colonel did not answer.

"Do you know a Detective Chad Kelly?" Tom pressed.

"Is he the one who told you I was at some party?"

Tom noted that the colonel was out to gather as much information as he could without revealing his hand. "It's come to my attention that you were seen at the party speaking with the young woman in question, Sharon Walsh, who went missing and was last seen that Tuesday afternoon at the party."

"And who was this person who said they saw me at this alleged party, I had asked you?"

"I'm not at liberty—"

The colonel laughed. "Liberty. You're 'not at liberty,' you say. You're at liberty today, Mr. McManus, because of men like me," the pompous colonel boasted. "Men like me who put our lives on the line and gave folks back home the greatest gift man can bestow upon his fellow man. The gift of freedom. And what if I were to tell you, Mr. Private Investigator Man, that whoever told you they saw me speaking to this missing girl is mistaken?"

Tom Bolton shook his head insistently, feigning irritation but inwardly remaining calm as a tranquil breeze. "The man was emphatic and described you and her to a T," he assured the colonel. Tom had led Colonel Oliver Davis into believing that the eyewitness was a male. It took the onus off of Betty Fraser and purposely misdirected it toward one of the colonel's comrades and would likely get Davis' tongue wagging. "He saw you talking to Detective Diego Ramírez, too."

"Listen to me. I didn't say one word to that young woman. I simply asked Detective Ramírez if he would introduce me to her. He said no, and she laughed, and that was that. If I had had her undivided attention and someone came up to me and asked me to introduce her, I'd tell that person to fuck off."

"So, you saw this Detective Ramírez and Sharon Walsh talking together."

"If that's what her name is."

Tom handed the colonel a photograph of the attractive 22-year-old.

"Yep, that's her."

"Can you tell me if you saw her with anyone else? Did she mingle? Did she come alone?"

The colonel was shaking his head.

"Can you tell me anything at all?"

"All I can tell you is she was there one moment and gone the next."

"Gone? Did she leave with someone?"

"Nope, she just left."

"How long was she at the party?"

"Oh, I'd say maybe ten minutes."

"And Detective Ramírez didn't leave with her?"

"Nope. Detective Ramírez said good-bye to her, and she left."

"Just like that?"

"Just like that."

"And Detective Ramírez remained at the party?"

"Yep," Colonel Oliver Davis lied.

"And how long did the party last?"

"Two, maybe three in the morning."

"And Detective Ramírez was there the whole time?"

"Of course he was."

"Why do you say 'of course'?"

"Why? Because he hosted the party That's why. You just don't up and leave a party when you're the host."

"Tell me what Detective Ramírez did right after Sharon Walsh left the party."

"Did?"

"Yes, what did he do?"

"Well, he went around to all us guests and made sure we were getting something to eat and drink and having a good time."

"And he didn't leave the party that you know of for a period of time?"

"Like I said, he was the host of the party. If you're looking for a reason why that young lady left the party so abruptly, it might have been because Detective Ramírez had asked her to leave."

"And why would he do that?"

"Maybe because she looked very young."

"Then why would he invite her?"

"He didn't."

"Then who did?"

"A Detective Chad Kelly from Suffolk County, who never showed up that evening. So maybe she left the party to go find him. Who the hell knows? All I can tell you is that it was a hell of a party and that Detective Ramírez is one a hell of a host."

"And he was there the entire time you're saying?"

"Absolutely."

"Well, then that's that, and I thank you for taking the time to see me and clearing this up."

"I'm sure that young lady will turn up sooner or later, Mr. McManus."

"George."

"Let me ask you something, George McManus."

"Colonel."

"You a Republican or a mindless, spineless, liberal Democrat?"

The imposter smiled. "About as far-right a Republican as one can be without being labeled a radical."

"Good man. Good man, by George, George McManus. This country is going down the shitter by the minute. Thank God we've got a man like Donald Trump at the helm who has a chance of pulling us out of the crapper. When we get this pandemic under control, we're going to get back to kicking some liberal donkey asses. Schiff, Pelosi, and Schumer need to be taken out. And you can interpret 'taken out' any which way you want. China is our enemy, but we have to deal with them we're told. North Korea is our enemy, and we shouldn't be dealing with them at all. Iraq is our enemy, but we're told to show restraint when we should be bombing the hell out of them. Russia is our enemy, and we should kill every last one of them goddamn Commie bastards starting with Bernie Sanders. We're building a wall to keep out the undocumented immigrants. I say we should build a wall to keep out immigrants, period. I say we should adopt a policy of national isolationism."

Whereas Colonel Oliver Davis fit the physical appearance of cartoon character Colonel Blimp, known for such nonsensical language such as, 'The League of Nations should insist on peace—except, of course, in the event of war,' Colonel Davis' language was couched in sheer hatred, prejudice and principle.

"The goddamn Jews and niggers ruined this country, too," the colonel continued. "The 'Final Solution' could have been the final solution to the first fucking problem. Genocide was a stroke of genius on the part of Hitler. Not that he was the first to implement such a practice. For that we'd have to go back in history to the Peloponnesian War. No, it was the way in which the Führer eventually carried out his plan. Gas chambers and ovens. And not just the mere occupation of a country like Poland and exterminating the male population. No, indeed. In deed he exterminated men, women, and children of both sexes. Ethnic cleansing in its purest form. The eradication of racial and religious groups. Now, that's what I call a bit of R and R. Yes, World War II.

"The niggers are the flip side of the coin in considering the ruination of this great nation immediately following the Civil War. Lincoln's Emancipation Proclamation fostered the Ku Klux Klan. Is it really any wonder? The newly enfranchised black freedman, my white ass. Our nation didn't get it back in 1865 when the Confederates secretly formed the KKK, nor its resurgence in 1915 when the organization not only denounced the niggers, but also the Jews, Catholics, and foreigners."

Lieutenant Tom Bolton believed the irascible colonel was lying to cover Detective Ramírez's tracks that evening. He based that belief on the colonel's demeanor during questioning. Where the colonel should have shown indignation at Tom's more challenging questions, grounded in the colonel's mercurial temperament, the colonel exhibited obvious restraint, remaining uncharacteristically calm. Of course, it was mere speculation, but he knew that something was not right. Tom's gut told him that Detective Diego Ramírez was the last person to see Sharon Walsh alive and knew what had happened to her. The fact that Tom knew that Detective Ramírez and Detective Kelly were friendly spelled out a lot, too. Maybe too friendly.

CHAPTER FORTY-EIGHT

Lieutenant Tom Bolton reported back to Detectives Brenden Reilly and Mike D'Angelo, relating his conversation with the bigoted, irascible retired army colonel. The three men were seated between two desks in the hallway. Tom told them of his gut reaction, that Colonel Oliver Davis was possibly covering for Detective Diego Ramírez's whereabouts during the Saint Patrick's Day party.

"We have eyes on Ramírez 24/7," Brenden made clear.

"Well, you may *think* you have eyes on him 24/7," Tom retorted, "but you'll only see what he wants you to see and when he wants you to see it. Let me tell you what I see. I see quite an age difference between the stalwart colonel and Ramírez, and that the detective is the colonel's protégé. I see a somewhat similar situation between Detective Chad Kelly and Mathew Hansen in that Kelly and Hansen were good buddies, Kelly protecting him at all cost, no different than the relationship between Thomas Spota and James Burke."

"What are you saying, Tom?" Brenden questioned.

"I'm saying to draw your own conclusions."

"You saying they're butt buddies," Mike inferred.

"Like I said, you can draw your own conclusions. But I'll carry my belief a step further. I think the colonel is the real power behind the throne. The wizard behind the curtain. I saw a photograph of a

211

young teenage male in shorts on one of the colonel's end tables who I believe to be Detective Diego Ramírez."

"While you were playing private investigator, Tom, our team tracked down four of the people at the party; two regulars, and two guests who Betty Fraser said were at that party. They all say that their host, Detective Diego Ramírez, remained at the party the entire evening."

"Likewise, the colonel claims that, too. And when we were later barraging Miss Betty Fraser with questions about the layout of that rental home in Gilgo Beach, she mentioned that one of the upstairs rooms has a staircase leading downstairs and out the back. So, it's possible that Ramírez slipped out, met Sharon Walsh outside, drove her off to some safe haven, incapacitated her, drove back to the party alone, and saved what he had in store for her at a later point."

"I guess it's possible but not probable," Brenden said.

"And why is that?"

"Because of the time frame, Tom. He'd have little time to do what you're speculating."

"Not if where he took her was but a stone's throw from Gilgo Beach; namely, Oak Beach. Eleven minutes; seven point eight miles along Ocean Parkway. I'm not suggesting that he took her home to his apartment. And as a point of information, our retired United States Army Colonel Oliver Davis just happens to own several pieces of real estate in Gilgo Beach and Oak Beach."

"Yeah, and without probable cause and the issuance of a search warrant we've got nothing," Brenden said, reminding Tom of the Fourth Amendment.

"I've got something far better than that," Tom assured them in all seriousness.

"And what's that?" Mike asked, already knowing what Tom's reply would be.

"My hunches coupled to a keep-out-of-jail-free card, which I mentioned to you earlier."

A call was put through to Brenden, who excused himself for a moment.

Both Mike and Tom watched and knew from Brenden's cold expression that the news was not good.

"When?" was the single word question that carried with it a

somber note of gloom. Brenden held back the tears welling up in the corners of the seasoned homicide detective's eyes. "Where exactly?" A moment later, Brenden quietly put down the receiver.

Mike sensed the situation. "Tell me, partner."

"Sharon Walsh. They found her."

"When?"

"Early this morning. Nassau notified Team Three."

"Where?"

"Along the side of a road. A motorist traveling along Ocean Parkway between Gilgo and Oak Beach stopped and found her bagged body. Not pretty what someone did to her."

"Someone, huh? Four days following the evening of the Saint Patrick's Day party," Tom stated gravely, getting up from his chair. "See you fellas later."

"Where you off to, Tom?" Brenden asked.

"Got work to do."

Mike nodded his understanding.

Brenden smashed a closed fist firmly upon the wooden desk.

"Easy, partner. We'll get the sonofabitch."

CHAPTER FORTY-NINE

Lieutenant Tom Bolton paid a second visit in two days to Colonel Davis' waterfront residence on Meadowfarm Road in East Islip. Only this time, he did not arrive by car. Tom completed the last leg of the jaunt by borrowed kayak, paddling up Champlin Creek, which lies between the hamlets of East Islip and Islip. The spring fed narrow body of water flows southward into Great South Bay. Tom had no trouble navigating north through the slow-moving current toward the colonel's dock, landing and securing the yak in the underbrush 100 yards east of the home. It was 8:30 p.m. and pitch black. Tom withdrew a penlight and peered through a window in the garage, checking to be sure that the colonel's car was there before continuing along the edge of the property to the back door. It was locked. He went around to the front door and rang the bell. A moment later, the colonel came to the door but did not open it.

"Who the hell is it at this hour?"

"George McManus, P.I. We spoke yesterday, Colonel."

Dressed in pajamas, the colonel opened the door ajar and looked around suspiciously. "Where's your car?" Only Detective Diego Ramírez's sedan was parked in the driveway.

"I broke down. Can I come in and use your phone, please?"

"A private investigator who doesn't have a cell phone? You

shitting me or what?"

"Lost it in the water."

In the lighted entranceway, the colonel looked down at the man's feet. "Your pants and shoes are soaking wet. Where the fuck were you, and what are you doing around here at this hour, McManus?"

"At this hour, Colonel, I'm Lieutenant Tom Bolton, Southold P.D. And actually, it's early." Tom had his revolver pointed at the man's head.

"What the fuck is going on here?" a voice from behind the colonel bellowed.

"Sorry to have woken you, Detective Ramírez," Tom said calmly. "Now take a seat over there," he directed, pointing to the overstuffed armchair he had sat in yesterday. "You, Colonel, take a seat over there," Tom ordered, gesturing to the matching Gurdon. "You can move it closer to one another if you like. It seems to me that the two of you are not too concerned with social distancing."

"You are making the biggest fucking mistake of your life, fella. Do you fucking understand me?"

"I'm hearing that a lot lately. Now, let me tell you about mistakes, Diego. There are a couple of great lines in the lyrics from a Willie Nelson song titled *Nothing I Can Do About It Now*, which also happens to be the refrain. It goes like this: 'Regret is just a memory written on my brow, and there's nothing I can do about it now.' It's a great song. I brought it along especially for both of you to hear." Tom removed his smartphone from an inner pocket of his yellow slicker. This LG G8S ThinQ smartphone is said to be the best for audio quality. You'll tell me later what you think."

"Listen to me you fucking asshole. You will fucking die—"

"No, you will fucking die, Diego, in the next few seconds if you don't shut up and listen to these lyrics."

Diego started to get up, and Tom thumbed back the hammer of his revolver. Diego sat back down.

"Nice underwear, Diego. Hearts and Flowers. That's also a song. It really doesn't do anything for me though. But then again, neither does your underwear." Tom pressed the power button and set the smartphone down in the center of a lobster trap table and selected the 3-minute, 17-second Willie Nelson recording.

Neither the colonel nor the detective moved a muscle until the song was finished.

Tom closed the screen. "The neat thing about this phone is that you can operate it with hand signals as you probably noticed. It scans the veins in the palm of your hand. Otherwise, it can be a bit awkward holding a gun on you and working the device."

"What is it that you want, Mr. Imposter?" the colonel calmly asked.

"The truth."

"The truth about what?"

"The truth about who brutally murdered Sharon Walsh."

"Ah, the girl at the Saint Patrick's Day party. So, we're back to that again. To tell you the truth, Lieutenant, I had no idea she was murdered." The colonel turned to Diego. "Did you hear anything about this, Diego?"

"You think you can come in here at gunpoint and threaten us?" Diego said with pure hatred in his eyes. "By morning, you won't have a fucking badge, a gun, or a job. I'll personally see to that."

"You think?"

"I know."

"I'll tell you what I know and what I think I know. I know you're both wondering where Detective Chad Kelly and his bosom buddy Mathew Hansen disappeared to. Well, let me show you." Tom reached down and turned on the smartphone. "See? I don't even have to push the power button. Hand signals and the unit's on. Recognize the two in the picture?" Tom slowly scanned the images of Kelly and Hansen lying stone cold dead on a bloody concrete floor in an outdated Montauk farmhouse. "They refused to talk, too, thinking that I was bluffing."

"You're crazy," the colonel declared, all color leaving the man's face, and in its stead, displaying a ghastly hue.

"I killed them both in cold blood," Tom continued. "Hansen suffered greatly before he died."

Diego Ramírez's face contrasted the colonel's in that the detective's countenance was a scarlet red, sitting on the heels of sheer rage.

"What I think, Colonel, is that Diego here murdered Sharon Walsh, a pretty twenty-two-year-old girl with her whole life in front of her. What I think, Colonel, is that you are today's Grand Wizard, father protector for a clan of serial killers, and a suspected fourth: former Suffolk County Police Chief James Burke. No different than Thomas Spota was father protector of Burke and Christopher McPartland. I've connected most of the dots, and this is the picture that emerges before me, Colonel. Tell me the rest of what I need to know to complete the picture, and I'll let you live. Who are the bad actors in an idiomatic sense? In other words, I need the names of the other players, like Diego here. Tell me who, Colonel. Tell me the truth. Lie to me, and I'll kill you on the spot. I know certain things that you don't know I know. Doubt me?"

"You're insane."

"Quote. 'In a mad world, only the mad are sane.' Akira Kurosawa. Japanese film director. I'm terribly mad, and waiting, Colonel. Did Ramírez kill Sharon Walsh? We'll start with that. I'll give you the next five seconds to answer me." Tom's finger was on the trigger with the slightest of pressure being applied. "Hair trigger, Colonel."

The colonel suddenly began to weep. "I told him he crossed the line, Lieutenant. I told him—"

"SHUT THE FUCK UP!" Diego screamed.

"I told Kelly that Hansen was stepping out of line and that we had to move him out."

"I said, shut the fuck up," Diego repeated, the veins in the detective's neck a bulging purple.

"No, you shut the fuck up," the colonel swore.

Diego sprang from his seat like a jack-in-the-box.

And in that second, Tom Bolton sent a bullet through Diego's skull and into his brain. "Maybe that will keep him quiet," the lieutenant calmly stated. "That's what I call my 'take no prisoners policy,' Colonel."

"Oh, my God! Oh, my God." The colonel scrambled out of his chair and onto the floor, crawling over to Diego who had fallen onto the expensive 10-foot square floral pattern Persian Nain wool and silk hand-knotted carpet, cradling the body in his arms. "Oh, my God."

"Would that happen to be a Christian God, Colonel, or just a figure of speech?"

"Oh, my God," Colonel Oliver Davis repeated, rocking Diego

back and forth. "What have you done, you bastard?"

"Killed a bad actor, Colonel. Now, where were we?"

"Look at what you have done, you fucking bastard."

"I could take a picture with my smartphone as a reminder if you like," Tom toyed, "but I don't think that would be very smart. So, you give me the names of those in The Administration and the key roles they play and you get to live, albeit in a prison after a jury of your peers finds you guilty of aiding and abetting, an accessory to the crime of premeditated murder. I'm sure you know the law. Fall short of my request, and you'll suffer Diego's demise."

"Listen to me."

"I'm listening."

"I could make you a very rich man. It doesn't have to be like this. I could make all traces of the body go away, and you could live a lifestyle most men only dream of."

"I don't expect you to get it, Colonel. I really don't. Serial killers like Mathew Hansen, Chad Kelly, and Diego Ramírez are less than human. People in power like yourself with a predilection for the perverse somehow wind up protecting these monsters while promoting such senseless violence. Not that these animals wouldn't kill anyway. It's in their makeup. Whether it's a matter of nature or nurture is immaterial to me. What matters to me is the path of destruction they leave behind, the lives they destroy, and the families that suffer forever. You are not a killer. You are an enabler, Colonel Davis."

"I will give you anything you could possibly want."

"I already told you. I want the names of those in The Administration and the key roles they play."

"Five million dollars deposited into an untraceable offshore bank account. I could set that up in a matter of several hours. By mid-afternoon tomorrow, I promise you."

Tom stared down at the costly carpet on which Diego Ramírez and Colonel Davis lie. One dead; the other alive for the moment. "How much did that carpet cost you, Colonel? Two, three thousand dollars? Chicken feed to a person of your wealth and power. Maybe I'll address you as Colonel Sanders, Oliver Davis. Note that I erased your rank—just like that—in a matter of a second with a wag of the tongue. All that's left is your name and serial number. In the next few seconds, I'll eliminate your name. All you'll be is a number. A statistic, to be more accurate."

The man held Diego's head close to his chest. "Go fuck yourself. I die a military man," he sneered.

"No, you just die." Lieutenant Tom Bolton sent a bullet between the man's eyes.

Tom slipped on a pair of heavy-duty nitrile gloves with a fingertip thickness of 10 mil before searching through the contents of the home. One item he found was especially interesting. After an hour, Tom exited the colonel's home through the back door. Using the butt end of his revolver as a hammer, he broke a windowpane then unlocked the window, leaving it to appear as though someone had broken in. It always amazed him at how so many homeowners had state-of-the-art security systems but did not set them unless they were leaving home for extended periods. Making his way back along the property to the water's edge, he untied the kayak from a branch of underbrush, paddled to a neighboring home and left the yak where he had found it. From there, Tom walked the short distance to his car and headed for home. He had been very lucky thus far.

CHAPTER FIFTY

Detectives Brenden Reilly and Mike D'Angelo sat with Lieutenant Tom Bolton in a conference room at police headquarters in Yaphank. The distance between the detectives and the lieutenant was now at least six feet apart. Social distancing was standard procedure where practical. Of course, it did not prove practical when Brenden and Mike rode together on assignment. Mike joked that he put in a request for a large transport van in lieu of their assigned sedan and that he would sit in the rear of the vehicle while Brenden chauffeured him around wherever they needed to be. After exchanging back-and-forth banter, the three got down to business.

Tom began by unfolding certain information relating to his contact with the colonel, leaving out specific details of what had eventually transpired among the three of them: Colonel Davis, Detective Diego Ramírez, and himself.

"An item I found of particular interest," Tom went on, "was the colonel's Rolodex." Tom took out his notes. "A file filled with the names, addresses and phone numbers of state-run maximum-security facilities like Kirby Forensic Psychiatric Center and the Manhattan Psychiatric Center on Wards Island in Manhattan; the Mid-Hudson Forensic Center, New Hampton, New York; city jails such as Rikers Island; and New York State's Department of Corrections and

Community Supervision. Specifically, the names of the agencies' executives. A numbered list of fifty-two prisons, all in alphabetical order from A to W," Tom elaborated: "Beginning with the Adirondack Correctional Facility, and ending with the Wyoming Correctional Facility, Wyoming County, New York, which is adjacent to the Attica Correctional Facility."

"Hey, do you recall the movie *Dog Day Afternoon* where Al Pacino, portraying the character of Sonny explains to John Cazale, playing Sal, that Wyoming is not a country when asked what country he'd like to go to as part of the couple's demands in a bank robbery gone amuck?" Mike interrupted with his bantering.

Tom and Brenden were not amused.

"Knock it off, Mike, all right?" Brenden chided.

"I was just pointing out how that all tied in with Attica. Remember how Sonny and the crowd were all chanting 'Attica, Attica,'?"

"Just stop," Brenden repeated.

"Jeez! Lighten up, will you, partner? Tom's always drawing analogies from books and songs and movies like he did *The Godfather* awhile back if you recall. I was just showing how—"

"Go on, Tom," Brenden cut in.

Tom continued. "The colonel had cryptic notations written on the back of several cards, along with inmates' names. What I keep running through my brain is why in the world he would have such a listing?"

"The colonel let you see this Rolodex file?" Brenden questioned.

"Let's just say that he didn't object to it and leave it at that for the time being. All right?"

Brenden and Mike exchanged telling glances.

"Go on, Tom," Mike said evenly.

"In addition to those fifty-two New York State prisons, he had file cards on facilities operated by the Federal Bureau of Prisons: Federal Correctional Institute in Otisville and Ray Brook, the Buffalo Detention facility in Batavia, Border Control, Customs. Nothing outside the state. Everything listed is in New York. Why would he have that? I kept asking myself. That and the fact Hansen had told me both he and Kelly had 'get-out-of-jail-free cards,' that I couldn't touch either of them. Those were his words. I believe they both believed that. In fact, I believe Ramírez and the colonel believed that, too. Ramírez's exact words to me were, 'You are making the biggest fucking mistake of your life, fella. Do you fucking understand me? You think you can come in here and threaten us?' Diego said that with pure hatred in his eyes. 'By morning, you won't have a fucking badge, a gun, or a job. I'll personally see to that.' Those are some of the things he told me."

"Come on, Tom. You know they all say shit like that."

"Not like that, Mike. He truly believed what he was saying. He had the power and the confidence in his eyes. Somehow this business is all connected with law enforcement. Twice I was offered a tidy sum of money to just walk away and mind my own business. Kelly was getting ready to move Hansen out of the country and wanted me to take his place and relocate, and I'd be set for life. The colonel on my last visit offered me five million dollars."

"To do what?" Brenden asked.

"To look the other way," Tom said, leaving out the incriminating part of allowing the man to live. "I believe—"

"Tom," Mike interrupted.

"Let me finish. I believe this whole business goes way deeper than any of us can imagine. I believe there is a corrupt network out there that is virtually untouchable. I say virtually because they fear no one or nothing except death. Whether it be death in the form of an invisible enemy such as the coronavirus, or death in the form of perhaps a very visible vigilante who has nothing to lose."

"Careful, Tom," Brenden warned. "Be very careful what you say here. Hear?"

"Of course, I'm speaking hypothetically," Tom hedged, smiling ever so sadly before continuing. "You'd never beat an organized and resourceful enemy like The Administration in a million years if you were to follow the letter of the law. Why? Because many of them are the law. Sure, you will have your sacrificial lambs who will not be sent to slaughter but rather held in a state of limbo and do penance in a low- to minimum-security federal prison for a minimum period of time like James Burke. And waiting in the wings are Thomas Spota and Christopher McPartland. One postponement after another. Sheer arrogance and pure stupidity were their downfall, otherwise they'd still be in the game. Sheer arrogance and pure stupidity were the big mistakes made by Mathew Hansen, Chad Kelly, Diego Ramírez, and the colonel. The way you beat them is to circumvent the law. They must be taken out of the game. Again, I'm speaking hypothetically, of course."

"What are you going to do, Tom?"

"It's not what I'm going to do, Brenden. It's what you and Mike are going to do next. You're the detectives. I'm just a sick and tired cop who has his boss doing double duty back in Southold while I'm dicking around with you guys. You find the connection between the list of state and federal prisons in New York and known members of The Administration and you'll likely uncover a viper's nest. Mark my words. What you two do with that nest is entirely up to you. Again, I would play this very close to the vest because there are probably pairs of ominous eyes on the three of us as we speak. If there aren't, there will be."

"Talking about eyes. Through a contact we have eyes on Detective Ramírez day and night. Nothing suspicious has surfaced. He goes to work; he goes home."

"Is that a fact? Have you been listening to me? I said to trust no one, and you wind up putting a contact from Nassau on his tail."

"It's a question of manpower, Tom. You know that. There's only so much we can cover on this end."

"He's one of the brightest bulbs in the department," Mike chimed in. "Highly respected."

"So was Kelly. Let me tell you guys something. The information you received from your contact is misleading. From work Ramírez may go home, but from his home he goes to the colonel's home in the evening. I just explained that to you. He's the colonel's boy, and I don't mean that in a filial sense. I don't give a crap about their sexual preferences. I care about the lives they ruined, and now the two of you are in a position to do something about it."

"And how do you propose we go about that, Tom?"

"I'm going to give you the Rolodex file after I'm done copying it. See what you two can come up with."

"And what are you going to be doing after that?" Brenden pressed.

"I'm going to be validating my keep-out-of-jail-free card."

"Meaning?"

"Meaning that I'll be checking into Memorial Sloan Kettering in Manhattan. Meantime, you can check out the colonel's residence on Meadowfarm Road in East Islip. I believe you'll find that someone broke into the home. You'll find that one of brightest bulbs, as you put it, has blown. Someone put the colonel's lights out, too. It appears that the colonel and his lover were interrupted by a third party."

Tom stood up and left the conference room.

Brenden and Mike remained seated, slowly shaking their heads with a degree of disbelief, digesting what they had just heard from the lieutenant.

Brenden was the first to speak. "I guess we'll take a little ride to East Islip."

"Maybe we should keep our distance and send another squad."

"No way."

"How do we explain our being there?"

"We don't.

"I mean afterwards?"

"Informant."

"Well, that part is certainly true enough—in part."

"We say we can't divulge the name, that it would prove unwise."

"That it would put the person in harm's way."

"Probably would, in fact."

"We stick to our guns."

"We stick to that story."

"Tom doesn't look good, Brenden."

"I know."

CHAPTER FIFTY-ONE

It was late evening when a handsome seasoned homicide detective from the Nassau County Homicide Squad rang the doorbell at the Billings' residence in Riverhead. Claire Billings answered the door.

"May I help you?"

The detective showed the woman his credentials. "Detectives Reilly and D'Angelo asked me to drop by and update you on a matter of importance, ma'am. May I come in please, and I promise to keep a safe six-foot distance between us," the man swore, smiling while putting away his credentials and crossing his heart. "You can't be too careful these days."

Claire nodded and smiled warmly. "Come in please, and we'll practice social distancing, although I'm sure this is not a social call. Have a seat over there," she directed, pointing to sofa. "You can put your coat over that chair."

"If it wasn't so important, I would have called instead of showing up on your doorstep like this. Is your husband at home?"

"No, Josh is out of town on business. Can I offer you a cup of coffee?"

"No thank you. I won't be staying that long."

Claire took a seat across from the well-dressed man. "What did you come to tell me that's so important, Detective?"

"It's really quite amazing how you homed in on Mathew Hansen, identifying him as well as the other fellow who was with him that night at the Iron Skillet Restaurant in Mattituck."

Claire smiled brightly. "Thank you. I never learned his name or who that other fellow was. Is that what you've come to tell me?"

"No, but if you'd really like to know."

"Well, sure I would. But before you tell me, I'd like to tell you that I've been following these cases very carefully. I'm sure Brenden and Mike told you that."

"Brenden and Mike, huh? You're on a first name basis with those two rascals, I see."

Claire presented an embarrassed smile. "They told me I was very helpful."

"Indeed. You certainly were. And that's why I'm here, Claire."

"So, are you going to tell me who this person was with Mathew Hansen?"

"His name's Detective Chad Kelly with the Suffolk County Homicide Squad in Yaphank."

"What?" Claire said with complete surprise, considering her next comment before she spoke. "Ah, he was working undercover and that's why he was with serial killer Mathew Hansen that evening?"

"Not exactly."

"Well, then what, if I may be so presumptuous?"

"He was a serial killer, too, working in their midst."

"What!"

"It's true."

"Where is this Detective Chad Kelly now?"

"Dead."

"Dead?"

"Yes, dead. And there are others out there."

"What exactly did you come here to tell me, Detective? That my husband and I have to fear for our lives?"

"No, not your husband."

Claire Billings stared at the detective in utter confusion, waiting for the answer, watching the man's manner change from pleasant to unpleasing in a matter of a single moment. She watched as the detective unbuttoned his jacket and withdrew a handgun from his shoulder holster. The extended barrel she recognized as a silencer that she had seen on many a television cop show. The scene she was in seemed surreal. The villain had almost always screwed the silencer onto the weapon for dramatic purposes. Here the man was pointing his weapon directly at the center of her chest.

"You're not a real detective, are you?" was all that Claire could think to say.

"Oh, I assure you that I am, ma'am."

Claire found it funny in her moment of pure fright that he called her ma'am for a second time in the minutes that had passed between them. She wondered if it might have made a difference if she had said 'Please call me Claire' . . . as if they were on a first name basis.

"Why are you doing this?" she questioned as the tears streamed down her pretty face. "Are you a serial killer, too?" she couldn't believe she was asking.

"I assure you that I am not, ma'am. I'm just a good solider doing what I'm ordered to do and to tell you why you are going to die."

Claire closed her eyes as she listened to the explanation.

"I am here to send a clear message, Claire Billings, to all those who interfere, in that they have The Administration to fear. I don't expect you to understand what it is that I'm saying here, but men like Detectives Brenden Reilly, Mike D'Angelo—in addition to Lieutenant Tom Bolton of Southold P. D.—will patently get the message."

Claire Billings had stopped listening and was reciting her prayers that she hadn't repeated since she was a little girl as a bullet struck her squarely in the chest. The Nassau homicide detective got up, grabbed his coat, then sent the second bullet into the side of Claire's temple. The woman fell to the floor.

It was a fifteen-minute drive from Riverhead to Speonk. Brenda Featherston was fast asleep and did not answer to the continued ringing of the doorbell and loud knocking. The old woman's cat, though, certainly heard the commotion and was hissing from behind the door. The homicide detective went back to his car to get a few tools then returned a moment later.

It took a good five minutes to gain entrance to the home. "Not as easy as what you see on T.V. or in the movies," he addressed the cat. As the stranger crossed the threshold, Tabitha attacked the man's leg.

"Motherfucker," he mouthed quietly, flinging the feline hard against a wall with his foot. Tabitha scurried off to the bathroom. The detective closed and locked the front door.

"Is that you, Tabitha?" Brenda Featherston called out, startled by the loud thump.

"Police, ma'am," the detective bellowed. "Please remain calm and stay where you are."

"Oh, my God! Where's my Tabitha? What is going on?" the old woman exclaimed and questioned as the man entered her bedroom. The widow pulled the covers up till they touched her chin.

The detective flashed his credentials. "Stay calm," he repeated. "I have a message to deliver, and then I'm out of here. Your meddling as a witness in the Mathew Hansen matter is your undoing. In your next life, ma'am, mind your own goddamn business." And with that remark, the detective withdrew his weapon and shot the widow in the face before walking around the bed and sending a second bullet into her temple.

Before leaving the home, the detective found the cat cowering in a corner of the bathroom. He raised the 9mm caliber pistol and aimed it at the feline's head. "Can't leave any witnesses," he assured her, squeezing the trigger and watching the coiled-up animal go limp.

The drive from Speonk to Addisleigh Park (St. Albans), Queens, took a little over an hour. The lights were still on when the detective pulled into Betty Fraser's driveway. He rang the bell and listened to the cadence of the chimes. Betty came to the door and peered through the peephole. Hesitantly, she unlocked the door and opened it to where the chain held it ajar. She was wearing a pure white full-length-hooded bathrobe.

"Betty," the handsome homicide detective greeted and smiled.

"Vincent," she said in surprise. "What on earth are you doing here?"

"Detectives Reilly and D'Angelo sent me here." He watched Betty's eyes narrow and jaw muscles tighten. "It's all right, Betty. Relax. We're working closely together. It's important and will only take a few minutes, then we'll be finished, and I'll be on my way. May I come in?"

"Of course, of course," she said, first closing the door then removing the chain from the slide. "Come on in and take a seat." Betty closed and locked the door. "I'd give you a hug and a big kiss, but this COVID-19 shit has me worried. I'm even wiping down grocery packages with alcohol swabs as I bring them into the house."

"Betty, why didn't you come to me instead of running to the Suffolk boys in Yaphank?"

"Please sit down, Vincent," she invited.

Betty and Vincent took up seats opposite one another in the spacious living room.

"I was scared," Betty explained. "Not of you, of course, but the people you work with. I didn't go to them, Vinny. The detectives came to me," she lied.

"Betty, Betty, Betty. How long have we known each other? Huh?"

"A good many years," she answered, lowering her eyes to the floor.

"You went to them instead of coming to me. We would have worked this out."

"I think Detective Diego Ramírez murdered that girl, Vinny. That twenty-two-year-old girl."

"Oh, he did, Betty. No question about it."

"I think some of the people at those parties are responsible for other murders."

"They are, Betty."

"Then why aren't you guys doing something about it?" she snapped.

"Because the some of us who you're referring to are instructed to look the other way."

"What? Why? What are you saying?"

"That I'm a good soldier who doesn't ask questions and follows orders to a T. I'm saying that a few of us are well compensated to keep our mouths shut. Big Christmas bonuses, junkets, parties that you've had a taste of because you were one of our finest party girls."

"Why are you here, Vincent? Why are you *really* here?"

"To make certain that you keep your mouth shut, Betty. To have you understand why it is you have to die this evening. To send a clear message to those who stand in the way."

Betty Fraser was sobbing uncontrollably. "To stand in the way of what?"

"The Administration." Detective Vincent Gomez slipped on a pair of nitrile gloves then withdrew his 9mm pistol, pointing it at Betty Fraser's face. "You will be the third person I shot and killed tonight, not including an attack kitty cat, can you believe?" Gomez laughed lightly. "You don't know the other two witnesses who upset the apple cart, Betty. But a Claire Billings will surely be missed by her grieving husband, Josh Billings. A widowed Brenda Featherston will be missed by no one except maybe her pussy cat if I hadn't shot it, too. And you, Betty, will be positively missed by your loving brother. But rest assured that I'll be in attendance and have some nice things to say about you at the funeral. Promise. This evening sends a strong message to folks to mind their own business and not get involved."

Betty was having trouble breathing and could barely get her words out. ". . . won't . . . I w-won't . . . I won't tell a soul. Pl-please don't hurt me. I'll k-keep my mouth shut. I swear it!"

The homicide detective was shaking his head. "It's too late for that now, but I'll help you seal your trap shut just the same." Detective Vincent Gomez squeezed the trigger and sent a 9mm Parabellum into the pleading woman's mouth. "The Administration is at war with those who interfere, Betty. There's part of a Latin phrase, Parabellum, which loosely translates to 'If you want peace, then you should prepare for war.' I believe detractors like Reilly, D'Angelo, and Bolton will get the message." Slumped over in her chair, the detective stood and went over to Betty. He fired a single bullet into her right temple. Removing one of the cartridges from a pocket, the assassin placed it on an end table. "As promised, I'm finished here, Betty."

CHAPTER FIFTY-TWO

Betty and her brother were very close. When she hadn't returned his phone calls in two days, he grew concerned and drove from Long Island to her home in Queens. She did not answer the door, so he let himself in with a key. He took no further than two steps into the living room to find his sister slouched over an arm of a high back wing chair. A crimson-stained white hooded robe and wide plank light-colored hardwood flooring with a coagulated pool of blood commanded his full attention. Terence brought a hand to his mouth, took three steps back and tripped going out the door, screaming bloody murder until Betty Fraser's neighbors came running.

On hearing the name of the woman who was murdered in her home in Queens, Detectives Reilly and D'Angelo flew into action. Phone calls were made to the Billings in Riverhead and the widowed woman in Speonk. Getting no response, units were immediately dispatched to those residences. Through a side window of the Billings' home, one officer reported that he saw a woman lying on the floor. He was instructed to break in straightaway.

When there was no answer at Brenda Featherston's door in Speonk, two officers were instructed to enter the premises immediately if not sooner. They found the woman shot to death in her bed, her cat dead in a corner of the bathroom.

Josh Billings was away on business. When he returned home, he learned about the murder of his wife. An officer said that he was deeply sorry for his loss. Josh Billings was shaking his head.

"I want you to give a message to Reilly, D'Angelo, and that fucking Southold cop, Bolton."

"Sir, I—"

"You shut the fuck up and listen to me. You tell those three fucks that they're fucking dead."

"Sir, you can't—"

"Now, you turn around and get the fuck out of my home."

The man left the Billings' home without another word, reporting the threat to Brenden and Mike's boss, Detective Lieutenant Steve Anderson.

CHAPTER FIFTY-THREE

Two days later, Lieutenant Tom Bolton died of stage 4 pancreatic cancer in a private room at Memorial Sloan Kettering Cancer Center in Manhattan. A key had been removed from around the cop's neck, placed in a narrow Manila envelope along with instructions, and given to Brenden by a duty nurse stationed at her desk. Mike had left Tom's bedside shortly before the lieutenant passed away.

Several hours later, Brenden and Mike drove out in separate cars to where Lieutenant Tom Bolton's body was brought to the Horton-Mathie Funeral Home in Greenport for cremation. There was no official memorial service held for the veteran cop in light of the coronavirus pandemic. However, Brenden and Mike requested then demanded a short delay just outside the columbarium where Tom's body lie in rest—entombed within the closed cardboard casket to be consumed by conflagration—so as to say good-bye to their friend and colleague. It was the way Tom wanted it, and all the arrangements were made well beforehand. The funeral director reluctantly acquiesced, handing Brenden a large locked metal briefcase filled with important papers and a large amount of cash.

Brenden had tears in his eyes. Mike's armor in putting on a brave face was his delivery at dark humor.

"Fucking Josh Billings had the gall to threaten the three of us like that—you, me, and Tom here? I think I'm going to arrest him after we leave here and tell him forensics found incriminating evidence that links him to our friend's death and all three witnesses: Claire Billings, Brenda Featherston, and Betty Fraser."

"Stop it. You'd probably behave the same. The poor guy's grieving the loss of his wife. He's venting."

"Then I won't arrest him. I'll simply tell him his threat and our preliminary investigation make him our prime suspect in Tom's death. How's that?" Mike pressed on in inane fashion, infuriated over the murders of their three key witnesses and the loss of their friend to an incurable disease.

"How about we focus on finding the killer."

"I got it narrowed down."

"Yeah?"

"Yeah."

"Like who?"

"Josh Billings. I'll arrest him on *suspicion* of murder and hold him for seventy-two hours. Let him sweat. Whattaya think?"

"I think you're a sick puppy."

"That's how I know we're going to nail this motherfucker. Come down to his level. Gunshots to the head like he did to the others. No court of law. No imprisonment. Just a gravesite that I can visit and take a piss on. This is an all-out war, Brenden."

"When you calm down, I'll ask you how you want to start."

"Let's start by brainstorming a list of ideas no matter how remote they may seem. Let's start by going over Betty Fraser's statement and putting eyes on every person at that party."

"We did all that."

"Yeah, we did that for *this* Saint Patrick's Day party. I'm saying we work backward to every fucking Saint Patrick's Day party Betty mentioned, dating back a decade. We were looking for the killer of Sharon Walsh. Tom found out who that was and took care of him and the colonel in the bargain. The anonymous phone call we got as to where we could find them either came from Tom or one of his friends. Tom as much as told us he killed them both, along with Hansen and Kelly. But now we're looking for the killer of three witnesses who helped us identify Mathew Hansen, Chad Kelly, and Diego Ramírez: two homicide detectives, one of who—or is it whom

234

—was Kelly's closest so-called friend."

"You're narrowing the witnesses' murders down to one detective."

"Likely a homicide detective."

"Who uses standard police issue ammo."

"Bonded hollow-points in this particular case."

"Nine-millimeter Parabellum."

"To let us know we're at war."

"Another mole in our midst like Chad Kelly?"

"I'd go with Nassau for openers."

"Reason?"

"You know as well as I that the incentive for a beat cop to look for promotion to detective or even remain a detective in Nassau is crushed because of all the politics."

"All that collective bargaining bull crap."

"Exactly. And some detectives are even requesting to return to patrol duty, turning in their shields."

"Because it's better to stay a police officer than to apply for a promotion and upgrade to detective."

"Inasmuch as the pay increases for detectives are not nearly an incentive for police officers to look for a promotion and upgrade to detective—or for detectives to remain detectives—because of the tremendous workload and loss in pay."

"You've got a handful of detectives handling a shitload of several hundred cases."

"Robberies, burglaries, drug trafficking."

"Extortion, murder, gangbangers from the hood."

"A group of African-American assholes."

"Central American scum from El Salvador, Honduras, and Guatemala. And on up and through Mexico."

"Who, by the way, I affectionately refer to as those mucho, macho, motherfucking Mexican mullets. You see those fucking hairstyles? Anyhow, as a result of all the political bullshit, bickering, bargaining, and other nonsensical negotiating—resulting in a piss-poor contract—the salaries, benefits, workload, and working conditions suck."

"Salaries for detectives actually went down on average, including overtime, by 18% percent. Where's the incentive to work your ass off and put your life on the line?"

"And is exactly why Nassau County law enforcement has a deficiency of competent detectives."

"Now, tell me something I don't know."

"I suggest we start by looking at those detectives who are quite satisfied with their detective status as opposed to those who were or are disgruntled and have considered turning in their badge to return to the street. I'd key in on those detectives most satisfied with their position as possible suspects in the assassination of our witnesses."

Brenden mulled over Mike's suggestion and played devil's advocate. "The problem with that idea is a disgruntled detective may still put prestige ahead of the negatives we just covered."

"But those negatives would easily be brushed aside if a detective was being well compensated in other ways such as perks and the possibility of being made the equivalent of a made-man, like a member of the Mafia. More specifically, in this case, a member of The Administration. Their own hit man."

"Sounds a bit far-fetched, Mike."

"So does having two homicide detectives turn out to be serial killers, and maybe an ex-police chief to boot."

"I don't know."

"Got a better way to approach this matter?"

"If we're playing this close to the vest, we don't have the time or manpower to ferret out this kind of information."

"How about womanpower? Cover a lot more ground in a fraction of the time."

Brenden smiled. "And who do you have in mind to recruit?"

"One of Tom's relatives. His niece. I think she'd do it in a heartbeat."

"You're talking about that strawberry blonde, what's her name?"

"Donna Carter."

"What a scene that was."

"Quite a performance. She'd be perfect, Brenden."

"We could be putting her in harm's way, you know."

"Brenden, it was Tom's last request for us to approach her and feel her out. If she accepts the assignment, we set her up with seed money from here." Mike was pointing to the metal briefcase. "We put her in an apartment near Nassau police headquarters. Their watering hole in Mineola is minutes away. Either way, the money's hers whether she takes the assignment or not. We get the papers, copies made from the colonel's Rolodex file—names, addresses, and cryptic notes. Tom was hoping that the three of us can work together as a team. You, me, and Donna Carter."

"And when were you going to tell me all this?"

"When did I have time to tell you? You were busy. I was busy. You distracted the nurse, and I got to say good-bye to Tom for the two of us before they threw us the hell out of there. And here we are, partner."

"What else did Tom say?"

"He said that the Double-Aught Bar on Mineola Avenue is a cop hangout and only three minutes away from police headquarters on Franklin Avenue. If Donna Carter were to get an apartment nearby, work the bar nightly, keep an ear to the ground, she might hear something, like those who are very happy campers, who are not, and the reasons why. One of them could possibly be our killer. If not, Donna might learn something that could point us in the right direction. In any event, Tom said he'd like us to coach her on how to handle herself, what to say and not to say. Whattaya think?"

"I think you took a separate car out here to keep your distance because of this COVID-19 crap," Brenden kidded. "And the problem with you and Tom's plan is that all the frigging bars are closed, good buddy, and no one knows at this point when things are going to turn around. Could be months from now."

"Not for cops they're not."

Brenden was looking at Mike like he had a screw loose for sure. "What are you talking about?"

"About an underground hush, hush operation, Brenden."

"Okay, I'll bite. Let's hear it."

"Tom knew for a fact that they're serving liquor at the Double-Aught Bar on the q.t. downstairs."

"Who's they?"

"They being a bunch of thirsty cops and detectives who will not be deprived of their beer, booze, and camaraderie. The owner's just turning his head and looking the other way. He sees no evil, hears no evil, and speaks no evil. The boys are running their own tab and keeping him afloat. Actually, he's making out better because he

237

doesn't have to shut down the business. Tom believed that if his niece accepts the assignment, she could worm her way in there to serve drinks, keep the books, and gather important information. Maybe we'd learn about a happy soul who wouldn't surrender his shield and become a beat cop if bureaucrats were to cut his salary in half. And that's because he'd somehow be well compensated and protected by The Administration is what my gut feeling is telling me."

"And Donna Carter is just going to somehow waltz in there and keep the books while serving liquor to a group of renegade cops. Would we have to coach her on how to mix drinks, too?" Brenden half kidded.

"Do you know what Donna does for income out in Greenport, Brenden?"

"You're going to tell me she's a bartender."

Mike was smiling and shaking his head. "Not exactly."

"I thought not."

"She's a certified mixologist and part-time bookkeeper."

"Again, this is such a long shot, Mike."

"So was staging that scene out in Southold, but it worked. It threw those fuckers off guard and got them buzzing and moving around. This time out will be even easier. Liquor served at a clandestine cop's-only bar will get them wagging loose tongues. And who particularly will frequent that bar? The younger officers and detectives who do not concern themselves with the pandemic because they believe themselves invulnerable or immune. Rules and regulations do not apply to them. They, in effect, feel themselves above the law. You know that's true for the most part, so don't give me one of those looks. What we'll have here if Donna Carter works with us is the perfect breeding ground for the killer to make a fatal mistake."

"Did Tom say how much cash is in the case?"

"A hundred grand plus. He closed out the account and wanted no paper trail to link back to Donna."

"Think she'll go for it?"

"The money or the assignment?" Mike kidded.

"Both."

"I do. Again, the money is hers regardless."

"And you think she'll convince the owner of the Double-Aught

Bar to allow her to work for him in this surreptitious situation."

"Pretty girl. Sexy figure. Unparalleled qualifications. Yeah, I do."

"Think this long shot plan will work?"

"We can only hope and pray."

"Let's set it up."

"Atta boy."

"One thing, though."

"Yeah?"

"Tell her to dye her hair."

Mike smiled. "What color?"

"Same shade of red as Sharon Walsh's."

"In memory."

"In memorial."

"Ah, here comes the funeral director followed by the woman of the hour."

Douglas R. Mathie made the introductions then politely told Brenden and Mike that they had to leave. No handshakes were exchanged or needed, just the key and the metal briefcase. Brenden entertained the idea of these casual customary greetings as the new norm.

"We waited for you before opening the case," Mike explained to the pretty woman. "We'd like to open it and remove the papers we need. The rest is yours, Ms. Carter," Mike explained.

"Donna, please," Donna said. "Of course, you may."

"Donna, when you have a moment, Mike and I would like to speak with you, alone."

The funeral director was shaking his head. "I'm sorry, gentlemen, but I'm afraid you're going to have to leave. Ms. Carter has—"

"It's all right, Doug," Donna interrupted. "Please give us a moment."

"Fine. If it's all right with you, Donna."

"It's okay, really. Thank you, Doug."

The director excused himself.

Brenden took out the key and opened the case, removing a large Manila envelope that contained the papers. He closed and handed the case containing the cash over to Donna. "You going to be all right with this?" he questioned. "It's a good deal of cash."

Donna brushed aside her open coat. "Licensed to carry. I'll be fine."

Brenden and Mike stared at the holstered weapon.

"Bet you will," Brenden said.

"What is it that you'd like to talk to me about?" Donna asked, looking them in the eyes.

"What we'd like to talk to you about will take more than a moment, Donna, but we wanted Mr. Mathie to give us some privacy. Tom planted a seed and hatched a plan to take down a very bad dude."

Donna was smiling. "I know all about the plan. Uncle Tommy told me all about it in the hospital before he passed away. But he didn't want you to know I knew in case I had second thoughts and changed my mind before you approached me. I told my uncle then, and I'm telling you now, I'm in."

Mike was nodding his head in understanding.

Brenden was shaking his head in disbelief.

Donna Carter's expression went from one of amusement to sheer seriousness. "After this cremation is over with, we'll get together and finalize our plan of action. I know I have a lot to learn from the both of you, so we'll get started. Just give me a day or two. Now, if you'll excuse me, I want to be alone with Uncle Tommy and tell him how much I love him all over again. And I don't want you two standing around to see me blubbering, or you may see it as a sign of weakness and change your minds altogether about handing me this assignment."

"Not in a hundred years, Donna Carter." Mike stated.

"Not in a thousand," Brenden echoed the sentiment.

"Go on, go." Donna began to tear, staring down at the cardboard casket.

The two men nodded their good-byes to the young woman, and as a farewell gesture to their friend Tom, brought the tips of their fingers smartly up to their foreheads in a sharp salute.

Cardboard. Pressed paper pulp or pasted sheets of paper. Yes, paper. A symbol of life's ephemeralness, Donna Carter entertained, taking a seat alongside her uncle's casket before it would be placed in a consuming furnace reaching temperatures ranging between 1,832°

– 2,372° Fahrenheit.

CHAPTER FIFTY-FOUR

The five-foot seven attractive redhead had been serving drinks and bar food to police officers and detectives for a solid uneventful month when a face she had never seen before descended the stairs. No one ever wore a mask or practiced social distancing. Two police officers were seated at a table and one detective was sitting on a stool at the end of the bar.

"Hey, Vinny," all three men voiced and greeted the detective warmly.

"Fellas," Detective Vincent Gomez acknowledged, strutting up to the bar and standing directly in front of the comely woman.

"So, you finally decided to take a walk over on the wild side," the detective at the end of the bar quipped.

"Yeah, I took a walk over to see what all the talk was about," Gomez said, staring directly into the barmaid's hazel eyes.

She smiled amicably. "First time here; first drink is on the house."

"And what if I have but one drink, leave, forget to leave a tip, then come back another time?"

"I'll remember you and charge you double for the round," Donna replied evenly.

"Hey, Vin. I think she likes you," one of the fellows seated at the table said then laughed heartily.

"Maybe they call this the Double-Aught bar because you *ought* to know better, Vinny," the other officer at the table kibitzed.

"Detective Gomez," Vincent said, extending an elbow across the bar toward the woman.

In a friendly greeting, Donna Carter simulated bumping elbows with the detective. It was the young woman's lame attempt at expressing social distancing. "Nice bumping into you like this, Detective Gomez."

The detective smiled handsomely. "Vinny; please call me Vinny. Your name?"

"Colleen."

"Nice Irish name. You Irish?"

"Only on Saint Paddy's Day."

"Last name?"

"Skrabanek. Father's Hungarian. Mother's Czechoslovakian. My parents fled Czechoslovakia during the German occupation and emigrated to Ireland. My father died early. My mother lives in Dublin and maintains an apartment in Prague. That's my whole life's story in a nutshell. What are you drinking?"

"Jack Daniel's Single Barrel Select."

"No got. For top shelf here, you'll settle for Jack Daniel's Old No. 7 and like it."

"I know. I just wanted to see if you knew your shit."

"Oh, you wouldn't want to bet against me when it comes to booze, numbers, or my feathered friends."

"Birds?"

"Yes birds."

"Well, let's see how you fare with liquor." Gomez leaned forward and placed his elbows on the bar. "All right, hotshot. Tell me how you would make a mojito."

Donna stepped back and folded her arms across her chest. "An authentic Cuban mojito, Detective Vinny Gomez, is traditionally made with five ingredients consisting of white rum, sugar cane juice, lime juice, seltzer, and mint, then topped off with crushed ice and a bit of sparkling water, which is different from seltzer. But for you, I'd make a Mexican version, swapping the traditional rum with smooth Don Julio Real Tequila from Jalisco, Mexico. That's, of course, if I had those ingredients here, Vinny."

"We're telling you, Vincent, that girl likes you," the other police officer at the table jabbered away with slurred speech.

"I'd ask her if maybe she has those ingredients at home, Vin," the detective seated at the end of the bar mockingly suggested.

Detective Vincent Gomez grinned. "What would be the most challenging drink for a bartender to make?" Vincent pressed.

"That would be The Commonwealth Cocktail, a drink made by mixing seventy-one ingredients, created by mixologist Mal Spence to commemorate the 20th Commonwealth games that took place in Glasgow in 2014, sourced from seventy-one Commonwealth nations competing in seventeen sporting events over eleven days. Kind of like a mini Olympics."

Vincent was quite impressed with Colleen. "Name me three exotic ingredients that go into that cocktail."

"Oh, there's just so many, Vinny."

"So, name me three," he asked, reaching for his smartphone and accessing the Internet for Commonwealth Cocktail.

"Three that immediately come to mind, and you'll probably note, are Belizean dragon fruit, Malaysian galangal, and Tanzanian cloves. Would you like me to name all the ingredients and the representative countries, Vinny?"

"You serious?"

"Deadly."

"I'll just bet you are."

"So, you going to just stand there testing me, or pull up a stool and tell me how you'd like your Tennessee Jack? Neat, or on the rocks?"

"Rocks, please."

"I won't even touch that line," the detective sitting at the end of the bar said and grinned, getting up off his stool and putting a fifty on the counter. "Keep the change, Colleen."

"Thanks, Bill."

"Take care, Vin."

"You, too, Bill."

Detective Bill Boyer bid the two officers at the table a good night. "You behave yourselves, boys."

"No fun in that, Bill," one responded.

The other officer picked his head up from the table and waved a good night, mumbling something unintelligible.

Donna turned her attention back to Detective Gomez and poured. "Jack Daniel's. A good masculine drink, Vinny. For a minute back there, I thought you were going to have me make you a makeshift girly mojito."

"Not a bad drink for summertime, Colleen."

"True." Donna was testing the detective's machismo sense of unrestrained pride. He passed. Over the next hour of making small talk with the man, she was learning to like him—a lot.

CHAPTER FIFTY-FIVE

Another month had passed when Detective Vincent Gomez asked Colleen Skrabanek out on a date. Their relationship up to that point had been one of customer/client. Nevertheless, a bond between them had grown considerably to where Donna trusted Vincent implicitly. She wished she could reveal to him her true identity and why she was really working at the Double-Aught Bar. Maybe he could even help her, she had contemplated on more than one occasion. But then she took a step back, remembering what Detectives Brenden Reilly and Mike D'Angelo had instilled in her: patience and perseverance. She would be violating those virtues that the pair had painstakingly drilled into her over the last two months via their weekly phone conversations and several meetings. Those qualities were the hallmark of a good undercover operative. Had she deviated from their course of action, she knew, too, that her Uncle Tommy would have been disappointed had he been alive to see the operation through. Following instruction and displaying loyalty were the elements of success. Loyalty was of paramount importance. Whereas Brenden and Mike had instilled in her forbearance and stick-to-itiveness, Tom had implanted in her the magnitude of faithfulness since childhood. Allegiance to a cause was at the core of her uncle's being. His word was his bond. A promise was to be kept at all cost regardless of the consequences.

On the other hand, Donna had struggled with the seeming hypocrisy in that her uncle had taken an oath to uphold the law but veered far from it. Had not her Uncle Tommy taken the law into his own hands? She knew that he was suspected of killing three serial killers and an accomplice who had knowledge of the others yet chose to look the other way. That person was retired United States Army Colonel Oliver Davis; guilty of aiding and abetting—but not murder. What the copies of the colonel's Rolodex file uncovered was that the man was a kingpin in an operation overseeing the distribution of many food products, snacks, soda and other beverages, toiletries, paper goods, clothing, and sundry items that were shipped to state and federal prisons throughout the State of New York. Contraband such as drugs was smuggled in surreptitiously. That is to say that the colonel had his hands in many pots and received a healthy percentage of the profits on virtually all goods sent to feed, clothe, and house inmates. The colonel had a virtual monopoly within the prison commissaries in New York State.

So, how had Lieutenant Tom Bolton rationalized his alleged actions, and just as important a question, how did Donna Carter justify her uncle's behavior in her own mind's eye? Very simply. When the law is broken and corruption is pervasive, one is justified to take the broken law into his or her own hands and try to repair it. The end justifies the means in such a situation.

She sat there in silence, listening to the sound of birds in the distance.

"You look deep in thought, Colleen," Detective Vincent Gomez said, interrupting her thoughts.

"Indeed," she replied, taking Vincent's hands into her own and giving the backs of both a tender kiss as she knelt before the picnic basket set upon a blanket in a closed off section of Mineola Memorial Park.

It was a warm sunny afternoon, but in the distance dark clouds were starting to roll in from the west.

"Tell me what's on your mind," Vincent asked, lying on his back and soaking in the last of the rays.

"That you had way too much to drink. Drinks before we left the bar. Now wine. And that I could easily take advantage of you," she scolded playfully.

"Promises, promises. And I noticed that you hardly touched yours. That's a very expensive red I bought."

"Brought, you mean. Not bought. I do the ordering and keep a precise inventory, remember? And if I find that a bottle of Campo Viejo Rioja Tempranillo is missing from the cellar, it goes on your tab, Vinny," she made clear.

"Guilty as charged," Vinny Gomez admitted and laughed. "I'll replace it."

"Nope, it goes on your tab at a full profit price as if you were drinking it at the bar. Marked up fourfold. That's eighty bucks, Vinny."

"Hey, that's not fair!"

"Neither is stealing."

"I didn't steal it. I borrowed it. I don't do anything illegal."

"No?"

"No."

"Sitting here in the park that's closed to the public because of the pandemic is illegal."

"We're not sitting. We're lying down. Or at least one of us is. And who's going to kick us out?"

"The police if they see us."

"I am the police, remember?"

"Think you have that kind of power?"

"Baby, you don't know the kind of power I wield."

"Really?"

"Really."

"Tell me about it."

"I'm a homicide detective, and I've put bad asses away for life."

"Ever shoot anyone? I mean shoot them dead."

Detective Vincent Gomez said nothing, sitting up and pouring himself another glass of wine. "Eighty dollars, you say, for a twenty-dollar bottle of wine. Highway robbery."

"If it were my bar and I had complete control, which I don't, I'd carry Campo Viejo Gran Reserva Rioja and mark it up sixfold. Hundred and twenty bucks. Cops would pay that to show off to their wives or girlfriends. Trust me. And don't try to change the subject. I want to know."

"Know what?"

"Did you ever shoot and kill anyone?"

"Only in the line of duty."

"Well, I hope that would be the case."

"Tell you a funny story, though."

"Yeah?"

"I once shot this fucking cat."

"In the line of duty?" she humored her date.

"More like in the line of fire." Vincent laughed. "Actually, it attacked me first."

"A cat attacked you?"

"I swear. I was on assignment when this cat comes out of nowhere, hissing, and went for my leg."

"And you shot it?"

"Nah, not right then and there."

"What is it with you guys and cats? My stepbrother hates cats for no apparent reason."

"See, that's the key word."

"What is?"

"Apparent."

"I don't understand."

"A dog is a pal, a good friend. A dog wants your attention. A cat is so fucking independent. It wants you to feed it, and that's about it. A dog, however, is man's best friend."

"I can see that you really don't know a lot about cats."

"Don't really want to." Vincent took a big swallow and poured himself another wine.

"So, tell me. What kind of cat was it?"

"Don't know, don't care."

"Tell me what happened."

"I really don't want to talk about it."

"You're the one who brought up the cat story."

"Are we having our first fight on our first date?"

"Did the cat have a name?"

"That part I can tell you. Its name was Tabitha."

Donna Carter fell silent and took a tiny sip of wine. She looked over and reached for her pocketbook.

"Cat got your tongue, Colleen?" Vincent asked and laughed

249

drunkenly. "You're not cross with me because I shot some stupid fucking kitty cat, are you?"

Donna Carter knew every detail relating to the murders of Claire Billings, Brenda Featherston, and Betty Fraser, including the unnecessary shooting of the widow's cat—named Tabitha. She had read the police reports that Brenden and Mike had handed her. She knew, too, the full firsthand accounts involving the shootings deaths of Mathew Hansen, Homicide Detectives Chad Kelly and Diego Ramírez, as well as Colonel Oliver Davis—learned at her uncle's bedside confession: Lieutenant Tom Bolton, Southold P.D. He had told her everything, instructing her to do what she wished with that information after his death.

"You're not answering me, so I guess you're mad," was Vincent's comment after taking another gulp, finishing off the bottle of wine.

"No, I'm not mad, Vinny. I was just remembering something. I knew *of* someone who had a cat named Tabitha. She was a Cymric, a long-haired breed. My uncle told me the story before he passed away. He was interviewing the widow in her home when she told him this because he showed an interest in her cat. You know my uncle's name because he was on the hit list of the three women you assassinated, but he died in Memorial Sloan Kettering Cancer Center before you had the chance to kill him. Isn't it funny that the cat you killed was your very undoing, Vinny? Isn't it fucking ironic?"

Homicide Detective Vincent Gomez stared in disbelief as Donna withdrew a handgun from her pocketbook and thumbed the hammer back on her .380 PPK Walther, pointing the weapon at the man's head. The detective remained speechless.

"Not as powerful a caliber as the nine millimeter you used to murder those three women, Vin, but this will do the job quite nicely."

Vincent was shaking his head. "They were orders, Colleen. Three witnesses who opened their mouths when they should have kept them shut. They had to be silenced to send a message to others. I had no choice."

"Wrong. You always have a choice. The upside to all this for you, Vin, is that I'll put in the money for your bar bill. You won't have to lay out a dime."

"Let me ask you a question. Do you even know how to use that thing?"

"Even better at it than mixing drinks, Vin."

Vincent was laughing lightly. "I'll ask you the same question you asked me. Have you ever shot and killed someone?"

"Let me get back to you on that in the next second." And with that remark, Donna Carter squeezed the trigger, sending a kurtz hollow-point bullet smashing into the man's skull. "The answer, Vin, is a definitive, yes."

The sound of the birds she heard just moments ago was suddenly gone.

Dark layers of cumulonimbus clouds swept in and covered what had a moment ago been a bright blue sky. Suddenly, lightening followed by thunder and a heavy downpour enveloped the park. Donna reached inside the detective's pants pocket and removed a set of keys, withdrew a gun from his shoulder holster, wiped her prints clean with a cloth napkin, then placed the weapon in his right hand. She grabbed the empty wine bottle and glasses, placing them along with utensils and trash into the picnic basket, praying that the ponderous rain would wash away any and all trace evidence. Carrying the blanket, picnic basket, and her pocketbook, Donna quickly headed for Vincent's car.

CHAPTER FIFTY-SIX

Detectives Brenden Reilly and Mike D'Angelo were parked in their vehicle when a call came through. Donna Carter was on her cell phone with Mike.

"It's all over," Donna said, just as calmly as she could.

"Where are you?"

"Heading east."

"That's not what I asked."

"I won't discuss it now. I need you to meet me."

Mike heard the urgency in her voice. "Where?"

"Someplace secluded. I need to tie up some loose ends."

"Everything's secluded these days. You remember where we met last time out? Not where we had breakfast, but where the three of us later talked?"

"I remember everything."

"We're about twenty minutes away from there."

"Perfect. I'm about the same distance."

"Raining by you?"

"Pouring."

"Same here. Drive safe."

Mike and Brenden were waiting in the rear parking area at an eatery in Brentwood, temporarily closed. Donna turned off the engine and immediately got out of Vincent's vehicle, walking briskly to the detectives' car, opening a door and climbing into the back.

"You're soaking wet," Brenden said.

"But alive, thank God." She was shivering but not necessarily from the cold.

"You said it's all over. You going to keep us in suspense?" Mike questioned impatiently, taking off his jacket and handing it to her.

Mike turned on the heater.

"Your killer of those three women was Homicide Detective Vincent Gomez," Donna stated emphatically.

"Was?"

"I shot and killed him, Mike." Donna shifted her eyes from Mike to Brenden.

"Holy shit!" Brenden exclaimed.

Donna related each and every detail that led up to that moment. When she finished, Brenden was shaking his head sadly.

"It wasn't self-defense, girl. You could have just reported back to us. We would have taken it from there."

"No, you wouldn't have, Brenden. Not in the way that it needed to be taken care of."

"Oh, so you're judge, jury, and executioner now. Is that it?"

"It is what it is."

Brenden looked at Mike. "How do you want to handle this?"

"Exactly the way Tom would have handled it," Mike answered his partner. "Exactly the way Tom would have handled it," he repeated. "We wipe the car down clean, likewise take care of her apartment in Mineola, then pray that this weather takes care of the rest." He set his eyes on Donna. "I don't think anyone is going to find his body that quickly from what you've told us about the location in the park. Right?"

Donna nodded. "Right."

Brenden was back to shaking his head. "This is nuts."

"Lighten up, partner. Everything's gonna be all right. His keys in the car, Donna?"

It was the first time in months she heard her own name. Donna Carter was no longer Colleen Skrabanek. "Yes, along with a blanket and picnic basket filled with incriminating evidence."

253

"I'll take care of his car for now," Mike said. "You drive her back home, partner, and we'll figure this out from there."

"You two upset with me?"

"Let's just say we liked you better when you were a strawberry blonde instead of a redhead and leave it at that," Brenden answered with a questionable smile.

"What you'll hear very shortly, Donna, is an announcement that another Gilgo Beach victim has been identified," Mike said.

"Referred to as the Manorville Jane Doe; that is, victim number six," Brenden elaborated.

"You're talking about the woman whose torso was found in Manorville back in 2000; then a year later, her head, hands, and right foot were found at Gilgo Beach."

"Exactly."

"We're working very closely with the feds, Donna."

"It's a new era, kiddo," Mike expanded. "She was identified by using advanced scientific techniques of DNA testing coupled with genetic genealogy. Several states are now relaxing their otherwise stringent policies of maintaining privacy/confidentiality issues when it comes to helping us solve egregious acts such as serial murders."

"Yeah, like it's about fucking time, wouldn't you say?"

"No argument here, kiddo."

Donna was doing a slow burn. "Dating back to 1974, it took law enforcement thirty-one years to learn that Dennis Rader, dubbed the BTK killer, was the serial killer they were after. Going back to 1970, it took law enforcement forty-three years to learn that retired California cop Joseph DeAngelo, called the Golden State Killer, was the serial killer they were hunting for. Okay. We're looking at a period of six decades. Fine. They didn't have all the tools in their toolbox back then that we have today. But you mean to tell me law enforcement can't find the serial killer or killers stepping back just two decades? That's pure bullshit. Suffolk County law enforcement officials didn't identify the killer or killers because law enforcement was covering up the crimes. Pure and simple. But with the public's help, people like Claire Billings, Brenda Featherston, and Betty Fraser pointed you guys in right direction. And with the indefatigable help from Uncle Tommy, his friends, and yours truly, we rid Suffolk and Nassau Counties of some real garbage."

"And in the course of events, you took the law into your own hands, Donna," Brenden put forth solemnly. "You shot and killed that man."

But Donna Carter was shaking her head. "I did no such thing, Brenden. Colleen Skrabanek shot and killed that assassin. The police will find a weapon in that killer's hand. Colleen was just quicker on the draw is all, fearing for her life when Detective Vincent Gomez suddenly realized that Colleen discovered who had shot Brenda Featherston's cat, Tabitha. That's going to be her official story, Brenden, and mine, too—come what may," she added coolly.

Brenden and Mike looked at one another and nodded in agreement.

EPILOGUE

The years flew by faster than a peregrine falcon was the mother's bird metaphor of the moment as Donna Reilly, the former Donna Carter, explained to her precocious 10-year-old daughter a fact of life. Darlene had been terribly upset and crying uncontrollably when she found a dead finch near the holly bushes in their Southold backyard. Donna comforted her child then elaborated on the natural life expectancy of an average finch, that being around five years.

"As a matter of fact, darling, some finches can live four times that long; that is, twenty years. But the average life span of a charm of finches is about five years."

"That's the age of my little sister, Debra."

"That's right, sweetheart."

"Which means that I've already lived twice that long. Ten years."

"Correct, you are. And you will live twenty times longer than the average finch if you take good care of yourself."

Darlene was adding up the number of years on her tiny fingers of both hands. "Wow! That's a hundred years."

"If you take good care of yourself," the mother of three daughters repeated.

"But I have you and Daddy to take care of me, Mommy."

"That's true, Darlene. But your father and I won't always be around."

"Why not?"

"Well, let's say you're twenty-years-old one day. You're going to want to start your own family, care for them, and teach your own children how to take care of themselves."

"Oh. How old are you, Mommy?"

"Thirty-two years old."

"So, when I'm twenty . . . you'll be forty-two years old."

"Correct."

"And when I'm forty . . . you'll be—wait . . . sixty-two years old."

"Yes."

"And when I'm sixty . . . you'll be—"

"Pretty old," Donna said and smiled.

"And Daddy?"

"Very, very old," she said and laughed.

"Mommy?"

"What, honey?"

"Debra is my little sister, and Dorothy is my older sister. Does that mean that Dorothy will die before either of us?"

"Life is filled with many uncertainties, Darlene. A person just never knows, dear."

"Does God know?"

"God knows everything, my precious bird."

"Can we go outside and feed the finches the sunflower seeds that Daddy bought yesterday?"

"Sure."

"Why do you call them a charm of finches?"

"Well, because birds are divided into groups. We say a flock or a bevy of birds, but then we use names to describe each group."

"Like when Daddy says a gaggle of geese?"

"Exactly. A gaggle of geese, a charm of finches, and so on."

"What do you call a flock of eagles?"

"A convocation."

"A flock of hawks?"

"A cast."

"Ah, a flock of crows?"

"A murder," Donna answered uncomfortably. "A murder of crows."

"Why do they call it a murder of crows, Mommy?"

"It generally refers to its scavenging nature."

"What's scavenging mean?"

"With respect to crows, it means that they feed on decayed matter, like the flesh of dead animals."

"Like vultures do, right?"

"Right."

"What are they called, the vultures?"

"In a group they're called a committee. In flight they're called a kettle. And on the ground when they're feeding on the flesh of another animal, the group is called a wake."

"Boy, this can get complicated. Right?"

"Right you are."

"What would you call a flock of penguins?"

"Penguins don't fly, precious, so they're not referred to as a flock. Remember? A flock pertains to birds. On land, a group of penguins is called a colony, a rookery, or a waddle. But when they're floating around in the ocean on a block of ice, they're referred to as a raft."

"Wow! How do you keep all those things to remember in your head?"

"I have what people call a photographic memory."

"Does that mean you remember pictures?"

"Pictures and other things."

"Like what?"

"Like what I read."

"You remember what you read?"

"Um-hum."

"How much?"

"Pretty much everything."

"How about what people say? Do you remember everything people say?"

"Everything."

"Then how come when Daddy asked you to pick up his favorite bottle of Scotch, you said that you forgot?"

Donna smiled and absently stroked her long strawberry blonde hair. "That's what we call selective memory, my inquisitive little trouble maker."

"What does selective memory mean, Mommy?"

"It means that I choose to remember certain things and that I choose to forget others."

"You mean like Daddy's Scotch?"

"Yes."

"And why do you choose to forget picking up Daddy's favorite Scotch?"

"Because he drinks a bit too much, and I'm trying to keep him alive till he's a hundred. That's why. Now, I thought you wanted to go outside and feed the finches."

Darlene ran to the closet and grabbed her coat then headed toward the front door when her father came through it and scooped his daughter up and into his arms. "Hiya there, my pretty little pigeon," her father greeted.

"Hiya, Daddy. Do you know what a group or flock of pigeons is called?"

"Nope."

"I don't either. But Mommy's going to tell us because she knows everything because she has a photography mind and—"

"Photographic mind," her father corrected.

"And, also a selective one, too, Daddy."

"Oh, she sure does," he agreed. "Your mom certainly does."

"Mommy doesn't forget anything unless she puts her mind to it, she told me."

"Did she, now? And did she tell you that Uncle Mike and Aunt Denise are coming over for an early dinner, or did she forget?"

"No, Daddy. Mommy didn't forget because she's making us and Uncle Mike and Aunt Denise a surprise dinner, and from there we're all going to church for a memorial service to honor Uncle Tommy."

"As we do every year, sweetheart," he said, setting his daughter down gently. "Where are your sisters?"

"Dorothy is helping Debra with her dress, but I'm all ready to go."

"Good girl."

"Uncle Mike and Aunt Denise are really not my uncle and aunt, are they, Daddy?"

"No, in name only, my little pigeon. But they're the greatest folks this family could ever hope to have. And so, out of respect, we call them your uncle and aunt. And your Uncle Tommy is actually your great-uncle."

"You mean he *was* a great uncle because he's dead and because I heard all the great stories. And that's why we're going to the church to honor him. Right?"

"That's not the kind of *great* I mean. I mean that—never mind. I'll explain it later, kiddo."

"Anyways, I like Uncle Mike and Aunt Denise a lot. Aunt Denise helped you and Uncle Mike solve a big criminal case. Right?"

"Right you are. That's what we do, darling. No more of those really, really bad guys like we had around here a long, long time ago. Just your garden variety criminals."

"And Aunt Denise married Uncle Mike because her first husband died of a virus a long, long time ago, too. Right?"

"Because he didn't take care of himself," Donna added. "That's why we want you and your sisters to wash your hands at least twice a day, just like you brush your teeth, and to keep away from large groups."

"But we don't have to wear masks like you and Daddy did a long time ago. Right?"

"Right. Because we have a vaccine now that helps protect all of us, which we didn't have before, sweetheart."

"Daddy?"

"Yes, my pretty little bird?"

"Do you want to help Mommy and me feed a charm of finches?"

"Absolutely."

"They only live to be five years old. Some can live a lot longer. But we're all going to live to be a hundred if we take good care of ourselves. Oh, and before I forget, what do you call a bunch of pigeons, Mommy?"

"They're called a flock or a flight."

"That's an easy one to remember, and I don't need to have a photography—I mean a photographic memory."

"No you don't," her father assured her. "No, you certainly do not" he repeated. "As a matter of fact, sometimes a photographic memory can get you in a heap of trouble," he reminded his wife while staring down mindfully at his gifted daughter. "Isn't that right, honey?" Detective Lieutenant Brenden Reilly questioned Donna heedfully.

"If you say so, dear."

"I say so, Mrs. Reilly."

Donna never told anyone of her Uncle Tommy's bedside confession. There was no need to. Mike and Brenden knew, unofficially, but it was not discussed. The annual memorial service that evening was, as were the previous services, poignant and positive in honoring a great man: Lieutenant Tom Bolton, posthumously promoted to captain, Southold Police Department.

Following the memorial service, Detective Lieutenant Mike D'Angelo had his arms around the shoulders of Donna and Brenden's three children as the group left the First Presbyterian Church of Southold, all walking toward the parking lot.

"Tomorrow we're all going fishing on Captain Tommy's boat," Mike reminded everyone.

"It's not Uncle Tommy's boat," Donna's eldest daughter, Dorothy, asserted. "It's our mother's boat because Uncle Tommy gave it to her before he died."

"Sorry, but it will always be Captain Tommy's boat," Mike argued, delighting in getting under the oldest girl's skin.

"No, it's not," Dorothy affirmed. "It has Mother's name, DONNA, printed across the stern, so there."

"Are you trying to give me an argument, young lady?"

"Yes."

"And what about you, Debra? Are you going to go against me, too?"

The youngest of the Reilly daughters simply shrugged her shoulders then nodded a yes.

"So, you're all teamed up against me, I see." Mike turned to his wife. "And you, my dear. Is it Tommy's boat or Donna's?"

"Possession is nine-tenths of the law," Denise offered with a smile.

"See?" Dorothy said. "Why don't you ask my mom whose boat it is?"

"But of course she's going to say it's hers."

"Then you're outnumbered by five to one," Dorothy persisted.

"Brenden, do you see what's going on here?" Mike protested. "I mean, how can you ever win an argument with all these females lining up against you?"

"You can't," was Brenden's succinct answer.

"Debra, Darlene, Dorothy, and Donna. How do you even keep their names straight? Even my wife Denise is against me. I see this all as one big conspiracy, Brenden. I'm afraid that if we go out on Captain Tommy's boat tomorrow, the girls might declare a mutiny."

"Won't happen," Brenden assured his partner.

"How can you be so sure?"

"It's the leverage you wield, Mike. The power that you have over them."

"And what, pray tell, is that?"

"Your clams casino, homemade pasta, and garlic bread that you always prepare for all of us whenever we head out and anchor up in Coecles Harbor."

"Yes, I guess that's true." Mike released his arms from around the shoulders of the three girls, taking a step back to look the trio in the eyes. "Is that true, girls?"

Dorothy and Darlene giggled and nodded in the affirmative. Debra got the gist of what was going on, smiled broadly, then nodded, too.

"All right then." Mike turned to Denise and Donna.

The two women laughed and gave Mike a mighty hug.

"At least we'll behave," Donna said. "Right, Denise?"

"Just so long as he offers all of us seconds," Mike's wife proclaimed.

"Well, this time out, I bought half a bushel of littleneck clams for tomorrow. That's approximately two hundred clams, divided by seven of us—that's what, Donna?"

"Twenty-eight, point five seven," Donna said in the blink of an eye.

"Well, that ought to do us quite nicely; that is, if Debra and Darlene don't wipe us out like they did last time," Mike exaggerated with a bright smile.

"I love clams!" Debra exclaimed.

"Me, too," Darlene seconded. "But I hate them raw on the half shell," she declared vociferously.

"Yuck! Me, too," Debra totally agreed, scrunching her face into an ugly frown.

"I could easily eat half a bushel by myself, raw or cooked," Dorothy assured everyone. "That is, if I don't first fill up on your homemade linguine and garlic bread, Uncle Mike."

"Oh, believe me, I know. You're the culprit and a trouble maker in the bargain—telling me whose boat this really is. So. I'll give you another chance. Whose boat is that?"

"Mother's boat."

"You know you're very stubborn, just like your mom. Half rations for you tomorrow afternoon, girly."

"Oh, yeah?"

"Yeah. But I'll tell you what."

"What?"

"If you agree that this is still Uncle Tommy's boat, and not your mom's, I'll teach you how to tie a worm knot with a real live worm. It's the secret to catching really big striped bass."

"That's not true, and you know it because you don't tie a worm in a knot. Besides, worms like sandworms and bloodworms are mostly used for smaller fish, not striped bass. If you want to catch really big stripers, you use bucktails tipped with strips of pork rind in the afternoon, then you switch to live-lining porgies as the sun goes down, then around midnight you fish with eels. That's how you catch really big stripers, Uncle Mike."

"And who taught you all that?"

"Mother."

"And who taught your mother how to fish in the first place?"

"Uncle Tommy."

"And on whose boat did she learn to do all that?"

"Uncle Tommy's."

"So, don't you think that boat should still be considered Uncle Tommy's boat?"

Dorothy thought hard before she uttered another word. "I'll tell you what, Uncle Mike."

"Tell me."

"I have to think about it, and I'll let you know sometime after we have lunch on Mother's boat tomorrow."

"You know, I think you're as tricky as your mother is what I think."

"You know, I think you just paid me what Mother calls a lefthanded compliment is what I think."

Mike smiled broadly then looked at Donna. "Raising them very wisely, Mrs. Reilly."

"Well, thank you very much, Detective Lieutenant D'Angelo."

"See you all tomorrow," Mike said and waved, taking his wife by the hand and heading toward their car.

"Tomorrow," Brenden said and smiled happily. "Tomorrow."

Brenden's cell phone rang loudly before Mike and Denise reached their car. Seconds later, Mike's cell phone also sounded.

Brenden glanced at the name and number. "Yes, sir," he answered, stepping aside and listening to the voice filled with urgency on the other end.

A long moment passed before Detective Lieutenant Reilly responded. "He's right here, Commander. From the look on his face, probably hearing the same report you're unfolding, sir."

"It's really, really bad, Lieutenant. We haven't seen anything like this in a decade. Multiple victims. All with the singular signature earmarks of serial killers Mathew Hansen, Detective Chad Kelly, and Detective Diego Ramírez, not to mention The Administration's assassin, Detective Vincent Gomez. Scenes at Gilgo Beach, Oak Beach, and Manorville. Virtually simultaneous! The latest in Riverhead less than an hour ago in back of the aquarium."

"Mike and I are leaving for the aquarium right now. We'll meet the team there."

"Copy that. I'll alert them."

Brenden and Mike ended the calls. "You hear all that, partner?" Brenden asked.

Mike was now standing next to Brenden. "I think this is a pretty good example what they call déjà vu," Mike said in a low voice. "I'll send Denise home. We'll take your car."

Brenden nodded. "It just doesn't end. Does it?"

"Oh, we'll find them and end it altogether, once and for all, good buddy. You know we will. We'll just have to adopt a few unorthodox methods as Tommy and your wife had."

"Got that right, partner. You got that oh, so right. Adopt and adapt," Brenden said quietly as the pair headed toward the car. "Monsters like that do not belong in prison, period."

"But in an early grave," Mike said assuredly.

"You no longer have to convince me of that."

"Amen to that, partner. Amen to that."

Both Donna and Denise knew from their husbands' expressions that serious trouble was on the horizon.

Donna's eldest daughter, too, suspected something was terribly wrong. "I have a sneaking suspicion that tomorrow's trip on Mother's boat is going to be called off," she surmised, looking down at her two younger sisters.

"Why? Is it going to rain tomorrow?" Darlene wanted to know, the look of sheer disappointment transforming her pretty face into that of abject sadness.

"I like it when it rains," the youngest child chimed in.

"You don't know what you're talking about, Debra," Dorothy scolded.

Donna knelt down and gathered her three daughters about her as one might cluster an arrangement of beautiful flowers. She spoke in a soft voice. "Listen to me carefully. Into each life, my three precious children, some rain must fall," Donna said so sweetly, paraphrasing Henry Wadsworth Longfellow.

"You see?" Debra said gleefully.

Dorothy rolled her eyes. "You're missing the point, little sister."

Donna smiled patiently. "Anyway, on the bright side, there's always the day after tomorrow."

"Absolutely," Mike's wife agreed and nodded emphatically. "And if the men are busy with work tomorrow or the next day, your mother will captain the boat, and I'll prepare lunch for the five of us. Girls' afternoon out. Won't be the same as Uncle Mike's, but it will do. How does that sound?"

"Sounds like I'm not going to have to worry about seconds or thirds," Dorothy said. "Lots of clams on the half shell for me will be just fine," she concluded with a grin.

Denise gave Donna and the three girls hugs and kisses then continued alone toward her car. Brenden and Mike were already on their way to the crime scene in Riverhead.

ABOUT THE AUTHOR

Robert Banfelder holds an M.A. ~ genre Creative Writing ~ and a B.A., English honors, from Queens College. He is an award-winning crime-thriller novelist and outdoors writer. His novels titled *The Author* and *The Teacher* both received the Best Suspense Novel Award from NewBookReviews. T*he Long Island Serial Killer Murders ~ Gilgo Beach and Beyond* is his 10th novel.

In addition to his novels, Robert has written five handbooks: *The Fishing Smart Anywhere Handbook for Salt Water and Fresh Water, The North American Small & Big Game Hunting Smart Handbook, Bull's Eye! The Smart Bowhunter's Handbook, The Essential Guide to Writing Well & Getting Published* and *On Your Way to Gourmet Cooking.* Additionally, Robert writes outdoors articles, which have appeared in national and regional publications: *The Fisherman, On The Water, Big Game Fishing Journal, Hana Hou! The Magazine for Hawaiian Airlines, Deer & Deer Hunting, New York Game & Fish*, to name but a few. He is a member of the Outdoor Writers Association of America and the New York State Outdoor Writers Association.

Robert also co-hosts, with Donna Derasmo, their YouTube Channel titled *Special Interests with Bob & Donna.* The channel is eclectic in that it covers numerous topics such as crime, politics, outdoor sports, quality knives and knife-sharpening systems, cruising, cooking, et cetera.

www.robertbanfelder.com
Facebook@Robert Banfelder
Twitter @RobertBanfelder

Made in the USA
Middletown, DE
05 January 2022

57893645R00152